TOGETHER
With Love

KENNEDY FOX ❤ CHARITY FERRELL ❤ EMILY GOODWIN
PIPER RAYNE ❤ K WEBSTER ❤ JIFFY KATE
ADRIANA LOCKE ❤ RACHEL BROOKES ❤ RED PHOENIX
D. KELLY ❤ REBECCA SHEA ❤ WILLOW WINTERS
SKYE WARREN ❤ K.K. ALLEN ❤ AMELIA WILDE
MANDI BECK ❤ PIPER LAWSON ❤ ROXIE NOIR

Together with Love
Bonus Scenes Collection

Cover design by Designs by Dana

AUTHOR'S NOTE

Hi readers!

Thank you so much for picking up our bonus scenes collection! We're so excited to bring you these stories of previous characters in various "stuck" together situations—from being in lockdown, to stuck on an island, to taking shelter from a tornado, to be locked in a wine cellar. We've teamed up to give you the escape you need when our characters can't escape each other. If you haven't read the book/series from the bonus scene, make sure to check out the original story. You can still read most of these for pure fun.

We know the world is going through some crazy times right now and even though we all have different circumstances at the moment, we wanted to show you that we're in this *together*. We hope this collection gives you a little escape of reality and hope you enjoy!

—the authors of *Together with Love*

CONTENTS

KENNEDY FOX

CHAPTER ONE

COURTNEY

DAY 1

DREW, the triplets, and I have been in beautiful Hawaii for the past fourteen days, and we've had the time of our lives celebrating my parents' wedding anniversary. The entire Bishop family is here, and we've done all the touristy things from visiting the volcanos, taking an island tour, and even went whale watching. It's incredible for all twenty-four of us to all be together and celebrate their love and the life my mom and dad made.

Convincing them to leave the ranch and get on a plane wasn't easy, especially considering they didn't even know where they were going. The only way I can describe it is like trying to help a stubborn old heifer give birth. The big surprise almost didn't happen because Mama is so damn hardheaded. She's always talked about visiting Hawaii, but she never had the guts to do it, so all the kids pitched in and made it happen.

My brothers promised me our parents would be there, especially after all the planning it took. While they're away, the ranch is being taken care of by our trusted workers.

Since Drew and I live in California, we met everyone at the Los Angeles airport, then announced where we were going before boarding a plane to Honolulu. To say Mama was shocked would be an understatement, but she and Daddy were really excited to have the whole family together for the first time in two years. The last time Drew, the kids, and I were in Texas was for Riley and the triplets' tenth birthday parties. They're twelve now with teenage attitudes and are glued to their iPads.

Though the California beaches are a huge improvement from the chocolate milk water on the coast of Texas, they don't even compare to the ones in Hawaii. The sand here is so white it nearly blinds me during the day, and the sky is so blue, sometimes I lose focus of where the water ends on the horizon. I've had the best time hanging out with my sisters-in-law and love that our kids get to play together again. My life is hundreds of miles away from everyone else. I don't get to visit them as much as I want, so I've soaked in every minute of the past two weeks.

As we all sit out by the pool, relaxing with a cocktail in hand, I realize how much I've missed everyone. Sure, they're loud and Southern to the bone, but I wouldn't trade them for the world. Jackson—no matter how old he gets—will always give us a run for our money, and this trip has been no different. I thought after he got married and had kids, his antics would settle down, but I was so damn wrong. He's a child in a man's body. Sometimes, he's worse than his own twin boys.

As I sit on the lounge chair drinking with my pinky out, he takes off running from the other side and does a cannonball right in front of me. Water rises and splashes in our faces. While I try not to say too many obscenities in front of my kids, Jackson has me cussing up a storm.

He kicks his feet, continuing to get all of us wet, and I groan loudly, but he's not fazed. He lives to annoy me, and everyone else too. But he loves getting a rise outta me because I'm not around very much, and I'm his only sister. I turn and look at Evan, who shrugs with a grin. He's the oldest and is supposed to help me, but he doesn't, and then Jackson splashes me again.

"Jackson Joel Bishop! Leave your sister alone," Mama yells from a chair under an oversized umbrella. She uses that tone that used to make the hairs on the back of my neck stand up. The grandkids get quiet, but he's immune and continues to antagonize me.

"She started it! Courtney gave me a dirty look," he whines like he's seven.

Kiera shakes her head and apologizes for him.

"I cannot believe you married him."

A sly grin spreads over her lips. "Sometimes, I can't either."

"Oh, you're trying to get my wife to help you? Sorry, Sis. She's Team Jackson *all the way*." He makes a thrusting motion in the water, and I gag with an eye roll.

I lift my eyebrows at him and chug the rest of my alcohol, hoping I didn't just suck down pool water, then set it down. He continues, so I sprint and dive into the pool after him. I dunk Jackson and push water toward his face when he comes up for air. That's one thing about growing up with brothers; I can take it, but I can *also* give it.

Jackson puts me into a headlock and pulls me under, and I try to fight my way out of his hold. When I come up for air, I call him every word under the sun. It doesn't take long for us to clear out the pool area until there's no one but Bishops around. While I want him to stop, I'm too stubborn to give up.

"Mom, I'm hungry," Anderson tells me, rubbing his palm over his stomach. As soon as one kid says they're hungry, then they all do. Considering there are so many of us, it's an enormous feat to sit together, but somehow, we've managed so far.

After we dry off and go to our rooms to change, we meet at the restaurant downstairs. Once we sit, Drew wraps his arm around me, and his fingers trail against my skin, causing goose bumps to form. I look at him and wink, then glance around the table at my family that I love so much.

There's a TV at the bar, and I see some warning flash at the bottom. I lean closer to Drew, and whisper, "What does that say?"

His eyesight is ten times better than mine.

"Says a tropical storm is coming soon and to take shelter."

I stare at the screen, keeping my voice low so I don't worry the kids. "What does that mean exactly?"

"If it's bad enough, I might need to call my boss because our flights could get canceled tomorrow."

My mouth falls open, and I suck in a deep breath, wanting to stay calm. Instead of alarming everyone, I try to focus on everyone chatting and decide I'll google it later.

Daddy smiles as he talks about the ranch and all the things he needs to do when he gets back. Mama chats about the B&B, and Kiera is deep in conversation about horse training with Jackson. John and Mila laugh about something with Emily and Evan. River and Alex are too busy reminiscing about meeting in Florida to pay attention to anything. All of our kids are at the opposite end of the table, sucking down sodas and chewing with their mouths open, but I can't even find the heart to demand they mind their manners because the moment is too perfect. Being together is all that matters, and I'm as happy as a hog in mud about it.

CHAPTER TWO

ALEX

DAY 2

THIS MORNING when I woke up, I got an alert on my phone that all outgoing flights from Honolulu were canceled because of a tropical storm making landfall. Courtney warned us about it late last night, so I expected it, but it still kinda sucks. There's no telling how long we'll be stuck here. Thankfully, the hotel has been nice about letting us stay longer.

The rain beats against the windows as if it wants to come in. The sky that's been blue is now the color of a dark bruise. River and I have been lounging around most of the day while Rowan and Riley have been with their cousins. It's been a quiet day for us, which is rare. All the grandkids decided to camp out in my parents' room tonight, which means we're kid-free for the next twelve hours.

River loops her arms around my waist as I stare outside. The wind has really picked up.

"After this, we're never gonna be able to get Dad to leave the ranch again." I laugh and turn around, then place my lips on hers.

"That's very true. But I also think they're enjoying spending time with the kids."

I kiss her again, almost getting lost in the moment. "I love you."

"I love you too," she says. "The ranch is gonna be fine. There's really nothing to worry about because Jackson's here, so there's no trouble at home."

That makes me chuckle. Just as I'm about to turn on the TV and watch the news, the lights flicker, and I get a text from Evan.

Evan: I've got tons of whiskey. Come over. Everyone else is already here.

This trip was a much-needed vacation for him and Emily. They've been working so much lately. He went all out and rented a damn suite that has several bedrooms inside, along with a table large enough to fit twelve. I ask River if she wants to go, and she agrees, then grabs her cranberry juice and vodka.

"Is Evan drunk or something?" she asks because he's usually so uptight.

I laugh. "Maybe. Having a party usually isn't his thing. Even in high school."

"Maybe he was blackmailed into it," she suggests. "You know how he gets when Courtney's around."

"Loose as a goose and only happens once in a blue moon. Might as well enjoy it." As the words leave my lips, lightning crashes and hail pounds against the windows.

We both jump, unnerved by it. I've never experienced a storm this intense. At home, we get the occasional rain or hail with high winds, but it's typically over in a few hours. This has been going on nonstop all day with no end in sight. I swear it's hovering above us by how low the clouds hang in the sky.

I interlock my fingers with River's, and we make our way to the end of the hall. Even if I didn't know where he was staying, it wouldn't be hard to find. Music and laughter lead us straight to the door. I knock, but no one answers. After a few more moments, it swings open, and Courtney's standing with a smirk.

"Hey, Sis." I grin at how chipper she looks. She's already a few drinks in and gives me a hug like she hasn't been hanging out with me for the past two weeks. "Ahh, my baby brother." I'm the only one she can say that to, which makes me laugh. Her eyes squint as she chuckles.

"You okay, Court?" River asks.

"Peeeeerfect. Never been better. C'mon, guys."

I snort, shaking my head. You wouldn't think we're in the middle of a horrible storm by the sounds inside.

River and I walk into a full room of Bishops. Drew's chatting with John as Jackson drunk dances to Garth Brooks.

"Oh shit, who gave Jackson tequila?" I glance at Evan, and he shakes his head, then points at Kiera, who's encouraging Jackson.

"We're all getting arrested tonight," I say.

River points at me. "Better not because I'm not bailing you out in this mess."

Lightning strikes again, and Mila shrieks. I join Drew and John at the giant window, and we stare at the flag that looks like a sheet that's been starched stiff and put on a pole.

My mouth falls open. "It's gotta be blowing at least sixty miles per hour."

"Sixty-five," Mila says from the couch, glancing up from her phone. "And it's supposed to get worse."

Courtney rounds us up and forces us to sit at the table. "We're gonna play a round of truth or dare."

A mischievous grin spreads across Emily's face. "This is such a terrible idea, but I'm totally in."

John agrees with her from behind us but sits anyway. You never dare a Bishop because we're all too stubborn to pass on it.

"Alright. Grab your booze. We're about to have some fun." Courtney fills her glass with more whiskey.

"Let's up the ante. We'll let the bottle decide who goes first," Jackson says, then leans over and whirls it. I think he and Courtney are on the same team, and I'm kinda scared.

The glass spins around, then stops on him. "This shit is rigged!" he shouts.

John claps his hands together and asks the question. "Truth or dare?"

"You know I ain't no damn chicken. *Dare.*"

Courtney grins like the Grinch. "Dare?"

"Ya heard me," Jackson says, puffing his chest out.

She nods. "I sure as hell did."

Tapping her finger on her lips, she pretends to think. Making a show out of it, she leans over and stares Jackson in the eyes. "I *dare* you to strip down to your underwear and go take a lap around the pool."

"Absolutely not," Evan chimes in, trying to be the voice of reason, but it's too late. Jackson has already removed his shirt and is going for his belt buckle.

"You could get hurt," Emily adds. "It's lightning out there."

"If I die, I'll make sure to haunt every single one of ya." He cackles, taking off each cowboy boot.

"The wind is blowin' like crazy. It's dangerous," John tries to convince him he shouldn't, but Jackson's already got his pants pushed down to his ankles.

Mila turns her head away, and Courtney crosses her arms with a smirk and waits.

"Gimme a kiss before I go, baby." Jackson captures Kiera's lips with his. When he pulls away, she tells him how much of a dumbass he is. Regardless, he exits the room, grinning like a dumbass.

The group of us huddle by the gigantic window because it has the perfect view of the pool. A couple of minutes pass, and we see Jackson down there, flipping us off and mooning us before running around the pool. He goes an extra step and jumps in and swims around. When he gets out, he continues laughing his ass off, and I know the rain has to hurt against his skin. Seconds later, John gets a call on his cell. He flips it around, and we see it's Mama.

"We're so fucked," I whisper, holding back laughter.

He puts the call on speaker, and Mama remains calm, but I know she's as furious as the storm outside.

"Please tell me that wasn't your idiot brother showing his rear end to God and country by the pool."

John sighs, and it's all the confirmation Mama needs.

"He better stay down there if he knows what's good for him," she warns with gritted teeth before ending the call.

We snicker until someone loses it, and we all hunch over and laugh our asses off. I'm nearly gasping for air 'cause I know Mama's gonna chew him up and spit him out. None of us are too old for a good old-fashioned ass whoopin', and Jackson has one coming.

CHAPTER THREE

EVAN

DAY 3

THE STORM HOWLED ALL through the night, wind and rain stirring up a mess outside. At some point, it was so loud that everyone shouted just to hear each other. Though, that could've also been because we were drunk as fuck.

Emily rustles beside me. I tighten my arm around her waist, pulling her closer as she wiggles against my erection.

"Good mornin'," I whisper in her ear and smirk when the corner of her lips tilts up. She arches her back, and I grip her chin, turning her face. "Don't start something you can't finish, sweetheart."

This vacation has been a paradise for us and healthy for our marriage. We get so stuck in our day-to-day lives and the monotony of working, being with the kids, and then going to bed. It's the same ole thing week to week. Though I love our lifestyle and going home to my family after being at the hospital all day, getting away from Texas was just what we needed. Emily and I are doctors and work long hours, and there have been days when we only get five minutes alone before passing out from exhaustion. Though we didn't expect canceled flights, I can't complain. Being stuck in Hawaii for a few extra days hasn't been the worst thing.

"Then you better stop your wandering hand…" Emily warns.

"For the love of Jesus, please stop." River barrels in, looking around. "You're not *alone*."

I blink and sit up, scanning the room. "What the hell?" Drew, Alex, and Jackson are scattered on the floor.

Emily starts laughing as she leans against the headboard and brings the sheet up to her neck.

"Why are y'all on the goddamn floor?" I ask. This suite has enough rooms for everyone to have a bed.

"That's a fuckin' good question," Alex grunts as he gets to his feet and stretches out his arms.

"Don't even act surprised. I saw Drew humping someone's leg last night." John chuckles as he and Mila walk in.

"I don't know whose leg he was humping, but it wasn't mine," Courtney chimes in from the couch next to them.

"It was mine, you cocksucker." Jackson stands and cracks his back.

"I need breakfast and four mimosas to deal with you pain in the asses for another long flight." Courtney stands up and kicks Drew before stepping over him.

I grab my phone, and an alert is on the screen. "Speaking of flight…" I draw out. "Airport is still closed."

"What?" John walks toward me.

Clicking on the app, I quickly read the announcement. "The storm damaged some planes and their runway. Could be another day or two before it's cleaned up."

"Oh for fuck's sake." Kiera waltzes in with a groan.

"Well, we better go tell Mama," River says. "I'm sure the kids will be happy, though." The girls head out except Emily, who's sliding her foot up my thigh under the covers.

"Yeah, why don't y'all leave so I can have my wife alone for twenty minutes?" I raise my brows.

"Only twenty, huh?" Jackson laughs, and Alex shoves him out the door.

"Keep laughin'. Kiera told me that's twice as long as you," Emily retorts.

"Fuckin' lies!" he howls from the other room. "Lies!"

When the hotel door slams shut, I blow out a breath. "*Finally.*"

I pull up the covers, climb over my wife, and make love to her for *much* longer than twenty minutes.

By the time we shower and get ready for the day, it's almost noon. The grandkids are all hanging out in my parents' suite, shoving junk food in their mouths and watching TV.

"About time," Courtney scolds when we enter.

"Had to prove a point." I puff out my chest and glare at Jackson.

He rolls his eyes and scoffs. "Fifty bucks he's a two-pump chump, then they fell back asleep."

"Jackson Bishop!" Mom rounds the corner and smacks him upside the head. "We don't talk like that, especially not in front of the children."

"Sorry, Ma." The sorry-ass rubs the spot she hit, then Mama walks away, shaking her head. You'd think she'd be used to this by now.

"If you want a real bet, we should have a race," Drew suggests.

"I'm not liking the sound of that." I sigh.

"I'm in!" Jackson fist pumps the air before we get more details.

"You're worse than the kids." Mila shakes her head.

"I'm not even surprised anymore." Kiera chuckles. "Children didn't make them grow up; they just have someone new to play with."

Before Drew explains, the little ones start getting antsy and want to go outside.

"Dad and I will take them to the inside pool soon," Mama tells us. River volunteers to tag along and help.

After we've finished eating and the kids have cleared out, Drew rubs his hands together. "Alright, ready? We're having a chair tag race."

Shaking my head, I cross my arms over my chest. "A what?"

Drew shrugs with a shit-eating smirk. "Yeah, my partner and I do it at work all the time."

"Oh really?" Courtney tilts her head. "All those 'long hours' of paperwork, right?"

Drew grins. "Right."

Moments later, we're standing in a long empty hallway with four desk chairs as Drew explains the setup. Mila volunteers to be the referee while the rest of us get into two teams of four.

"One person sits, and the other pushes until you reach your other teammates, then they continue to the finish line. First ones there win," Drew says with a nod

When we're all ready, Mila raises her arms and announces, "Ready, set, go!"

I push Emily's chair as fast as I can with Drew and Courtney next to us. We're on opposing teams, so I bump my body into Drew's, hoping to slow him down.

"Quit being a cheater!" Courtney shouts as she holds on tight.

"Go, faster, faster!" Emily laughs, keeping her legs up as I speed forward.

As soon as we get to John, Alex takes off like lightning. Then Jackson charges Kiera's chair, and soon, they're racing toward Mila.

"Better watch out," John warns Mila as Alex body bumps Jackson into the wall.

"Motherfucker," he hisses, pushing right back.

Alex's legs slide out, causing a ripple effect when he trips Jackson and loses his balance. The entire scene is hysterical, and Courtney and Emily are buckled over laughing.

"Fuck." Jackson gets to his feet before Alex, and Kiera squeals as he sprints.

"Go!" John shouts at Alex.

A few feet before the finish line, Alex pushes the chair into the other, and they flip over. All four of them fall to the floor, struggling to get back up.

"You asshole." Kiera swats at Alex. "Coulda killed me."

"Screw this," Courtney says before rushing forward. Drew

quickly follows, and the two of them grab one of the chairs. He pushes her to the finish line, and she raises her hands in victory.

"Yeah baby! Eat cow shit, suckers!"

"That's cheating!" John holds out his hand at them. "Doesn't count."

Courtney stalks back, shaking her head with a grin. "Didn't say in the rules I couldn't take their spots if they fell, now did it?"

"There weren't any rules," Emily argues as we make our way toward them.

"Exactly." Courtney shrugs.

Before we can continue arguing over who won and who cheated, a guy in a suit rounds the hallway and comes toward us. "Hey!"

"Shit." I grab Emily's hand. "Time to go!" We run away from him, leaving the chairs behind.

"Get back here!" the guy yells.

The nine of us take off like we're teenagers who snuck into an abandoned building. We rush around another corner and sprint toward my suite.

Once we're inside and the door closes, laughter fills the room as we catch our breaths.

"Mama's gonna kill us for good this time," Alex says.

Jackson chuckles. "Wouldn't be the first time."

CHAPTER FOUR

JOHN

DAY 4

BEING in Hawaii with Mila and the girls has been an amazing family vacation, but I'm ready to go home. Back to my B&B, my own bed, and Mama's Southern home cooking.

We should've been on our flight to Texas two days ago, but now we have to try and reschedule as soon as the airport reopens.

"I'm bored," Maize tells me for the fifth time in an hour. You'd think at eleven, she'd take advantage of the endless screen time, but she's eager to get back into a routine like the rest of us. She loves baking and helping the cooks at the bed and breakfast.

"I'll play with you," Mackenzie says sweetly.

"Go away, rat."

"Maize," I scold. They're only three years apart, but for the past six months, Maize's been in a whole mood. The girls used to play together all the time, and we'd have to constantly remind them to stop talking and go to sleep, but things have changed.

"Well, I don't want to play *baby* games." Maize crosses her arms with an eye roll—another new gesture of hers we've been gifted recently.

"I'm not a baby!" Kenzie whines.

"Then stop acting like one." Maize sticks out her tongue.

I scrub my hands over my face, blowing out a frustrated breath.

"Okay, you stay here and pout," I tell Maize. "Kenzie and I are gonna find something fun to do."

"Whatever," she mutters.

"Put on your shoes, and we'll go out."

Kenzie smiles wide, then rushes around to look for them.

"Girls bickerin' again?" Mila asks as I walk into the other room, wrapping her arms around my waist. "Pre-teen hormones are fun, aren't they?"

I pull her against my chest and kiss her forehead. "Yep. What terrifies me the most is that in a few years, we'll have two of them with attitudes."

"And then our house will be filled with doors slamming and high-pitched 'I hate you's.'"

"Can't we just make them live with Mama during those years? She's more experienced and would whip them into shape."

Mila pulls back slightly. "Please. We know how well that worked out for y'all. Also, she's a softy for her grandchildren."

My shoulders shake with laughter. "Got that right. Twelve of them and she's *still* begging for more."

"Don't worry, school starts in two weeks." She winks, and I press my lips to hers.

"Ooh yes, I love it when you talk dirty to me."

Mila giggles as we get lost in each other. I capture her mouth and slide my tongue between her lips.

"Ew, gross. Get a room."

We break apart and see Maize in the doorway.

"We're in a room," I mock.

"Kenzie is looking for you. Hurry up before she blows a blood vessel," she says, then spins on her heels and leaves.

"Lord, bless the man who's able to take all her sass." Mila shakes her head.

"Don't even talk about that. She's not dating till she's thirty, and that's final."

Mila snorts and pats my chest. "Okay, we'll see about that."

"No," I say firmly. "The boys back home are all little shitheads who're only after one thing."

"Just like you and your brothers were," she sing-songs as she walks to the vanity and sits.

"No, that's different," I argue, my hands balling into fists at the thought.

Mila glares at me in the mirror. "I don't know what you're even worrying about. Maize will chew any boy up, then spit him out. Plus, I'm pretty sure I overheard Riley telling his friends that his cousins were off-limits to tease or crush on." She laughs. "In fact, it was quite cute."

I narrow my eyes at *cute*. "He's twelve. What does he know about girls?"

"He's Alex's son. Don't be surprised if he's married with a baby in ten years."

I nearly choke at the thought because that means my girls aren't too far behind. "Fuck that. We'll lock down the ranch and homeschool them all."

Mila stands, then turns toward me, patting my cheek. "I think you've been cooped up for far too long. You need some fresh air, so why don't you take Kenzie for a walk through the inside garden?"

"Dad!" Kenzie yells as if on cue. "Are you comin'?"

"Be right out, baby."

I slide on my shoes and grab a new shirt. "Maybe perform an exorcism ritual to bring back my nice little girl before I come back?"

"Don't worry. I know the cure for hormonal blues. We'll watch a chick flick and talk about boys."

"Mila," I growl, wrapping a hand around her neck.

"Kidding. Go. Have fun." She shoos me away.

I kiss her, then find Kenzie in the living area clicking through the channels. "Ready?"

She jumps up eagerly. "Yep!"

Grabbing her hand, we head for the door and walk out into the hallway. "You're not gonna turn boy crazy and start hating your parents too, are you?"

Kenzie wrinkles her nose. "Nah. Boys are dumb."

I give her a high-five. "That's my girl. Promise to remember that in a few years, alright?"

She giggles. "Okay, Dad. Whatever you say."

CHAPTER FIVE

JACKSON

DAY 5

KIERA CLOSES her eyes and hums as I scrub the soapy washcloth over her soft skin. The stream of hot water falls on us as we take a shower and enjoy the only alone time we'll get today. We'll be boarding a plane back to Texas shortly and will be in work mode.

"Lower," she whispers, my chest to her back.

I smirk at her demand, then bring it between her legs. "Here?"

"Mm-hmm."

Dropping the cloth, I cover her pussy with my hand and slide a finger up her slit. "Very, very dirty."

"Yes, *very*."

I circle her clit with one hand and cup her breast with the other. She rocks against my erection, driving me insane.

"Dad!" The door whips open. "I can't find my iPad." Knox stands in the doorway.

I yank my hands off Kiera and do my best to cover her while shielding myself.

"Dad!" Kane waltzes in next, then grimaces. "You're in there together? Yuck!"

"Boys, get out," I say firmly. Their seven-year-old eyes don't need to see their parents naked in the shower. "You don't just barge in when someone's in here."

"Why not? Mom does it to us all the time," Knox argues.

"Boys, go help your sister get dressed," Kiera chimes in from behind me.

"I'm already dressed. See!" Kaitlyn enters next wearing a princess tiara and pink cowboy boots in only her underwear. At only four, she basically runs our household. Not only is she the only girl of the three, but she's also the youngest grandchild.

"Kids, out," I say sternly. "We'll be done in five minutes."

"Geez, fine," Kane mutters.

Once they finally leave, I turn to Kiera, and she's full-on laughing.

"What?"

"They're just so damn cute; it's hard to yell at them."

"That's your fault. They all got your looks." I wrap my arms around her waist and pull her closer.

"But they got your crazy personality."

"Fuck yeah, they did, which is why it's so hard to discipline the little shits when they do the same stupid stuff I did at their ages."

"Sometimes, I think they just like to test you to see how much they can get away with, or it's payback for all the heart attacks you gave your parents over the years."

"Or the rascals just like hearing me yell because they think it's funny to see me lose my temper."

"Hmm...maybe. You do have a pretty sexy dad voice, though. I'd let you put me over your lap and spank me," she taunts, waggling her brows.

"Don't even start..." I warn. "We have thirty seconds before they barge in here again."

"Then you better make those seconds worthwhile, cowboy." She licks her lips, taunting me with her beautiful eyes and sexy body. Kiera lowers her hand to my cock, strokes it a few times, and then I give her the fastest orgasm of her life.

Once we've finished packing, we meet everyone in the hotel lobby. I look around and soak it all in. It's been a crazy couple of weeks. We did something new or adventurous every day besides the four we were stuck inside. The tropical storm took out a couple of windows near the front entrance and downed some surrounding trees, making a huge mess around the resort, but at least the airports are open. I actually didn't mind the added days to relax before going back to the ranch. The second we get home, it'll be a complete one-eighty. Spending this quality family time was a nice change.

"Let's do one last family photo before the bus comes," Courtney suggests.

We gather around the fountain in the front while she asks one of the staff workers to take a picture for us. I wrap my arm around Kiera's waist and pull her in close while we wait. "Too bad we weren't stuck here for one more night."

"Why? I thought you were eager to get back to the ranch?"

"Because I'd pay Maize and Elle twenty bucks to babysit, so we had one more night alone," I tell her.

She arches a brow. "Oh really? And what would your plans for us be?"

Leaning in, I brush my lips against her ear. "I didn't pack lube for nothing…"

"Jackson!" She blushes.

I lick my lips. "And then I'd—"

"Dad! Look!" Knox yanks on my shirt, and I pull away to look at him, grunting.

Kids. The biggest cockblockers.

"What?"

He points up at the sky. "An airplane! Is that one ours?"

Inhaling a breath through my nose, I remind myself not to be upset that my son just interrupted sexy talk with my wife to ask about a goddamn plane.

"I don't know, buddy. Maybe."

"Alright, y'all...get into position." Courtney claps her hands as she returns with someone to take the shot. "We only have a few minutes, so look at the lady, smile, and don't move."

It takes at least five tries before everyone gives up and parts. Courtney texts it to us, and then moments later, the bus arrives.

"I'm gonna miss this place," Kiera says as we board. "We made such great memories here."

"Sure did, baby," I say as we find our seats. "But don't worry. I promise we'll make many more."

She smiles sweetly at me as she puts Kaitlyn on her lap. "I love you."

"I love you too." I lean in for a kiss.

"Blech." Kaitlyn wiggles between us.

She jumps into my arms. "Blech? You give Mommy kisses. Why can't I?"

"Because you're a boy."

My brows raise. "Remember that in ten years, Katie Kat."

"She has two older brothers. Boys would be stupid to mess with her or break her heart." Kiera chuckles.

Thinking back to when Courtney was younger and how we scared guys off has me cracking up. "Yep. She'll wanna kill them for it, but they'll protect her as though their life depends on it."

"I don't doubt that one bit. In fact, I almost feel sorry for her, knowing what's to come."

"Well, let's hope we don't have to find out anytime soon. You stay little, okay?" I tell Kaitlyn.

She giggles. "Okay, Daddy."

"That's my girl." I kiss her chubby cheek.

After an ungodly number of hours later, we finally make it back to the ranch. We're exhausted but have to get up at five a.m. for morning duties. However, looking at my three precious kids happily passed out in their beds with sun-kissed cheeks makes it more than worth it. Hawaii was an experience of a lifetime.

ABOUT KENNEDY FOX

Brooke Cumberland & Lyra Parish are a duo of romance authors who teamed up to write under the USA Today Bestselling pseudonym, Kennedy Fox. They share a love of Hallmark movies & overpriced coffee. When they aren't bonding over romantic comedies, they like to brainstorm new book ideas. One day, they decided to collaborate and have some fun creating new characters that'll make you blush and your heart melt.

www.kennedyfoxbooks.com

TWISTERS, CAVITIES, AND
Dirty Little Secrets

CHARITY FERRELL

CHAPTER ONE

WILLOW

"Move to Iowa, you said," I tell Dallas when he joins me in the basement. "There will be tornados, you didn't say."

My husband scratches his scruffy cheek while tornado sirens blare outside. "That part must've slipped my mind."

"A heads-up that I might get *Wizard of Oz*-ed here would've been nice. It sounds like the wind is ready to blow the house down."

"Baby, I wanted you to move here." A smirk plays at his lips. "Twister stories wouldn't have benefitted my argument."

"I want a refund."

He wraps his muscular arms around my waist and pulls me toward him. "You love me too much to leave, *and* you love Blue Beech—even with its lack of Starbucks and sushi restaurants. Not once in ten years have you mentioned moving back to California."

"Eh, I think it's the cupcake shop keeping me here. Your girl does love her sugar."

He chuckles, cupping my jaw to tilt my head up, and presses his lips to mine. "We both know that's not the best thing keeping you here."

Tingles sweep up the back of my neck, and I smile against his mouth.

Even after ten years and two children, this man—with his smooth sexy voice, his rough hands that have explored and pleased every inch of my body, and the way his dark eyes meet mine, as if I own his world—will never fail to turn me on.

Never fail to remind me how much he loves me.

How much I love him.

How even after the obstacles we've gone through, no matter what, we have each other.

My tongue slides along the crease of his lips as I return his kiss.

"Ew! Gross!" Maven says, walking out of the den. "What did I tell you about the basement? It's a PDA-free zone." She shudders, signaling between her father and me. "That smooching is most definitely PDA."

Dallas gives me a quick peck before pulling away and smiling at his daughter. "My bad, my bad."

Maven grins, pulling her brown hair into a high ponytail. "I'll let it slide just this once since you're buying me a Mustang for my birthday next month."

"You're not getting a Mustang as your first car," Dallas argues.

Maven glances at me, and I draw a line across my throat, telling her to shush—fully aware I'm about to be called out. "Willow looked at different models with me and said she thought I deserved it."

I throw up my arms when Dallas's attention shifts my way. "What? She has all A's, stays out of trouble, *and* she's student body president." I'd planned to discuss this after a night of wining, dining, and a blowjob, but here goes. If I get swept away like Dorothy, at least Dallas will know my opinion on getting Maven her dream car.

Since I started dating her father, my mission has been to become a great mother for her. She isn't just my stepdaughter. I see her as one of my own and love her just as much as my boys.

"I'm not buying you an expensive car to wreck," Dallas continues.

Maven crosses her arms. "I won't wreck anything, Dad! I aced driver's ed, and Willow lets me drive her car nearly every day since I got my permit."

"It's true," I say with a nod. "She's turned into quite the chauffeur for me."

"How about we discuss this when there isn't a tornado possibly headed in our direction?" Dallas asks.

"Agreed," I reply, and Maven gives us a thumbs-up.

He'll cave. Maven will have a shiny *used* Mustang on her sixteenth birthday.

Unbeknownst to me, and my lack of Iowa research, I had no idea I was moving into tornado fucking alley when I agreed years ago. The majority of Blue Beech residents, excluding the dramatic yours truly, didn't freak out when the sirens wailed through the streets. That changed last year when two twisters touched down and damaged several homes. My tornado anxiety increased, and I've become the president of the Twister Preparedness Club.

Club Members: 1

Rather be safe than sorry.

"I'm off to go look at Mustangs on my iPad," Maven calls over her shoulder as she strolls back to the den. "Samuel and Easton are watching TV with me."

"Thank you." I smile. "They love being with you. It takes their mind off the situation."

Samuel and Easton, our sons, love their big sister, and Maven doesn't mind them tagging along with her. Samuel recently turned ten, and Easton is five.

"One more thing," Dallas says, and Maven peeks back at us. "No shows over PG. Samuel ratted you out on watching *Sons of Anarchy*."

"Fine," Maven groans. "I'll put on some old Disney movies and lecture my little brother on not being a snitch."

She asks the boys what they want to watch when she returns to the den. Last year, we allowed her to move into the basement bedroom, and the basement has become her personal space, with the exception of tornado events. There's her bedroom, a full bathroom, den, and TV area—all perfect places for her to hang out with her friends.

I grab my bottle of water from the table, plop down on our white sectional, and sigh. "Fingers crossed this storm blows over."

Dallas falls down behind me, his strong chest pressing into my back, and I relax against him—his presence like a lavender bath to me. "From what it looks like, it'll pass us."

"Party is here!"

Lauren comes strolling down the stairs with her husband, Gage, and their daughters, Ruby and Ava, behind her.

Dallas's mouth hits my ear. "You invited my sister?"

"Lauren invited Lauren," I reply. "She doesn't have a basement, remember?"

"Yes, but she usually goes to my parents'."

I shrug. "She texted and said she was coming here tonight."

Maven skips out of the den and hugs Lauren before grabbing Ava and Ruby by the hands. "You want to hang out with us? I made a pillow fort, put down sleeping bags, and we're watching movies!"

Ava, their youngest and the same age as Easton, shyly peeks up at Lauren before biting into her lip and nodding. Lauren kisses the top of her head, and the three girls retreat to the den.

"She gets a little spooked with the sirens," Lauren says as she and Gage walk toward us.

"Easton was the same when we used to make him stay in here with us, but once we allowed him to be a *big boy* and hang out in the den with Maven, he's relaxed," I say.

"The girls love hanging out with Maven," Gage says, wearing a black *Blue Beech PD* tee. "They were ecstatic when we told them we were coming here."

Dallas rests his chin in the crook of my neck. "Speaking of that, why didn't you go to Mom and Dad's?"

I nudge him with my elbow.

"What?" he asks. "Not being rude. They're welcome here whenever, but Momma Barnes might take it personal."

"Your sister is …" Gage pauses while glancing at Lauren. "Avoiding your parents at the moment."

"What? Why?" I ask.

Lauren rummages through her big ass purse and drags out a bottle of whiskey, causing a tampon and her nurse ID badge to fall onto the floor. "I brought the goods. There's no way I can answer that question sober."

"You took the time to grab the booze before a tornado?" I shake my head and laugh.

"Nope, I snagged it on my way to the basement from your kitchen."

"Sorry to intrude," Gage says, tipping his head toward his wife. "And for the theft of liquor."

"Lauren has been stealing my alcohol since she was a freshman in high school," Dallas replies. "No shit has changed."

Lauren holds up the bottle. "Whiskey anyone?"

"It wouldn't be a Barnes hangout without whiskey." I tip my head back, grin, and press my lips against Dallas's jaw.

Dallas pulls my head back farther, his gaze hitting mine. "Mmm, I love when you drink whiskey."

"Uh, do you remember the first *and only* time I drank whiskey with you?" My stomach tingles as memories of that night flash through me—the good and bad ones.

"Yes, baby." He drags a finger across my lips and smirks. "I knocked you up."

"Those are some memories," Lauren says. "I almost got evicted the night you found out and came pounding on my apartment door." She twists open the whiskey cap. "I believe that deserves a shot for me."

Gage shakes his head. "As you can see, my wife is being quite the adult this evening."

Lauren glares at him. "I'm grieving, thank you very much."

"Grieving what?" I ask.

"My relationship with my parents."

"You need to elaborate on that," Dallas says.

"Not sure if you want her to elaborate on that, man." Gage scrubs a hand over his face.

Lauren takes a long swig of the whiskey and squishes her face together as she pulls the bottle back.

"You do know there's a possibility of a tornado?" Dallas asks her.

"Sure do," Lauren replies.

"Why are you drinking like you're back in college?"

"Should I tell them?" Lauren's attention snaps to Gage.

"Are you sure you want to tell anyone?" he replies.

"I think you should tell us," I input, squirming in my seat. I love me some good gossip.

"Get this." She takes another drink, and just as she's about to explain herself, the power flickers.

Flickers again.

Goes out.

"Shit," Dallas hisses before glancing around. "I guess we finally have a plus side of you spending thousands on candles."

"Told you it'd pay off." I have dozens of candles lit around the room, and a few battery-operated ones in the den for the kids.

"Let me grab the radio." Dallas squeezes my waist before gently moving me off his lap, stands, and walks to the utility room.

Maven comes out, nearly tiptoeing, the light of her iPad shining through the dim room. "Lights and the TV are out in the den, but we're good."

"Are the kids scared?" I ask, jumping to my feet.

"Nope. Everyone except Samuel is asleep, and he'll watch a movie with me on here." She holds her iPad in the air as she returns to the den.

"No surprise there," Gage says. "Storms make our kids sleepy."

Dallas sets the radio on the coffee table and plays with the knob until our local station is static free. The newscaster rambles about reports of power outages but confirms no tornados have touched down near us.

Dallas grips my waist, pulling us to back to the couch, and I fall onto his lap, his arms circling my hips. "You good, baby?"

I nod, biting into my lip, warmth spreading through me. He knows how much storms scare me, and he never fails to make sure I'm comfortable during them.

Lauren and Gage join us on the other end of the sectional. Lauren cradles the whiskey bottle in her arms like a baby and stretches her legs across Gage's lap.

"You guys were going to tell us something." I wiggle my fingers toward them.

"I think the power going out was a sign it shouldn't be said." Gage squeezes Lauren's ankle before massaging her bare feet.

"By the way you're drinking, I'll drag it out of you sooner or later," I tell her. "You might as well spill the tea now, sis."

Lauren points the bottle toward us before blowing a loose strand of her dark hair away from her face. "*Well,* Ava has to drop out of kindergarten, and we can no longer see my parents."

"Elaborate please," Dallas says, fully interested on the *parent* part. The Barnes family is as tight-knit as they come.

"We had a situation," Gage drawls.

Dallas cocks his head to the side. "What kind of situation?"

"Two nights ago …" Lauren clears her throat. "Ava walked in on us … uh …"

"Banging?" I ask.

"New fucking subject if that's the case," Dallas hisses.

"We weren't exactly *banging*. She walked in on us while his penis was in my mouth."

"New fucking subject," Dallas grits out, his back straightening behind me. "Big brother over here."

"I already have the bad part out of the way," Lauren says with another drink and shrug.

"No, it gets worse," Gage inputs.

"Do you know how hard it is explaining why his dick was in my mouth?"

Dallas's arms leave my waist, and he covers his ears while cursing under his breath.

I grab my water and take a gulp while giving her my full attention. "So, what did you do?"

Lauren's face scrunches up before she answers. "I told her that Daddy was giving Mommy a cavity check."

I spit out my drink, water drizzling from my mouth onto my shirt and Dallas's pants. "You're joking?"

Dallas, who obviously wasn't covering his ears fully, bursts out in laughter.

Lauren throws her arms out. "I didn't know what else to say! It's the first thing that came to mind. I told her and then walked her back to bed, hoping she'd forget it in the morning."

"I've heard shit like that happens all the time," Dallas says, his tone comforting. "She'll forget about it. Hell, she probably has already."

"Leave it to our daughter not to forget," Gage says with a chuckle.

"What happened?" I ask.

"Ava goes to school, and I get a phone call from her teacher asking us to come in. We do, and she says that Ava told her that her daddy was giving Mommy a mouth check with his private parts, and she hoped I didn't have any cavities."

I spit out my water again. Jesus, *I need to give the water a rest until this story is finished.*

"Yes, so not only did I have to figure out a believable story to Ava when she walked in on me giving her father a blow job, but then I had to explain why my child knew what a blow job was to her teacher." She takes another drink. "Talk about humiliating."

"Oh, it gets better," Gage says, sounding like the guy in those cheesy infomercials.

"No, it gets worse," Lauren grumbles.

"How can it get any worse?" is my next question.

Lauren sets the whiskey onto the coffee table, takes a deep breath, and relaxes her shoulders. "Last night, we had dinner at Mom and Dad's. Before we left our house, I made it clear to Ava that she was never to speak about what she saw again. If so, she'd be grounded from her iPad and any playdates. Everything was going great. Ruby talked about school, and Ava told them what she wanted for Christmas, but once dinner started, it went to hell. Dad, being a strict dad, asked her to put her iPad away. You want to know what she told him?"

My hand flies to my mouth. "Oh, God."

"She told him that Mommy said she can have her iPad as much as she wants as long as she doesn't tell anyone Daddy's private parts were checking Mom's mouths for cavities."

"Holy shit," Dallas says while I double over in laughter.

Thank you for bringing the entertainment and letting me forget about the twisters that could roll through the house.

"I almost died, not even lying," Gage says, struggling to hold back his own laughter.

"Mom choked on her wine, and Dad's face looked like he wanted to murder Gage. I stood, told Ava we needed to speak in the bathroom, and agreed to buy her a new iPad, shoes, whatever the fuck she wanted as long as she never said those words again. I'll be praying to God every night my bribing worked." Lauren laughs. "On the plus side, Gage says I'm cavity free."

"Gross," Dallas says, throwing a pillow at her. "Thank fuck we've never had to worry about the kids walking in on us."

I waggle my finger in the air and smirk back at him. "No, we've only been busted by the town preacher."

"What?" Lauren gasps.

"I doubt my sister wants to hear about this," Dallas mutters.

"Gross that it's my brother, but preacher and walking in on sounds intriguing enough that I'll act like we're not talking about my sibling here. When, where, and how did this happen? I need all the deets."

A blush creeps up my cheeks, and I'm thankful for the lack of light in the room. "I visit Dallas at work sometimes."

"Okay," Lauren drawls. "I visit Gage at the police station sometimes, but we've never had a preacher walk in on us."

Dallas clears his throat.

"Gross," Lauren says around a gag. "You bang there? In the business that's been in our family for generations?"

"Don't even start, Ms. Cavity," Dallas fires back.

"I'm telling Mom and Dad," Lauren says. "Or I'll send them a letter since I can't look my mother in the eye."

"What?" I throw up my arms. "It's secluded, and Dallas usually works alone because Hudson travels with Stella so much."

"He still has customers," Lauren counters.

"People schedule their pickups or deliveries, so with the exception of my lovely wife, I rarely get visitors."

My cheeks warm, and I rub my thighs together at the thought of the day I'd gone there. I'd been in a mood and on a mission to get fucked well by my husband.

Dallas shifts underneath me, his arm circling my waist, and his nails sinking into my skin.

"Problem is," I say, wiggling against him. "Dallas failed to mention he was working on the preacher's car as a favor."

"My bad that didn't come to mind when you walked in, took off your clothes, and dropped to your knees."

"You also like to be checked for cavities, I see," Lauren says.

"One thing led to another—"

"And you checked for cavities in other places?" Gage asks.

Even though they can't see me, I lower my gaze, and Dallas's lips brush along my neck. "I'm naked. Dallas is naked. We're ..."

"Banging?" Gage inputs.

"Yes, banging," I squeak out.

"And someone forgot to lock the damn door," Dallas says, eyeing me.

I draw back and turn to push his shoulder. "Sorry that wasn't on my mind! I walked in, and you were all sweaty and yummy looking."

"Gross, I don't want to hear that my brother is yummy looking," Lauren groans.

"Oh, but you want to hear a sex story with him?" I fire back.

"I'm pretending it's not him because I know this will be a great, embarrassing story that I don't want to miss out on."

"Our ... exercising led us to the hood of a car. We're naked, I'm bent over, your brother is behind me—" My voice turns into a hiss. "And the fucking preacher walks in."

It's Gage's and Lauren's turn to burst out in laughter.

"We didn't hear him at first, but then suddenly, Dallas stopped. When I glanced back at him to bitch about it, his eyes were wide. I nearly fell to my knees when my gaze followed his … to the preacher."

"Dude, no one thinks it's weird that the preacher didn't leave?" Gage asks. "Not being a dick, but just saying."

"I waited for him to," I answer. "It was like we were all frozen in place."

Dallas scoffs. "Frozen in place? I pulled out of you, and my amazing, has my back wife ditched my ass and fled to the restroom, leaving me to apologize while stuffing my dick back into my jeans."

"I'm sure that wasn't at all awkward," Lauren snorts.

"Not at all," Dallas says, his fingers trailing up and down my arm.

I shiver in his hold, goose bumps popping up along my skin. "You didn't tell them the best part, babe."

"Right," Dallas groans. "The cherry on top was that the car we were fucking on was his."

"Stop!" Lauren squeals. "You're making this shit up."

"I wish we were," I grumble.

Our secrets are helping ease the anxiousness of our storm situation, and the lack of light has allowed us to be more open. Not that Lauren and I aren't close. She's like a sister to me, but since I'm married to her brother, sex talk doesn't make its way into our conversations much.

"He was speechless as I apologized," Dallas continues. "I told him the repairs were on me and that I'd drop off the car to his home after having it professionally washed. I also threw in a complimentary oil changes for the rest of his life."

"What's more embarrassing?" Lauren asks. "Your kid telling everyone they walked in on me giving my husband a blowie *or* you being caught being pounded from behind on the preacher's car by the preacher."

"The preacher, nine thousand percent the preacher," Gage answers.

"Our daughter told people I was sucking your dick," Lauren shrieks.

"We're married. She told *grown-ups* who I'm sure have either sucked a dick or had their dick sucked. As long as Ava keeps it to herself going forward, we're good."

"Preacher fucking it is then." She narrows her eyes at me. "I'm a little disappointed I wasn't told this before. How long ago was this?"

"About what … two years ago?" I ask Dallas.

He scratches his head. "Somewhere around there. I've tried to forget about it."

"Is that why you always bail on church on Easter?" Gage asks.

Dallas nods. "Sure is."

"Cool," Lauren chirps. "Tell Mom that so maybe she'll forget about Ava's lovely dinner conversation."

Gage snakes his arm around Lauren's shoulders, and she laughs as he playfully drags her closer to him. "I'm just glad your dad didn't shove his knife in my throat."

"We're married. He obviously knows that we have sex," she says.

"Doubt he wants to hear about it, though," I comment before signaling to the bottle of whiskey. "I need some of that liquid memory blocker after that confession."

Lauren clicks her tongue against the roof of her mouth. "Sucks you can't go confess your sins to the preacher now, doesn't it?"

I flip her off. "Okay, Wannabe Dentist Perry's wife."

Since our minds have been on sex talk, I hadn't realized that the sirens went off, and then the room lights up. Dallas plants a kiss to my shoulder before lifting me off his lap, grabbing the remote, and turning on the TV. A newscaster stands in front of the Iowa map while spewing off updates and storm arrival times. The storm has moved out of Blue Beech, *thank God,* and we're in the clear.

"Phew," I mutter.

"Call Mom and Dad and make sure they know. I'm sure they've fallen asleep in their basement since they don't have our rug rats keeping them awake," Lauren tells Dallas.

"Why?" Dallas points at her with the remote. "You afraid to call them?"

"At the moment, yes."

I stand at the same time Lauren does. "I'll check on the kiddos."

She's behind me as we peek into the den. They're all sleeping, and I smile at the view. I love my life—the family I've created here. I've never been happier, and I thank God every day that Dallas knocked me up on our one-night stand.

Was I happy in the beginning? Hell no.

It was more along the lines of scared shitless.

I took a risk, and that risk changed my life.

Gage collects Ruby in his arms as Lauren gently picks up Ava.

"Good night guys," I whisper to them. "Be careful going home. Text me when you get there."

They agree and say good night.

"Ugh," I say to Dallas. "Have I told you how much I hate tornado nights?"

"Every single time," he answers, kissing the tip of my nose before chuckling. "You know, I forgot all about the pastor story."

"At least one of us did. That will haunt me until the day I die. Hell, it'll haunt me after death. God will shake his head in disappointment when I make it to heaven and label me a troublemaker."

"Looks like I'll be a troublemaker with you."

"Should we let the kids stay down here?"

"I'll carry Easton to his room, but I think Samuel is fine with Maven."

He quietly gathers Easton, and we walk upstairs. I kiss Easton's forehead before Dallas tucks him into bed, and I walk to our bedroom to undress. I peek up when the door clicks shut, and Dallas leans against it, wearing a devilish smirk on his face.

He runs his hand over his mouth, taking me in wearing only a bra and panties. "Now that you've refreshed my memory about the garage. I remember you saying you'd make it up to me for bailing on my ass."

I tilt my head to the side, fighting my own smile. "Oh, I did?"

He takes two long strides, meeting me in the middle of the room, and turns me around. "I love you." He swipes the hair off my neck and rains kisses along my sensitive skin. "Every damn thing about you. The life you've given me, given our children, it's perfect."

I shiver when his fingers dip into my panties. "Jesus, you're soaked for me."

"I'm *always* wet for you."

He wraps the string of my panties around his fist and jerks them down my legs. Just as he's about to bend me over the dresser, I stop him.

"You better go lock that door before Easton tells people you feed me your cock at night."

He chuckles, throwing his head back. "Good call."

He locks the door and undresses on his way back.

His hand wraps around my throat as he slides inside me, and my body ignites with each stroke of his cock.

He catches my mouth in his. "I love you, baby."

I moan. "And I love you."

ABOUT CHARITY FERRELL

Charity Ferrell resides in Indianapolis, Indiana. She grew up riding her bicycle to her small town's library and reading anything she could get her hands on. Angst is her happy place, and she loves writing about flawed people finding love. She loves the basics: books, shoes, and online shopping.

www.charityferrell.com

EMILY GOODWIN

CHAPTER ONE

QUINN

"I HAVE GOOD AND BAD NEWS." Archer lowers his phone, blue eyes zeroing in on me. I take another sip of my mojito and set it down on the wooden table next to my lounge chair. Waves crash against the shore, and I'm at that point where I'm just hot enough I'm starting to sweat, and the breeze coming in from over the ocean feels so fucking good.

"Give me the bad news first," I say, having an inkling of a feeling that I already know what it's going to be. We've been trying to live in blissful ignorance for the past few days, but it's been in the back of our minds, I know.

"Bad news isn't allowed when we are on vacation." Scarlet peers over the top of her large aviator sunglasses, a look only she can pull off.

"What is it?" I sit up, brows furrowing as the bad feeling in my stomach rises. My four brothers stand behind Archer, casting a shadow on my sisters-in-law and me. They just got back from some sort of fishing excursion while we relaxed on the beach.

"There's talk of international flights being halted," Archer says, keeping a straight face and a level voice. He's no stranger to delivering bad news to people. "Our return flight has already been delayed, and it's looking like they might cancel it outright."

"How long will international flights be canceled?" Danielle asks, sitting up from her lounge chair. Logan, my brother closest in age to me—even though Owen is just a few seconds older—goes around and sits next to his wife.

"The rumor is the rest of the month," Archer tells her.

"Should we try to leave now so we don't get stuck here?" she asks, taking Logan's hand. "If we can't get on our returning flight, it might be two weeks before we can get home."

"Oh, damn," Owen says sarcastically, dramatically rolling his eyes. He and Logan are identical twins, but their personalities couldn't be more different. "Two weeks stuck on a beach in Bali. Without children. How will we ever survive?"

Charlie, his wife, elbows him in the ribs. "I don't want to be away from our kids that long, and I know you don't either."

Owen wiggles his eyebrows and plops down next to her, sliding his hands under her waist. "That's not what you were saying last night. If I remember correctly, you were—"

"Stop!" She laughs, but I can see the tension on her face. "And I'm serious! I missed the kids the second we got on the plane. But then I was glad to have a break, and then I missed them again."

"I don't miss mine," Scarlet says, and Weston stifles a laugh. We all know she bawled like a baby the entire way to the airport even though she proudly labels herself as someone who "doesn't waste time with tears."

"At least I have one of mine with me," Rory says, patting her stomach. She's almost five and a half months along with her second child.

"What are we going to do?" I ask my husband, sitting up and swinging my legs over the side of the lounge chair.

"We'll figure it out," he assures me, coming over and taking both my hands in his. Even after five kids and many years later, he still makes my heart flutter just as much as he did on our first date…which he still insists wasn't actually a date even though he got me pregnant on said non-date. Closing my eyes, I can see us walking along the Chicago River and remember how neither of us wanted to admit just how strongly we felt for each other.

He was my older brother's best friend and totally off-limits. I was underage when we met. Yet somehow, through all the years, our feelings for each other never faded, no matter how hard we tried to ignore them. Little did we know we were fighting destiny.

"You said you have good news?" Charlie reminds Archer, pushing Owen away.

"Oh, right." Archer looks around at our large group. Even though this trip has been years in the making, it almost didn't happen when Rory found out she was pregnant, but both she and Dean insisted it would still be fun to finally take that big Dawson Sibling Trip we'd been talking about forever. "The good news is that the hotel isn't closing yet. They're allowing guests to stay until accommodations have been made."

"So basically, what you're saying," Owen starts, throwing himself on Charlie again. She acts annoyed and pushes him away, but we all know how crazy in love they both are—how crazy in love they have been since they started dating way back in high school. "We can stay for another two or three weeks."

"Yeah," Weston snips. "And we've put your credit card down to cover the cost of two more weeks at this swanky-ass hotel."

"Are we going to be okay?" I ask, chest immediately feeling tight. Archer had the news on this morning while we were getting dressed, and the symptoms of the virus sweeping the world were repeated over and over.

Maybe I'm not as out of shape as I thought, and my shortness of breath while trekking from the woods was from me being sick. Maybe it wasn't actually a sunburn making me hot and uncomfortable two days ago. It could have been the onset of a fever, and now it's too late. And if I'm infected, so is everyone around me.

"Quinn." Archer squeezes my hand. "It's going to be fine."

"What about the kids?" I ask, voice thinner than I'd like. Our five children are back in our hometown of Eastwood, staying with Archer's parents. His brother Bobby and his girlfriend Becca are helping wrangle our crazy gang, and even though it was so fucking hard to leave them, I know they're all right. "And the cats?"

Archer's family has been going to our house daily to feed my pride of house-lions. I might be checking in on them via the video surveillance on our security system more than I'm checking in on the kids.

This is the first vacation Archer and I have been on since our twins were born last year, and we have plans to go on another big family vacation to Disney World later this summer...if that will happen at all.

"They are fine," Archer says slowly, turning so he can look at the rest of our group, reassuring them too. Owen and Charlie's two children are at Charlie's parents' house, and my parents have Wes and Scarlet's son and daughter as well as Logan and Danielle's two kids and Rory and Dean's son. "We have dinner in about half an hour. Let's get cleaned up, and then we can talk more about it when we sit down to eat."

"And drink," Scarlet quips, and I look over, seeing her tightly gripping the rim of her sunhat in her hands. So much for not being nervous or missing her kids.

"It's five o'clock already?" Danielle asks, squinting in the sunlight as she reaches for her phone. We had a girls' day today, starting with the five of us getting our nails done. Then we had massages, a fancy catered lunch, and now we're still relaxing on the beach, sucking down cocktails. Well, everyone but Rory is, and I almost felt bad that she's been the DD...even though we don't have to drive anywhere. She didn't drink much before she got pregnant, at least, so it's not a big thing for her, and thankfully, she doesn't feel left out.

"You're looking a little red," Logan tells her and playfully moves the strap of her bikini over her shoulder. "Oh shit, you're burned."

"Ha. I'm not the only one," I counter.

"I don't have any tan lines," Scarlet tells Weston, sinking her teeth into her bottom lip.

"I'll be the judge of that," my eldest brother says, and I make an over-exaggerated gagging noise. I'm so fucking glad to be friends with my sisters-in-law, but it's *not* fun at all when our talk shifts from complaining about the kids to our sex lives—or lack thereof—now that we're all mothers.

Those are my brothers they're talking about, and I don't want to know a single detail about them in the bedroom. No, thank you. Gross…excuse me while I go barf now. Though Archer swears they don't discuss stuff like that, I know the situation is the same for him. And I'd be lying if I didn't have fun poking at Dean more than my other brothers. It took him long enough to stop being a big old baby and accept the fact his best friend actually wanted to fall in love with someone other than him.

"Should we call your parents and check in on the kids?" I ask, letting Archer pull me to my feet. His arms immediately go around me, and my hands settle on his waist.

"You are so fucking hot," he whispers, coming in for a quick kiss. My body bounced back pretty quickly and effortlessly after Emma, our first baby. And then Arya was born, and I was running around like a chicken with its head cut off, chasing a toddler and raising a newborn. It took longer to fit into my clothes again after the birth of our son, Aiden, and then after twins—forget it.

But my high-waisted swimsuit bottoms look better than I expected, and Archer hasn't been able to keep his hands off me since we landed in Bali five days ago.

"Get a room," Owen teases, and I laugh, resting my head against Archer's chest.

"Don't encourage them," Dean grumbles. "You're not in the room next to them, and it's not like they need any more kids."

"We're not having any more," I assure him. "We wanted four and got a bonus baby. Trust me. This uterus is closed."

"Gross, Quinn," Dean sneers, and I laugh. "You always overdo it."

"Oh please. You've got one growing in Rory's uterus right now."

Dean makes a face. "Why do you have to ruin everything?"

I laugh harder. "It's my specialty." Taking a deep breath, I reach for my mojito as I look out at the ocean. Things will be okay…I think. Until then, I'm going to need a few more cocktails.

I step out of the shower, water dripping down my wet hair. After wrapping a fluffy white towel around my body, I flip my head over, then use another towel to sop up the water from my hair. My heart has been in a constant flutter in my chest since we got back to the room, and I cannot get to dinner soon enough so I can order another cocktail.

Because I'm scared.

I'm thousands of miles away from my children and my cats, and we still have a plane ride home—assuming we can get one, that is. What if we get infected with this scary virus everyone is talking about? Our twins, Eliza and Adeline, are only a year old, and Emma is starting to show signs that she might have asthma.

My eyes fall shut, and I throw out my hand, feeling my way to the sink. I lean over, sucking in a breath. I want to go home and hug my babies and then never let them out of the house again.

Only…Archer is a doctor. He goes to the hospital five days a week, if not more. And sick people go to the hospital. I bring my hand to my face, rubbing my temples and trying not to panic. But I think it's too late.

At that exact moment, the bathroom door opens, and Archer steps in. He's wearing only boxers, having waited for his turn in the shower. He was on the phone with the chief of surgery from the Eastwood hospital while I got in, needing a head start, so I'd be done doing my hair and makeup in time for dinner.

We're eating at the resort tonight, so at least we don't have far to go. Because I took longer than I should have in the shower, doing my best not to freak.

"You okay, babe?" Archer asks, coming to me right away.

"I'm scared," I tell him and feel better right away from being honest. "I want to go home."

"We will."

"What if they don't let us come back into the country?"

"They won't do that."

"But they can," I say, words falling out of my mouth quickly. "I've seen it happen in movies. And I took a look at the virus data, and the numbers are steadily rising. If I compute them—"

"Quinn," Archer says calmly, brushing my wet hair back out of my face. He steps closer and looks into my eyes. His tall, muscular frame towers over me, making me feel safe wrapped in his embrace. "Everything is going to be okay, and I'm not just saying that. It really is."

"Can we get the kids and come back here? Say we got stuck so you don't have to go to work?"

He laughs softly and puts his lips to my forehead. "I'll be fine at work."

"How can you say that? You're a doctor! People only go to the doctor when they're sick."

"I know," he soothes. "But remember…I'm a surgeon. Elective surgeries are going to be postponed, so I'll only be operating on those who really need it, which will cut down on my interaction with patients by a lot. And I'm always wearing proper protective equipment. I'll be fine. I promise."

I blink, and tears roll down my cheeks, and we both know there's more he's not saying. Yes, Archer is a surgeon, and a great deal of his surgeries are scheduled. He'll still be needed in the OR, but if things get really bad, he'll be called to other parts of the hospital to deal with this virus head-on.

"If anything happens to you, Archer…" I can't finish my sentence. My throat tightens, and if I keep talking, I'll cry.

"Nothing will." Archer cups my face and turns it up toward him. "We're in a small town, and we haven't had many reported cases of this virus in our area yet. It's going to be okay. I promise."

Taking a deep breath, I nod. "I believe you." I put my lips to his and try my hardest to feel it deep in my soul. Because it will be okay as long as we're together.

CHAPTER TWO

SCARLET

Fuck this shit.

After working my ass off to be able to afford this luxury vacation, I'll be damned before anything ruins it, albeit we're on the last full day of lavish relaxing anyway. The kids are fine, and I keep repeating that to myself a million times an hour.

Smoothing out my black dress, I check the temperature on the curling iron. It's finally heated up, and I start curling my hair, all while repeating to myself that it's going to be fine.

Just fine.

Totally peachy.

Fucking fantastic.

I'm a master at repressing my feelings. At doing shit I shouldn't be doing and not batting an eye at it. If anything, it gives me a rush, and I find myself wanting to put on my best push-up bra, go to the bar, and charm the pants off some poor sap, then steal his wallet.

Well, I'd stop before I got his pants actually off.

Because I have my own sexy sheriff right here in this hotel room whose pants are already off…and have been off since we got back to the room and showered together. I'm running behind on getting ready because of said lack of pants, actually.

But I want to do something—anything—that distracts me from

what's actually going on. I heard Weston talking about it to Dean on the way back to our rooms. The virus isn't what he's afraid of. He's afraid of the way people will react once they're forced into lockdown and made to follow rules that only weeks ago you wouldn't ever dream.

It's for their own protection, but we all know people won't see it that way, and it terrifies me that Weston will be out there on the front lines, responding to any calls that come into the station.

But it's going to be okay.

Because it has to be. If it's not…fuck, I don't know. I can't think about anything else, which is why I want to go downstairs and swindle some cheating loser out of his last hundred-dollar bill. I'd rather worry about getting caught scamming some asshole than worry about my family falling ill, or someone going after my husband because he was trying to uphold the law.

Weston has a heart of gold and wouldn't hurt a fly—unless it was going after his family. He'll protect me until the bitter end, and he takes his oath as sheriff of our county seriously.

"Hey," I call as I wrap my hair around the curling iron. "What if we said we got stuck here but actually went home and just didn't leave the house? You wouldn't have to go into work or anything then."

"I think people would notice," Weston says, forcing himself out of bed. He's tired, I know, because I'm the one who wore him out. "We live in the middle of Eastwood."

"They'd only notice if you left the house."

"I would go crazy not leaving the house," he counters.

"But you're also the one who said we might be under quarantine," I shoot right back. I need to remind myself not to get defensive. I'm not mad at Weston, just at this state of the world . I don't deal well with pressure or stressful situations like this. Before, when the going got tough and someone came close to figuring me out, well, I'd threaten to tell their wives they were cheating on them —with me—and then I'd take my final payment and get the hell out of dodge.

I don't want to go away from Weston, the love of my life and the father of my children. But I don't want to go back to Eastwood and have him rush into work, risking his life *and* exposing himself to the virus. Now that Violet, our youngest, is in school, I'll be returning to work as well, answering phones and taking messages for the Dawson's construction business. I'll be safe in an office, away from the public, at least. Over the past year, I've slowly taken over my mother-in-law's job as she gets ready to officially retire.

"We will be under quarantine." Weston appears in the doorway, wearing only gray sweatpants, and Lord have mercy, I'm about ready to throw my curling iron on the counter and have my way with him again. "But it's going to be okay. Don't panic, Scar," he soothes, moving behind me and wrapping his arms around my waist. "I've been in contact with guys at the station back in Eastwood, and we haven't any positive cases in our county yet. And don't forget that Archer and Rory work at the hospital and will be able to keep us informed."

Wrapping another section of hair around the curling iron, I nod, blinking rapidly to keep tears from coming to my eyes.

"I know."

Weston carefully kisses my neck, avoiding the curling iron. "We have each other, Scar. No matter what happens, we're going to get through this."

CHAPTER THREE

DANIELLE

WE ARE *all going to die.*

I run a brush through my long hair, staring out at the ocean. My nerves are shot, and I can't shake the feeling that something terrible is going to happen. The feeling started slowly creeping into my bones yesterday. I thought maybe I was nervous about the plane ride home since I'm a nervous flyer, but I knew then it was an overall bad feeling about the state of the world.

Because it's pretty fucking bad. I'm scared of getting sick, of Logan getting sick, and of course about our children getting sick most of all. Logan and Owen spoke in whispers, door to our adjoining rooms open, as I got dressed to go to our last fancy dinner. If things get shut down, we can't run our businesses.

I'll have to close down the bakery, and I won't be able to pay my employees. Logan and Owen might be able to serve food for curbside pickup, but we have no idea if people will feel safe doing that, or if enough orders will come in to afford to keep the cooks at Getaway.

They want to keep paying their servers, but we know we won't be able to for long if the orders aren't coming in. All around, this fucking sucks. I'm scared of getting sick myself, of my family getting sick, or of us spreading the illness around, all on top of worrying about how we're going to make ends meet and continue to provide for our employees.

Things have been fine—more than fine, really. The bar is as busy as ever, and my bakery has really picked up business in the past year, finally establishing itself in Eastwood. I was an outsider, almost viewed as someone who turned their back on their roots in the town. But once Logan and I got married, the entire town accepted that I was here to stay, and I could finally fulfill my grandmother's dream of opening a bakery.

Setting the brush down, I head to get my dress that's hanging in the bathroom. I needed the steam from the shower to help loosen the wrinkles, and as soon as I put it on, Logan grabs me and throws me down on the bed, immediately wrinkling the fabric again.

But this time, I don't care. Not at all.

"You know we're going to be okay, right?" he says, eyes meeting mine.

I bend my legs up and nod as a breeze blows through the open balcony doors. It reminds me of our time in Hawaii, back when we were pretending to be in a relationship all while denying our real feelings for each other.

And I thought things were complicated then.

"I know." I hook my arms around his neck. "And they will be okay. Because I have you."

CHAPTER FOUR

CHARLIE

IT'S GOING to be okay.

"I don't know what people are freaking out about," I tell Owen, putting my last hoop earring in. "If you look at the statistics, it's not really that bad. Not yet, at least."

"I agree, babe," Owen says, running his hands through his wet hair. "But you know how people are. They freak the fuck out and take to social media to chastise anyone who isn't freaking the fuck out along with them."

"I'm going to be cautious," I go on. "But I'm not going to panic until all the evidence has been presented to me that would indeed cause the need to panic."

"Spoken like a true lawyer."

I put the back on my earring and give Owen a pointed look. "Fine. Maybe it is a little. But we have to be pragmatic about this, or we will fall into chaos."

Which is what I'm madly trying to avoid, because Owen and I both know I don't handle that very well. I've been through my share of shitshows before, though to be fair, the last time everything crumbled to pieces at my feet, Owen wasn't back in my life yet to pick it back up.

I'm not worried about that now, because I know he'd dive to the ground to catch the pieces before I even knew they were falling. And he'd put them back without me even asking him to.

"I know one way we can avoid all that nonsense." He wiggles his eyebrows and grabs me around the waist, spinning me and pushing me against the wall. Heat rushes through me, and I want to relent, to give in to him…just like I did only minutes before.

"You do?" I test, running my hands over his firm chest. "And whatever could that be?"

"We should make another baby."

My eyes actually bulge out of my head. Okay, maybe not, but if fucking feels like it. The subject of baby number three has been up in the air for some time, and we've always put it off, coming up with reasons *not* to try for a third and final kid. Last month, I had a particularly emotional moment when my period started, because I thought I was pregnant, and Owen was so relieved to see I wasn't.

"That's not funny," I tell him.

"I'm not joking, Charlie." His lips go to my neck, and my eyes flutter closed. "Thinking about the world going to hell in a handbasket…it made me realize even more how much I fucking love you, and how much I love our family." He cups my face in his hands. "And how I agree that it doesn't feel complete. I want another baby, and I want to put one in you tonight."

I swallow hard, overcome once again with desire. "The timing might be a little off, but I'll gladly toss my birth control pills."

"You want this, right?" Owen asks, kissing me.

"I do," I pant between kisses. "Are you sure you do?"

"Yes," he says firmly. "I love you, Charlie, and I know now more than anything, just how much family means to me. Let's go to dinner, and then come back to the room and get a head start on making that third baby."

"I love you too," I whisper, blinking back tears from my eyes. It hits me then, that no matter what happens, I have Owen, our two children, and hopefully one more on the way soon. Our family.

And we'll get through this together.

CHAPTER FIVE

RORY

I SHOULD HAVE SEEN this coming.

Everything in my life is finally going right. I'm in love. Married. We have one kid and another on the way. I have a good job, and I couldn't ask for a better boss. I get along with all my sisters-in-law, and my in-laws are the best fucking ever.

Figures it would all go to hell, right? It's what happens, and I should have been prepared. Any good story has at least one major battle in it, and maybe this is ours. Though being told we should come home from a tropical vacation only to sit on our couches while we watch TV and order takeout doesn't seem like much of a fight.

There are no demons. No orcs. Not even a single zombie. After much discussion and a collective hour searching online for flights during our last nice dinner at the resort, we were able to book a flight for the following morning. It cut our vacation a little short, and I'll admit the thought of being trapped on a tropical island for another two weeks was a little nice.

But I miss Alexander, our pets, and our house. I want to go home and have our son in our arms again, but I'm scared too. I'm a nurse —a pregnant nurse—and I'll be returning to work soon. I'm in the OR, though, and Archer and I went over the new procedures while we were waiting to board the plane. We have no reason to believe an outbreak in Eastwood is imminent, and we'll probably end up being bored in the OR, waiting for an emergency appendectomy to come in.

I did have a momentary freak-out about my brother, Sam. As an anesthesiologist, he can't really get more up close and personal with people who have a terrible respiratory illness. He's the one intubating them, and then hopefully extubating them as well. I called him crying, blaming my nonstop sobbing on pregnancy hormones. But he's not scared, so I shouldn't be either.

Now we're on the plane home and will be landing in Chicago soon. I look out the window and see Lake Michigan in the distance and feel the change in the dropping pressure in my ears.

"You okay?" Dean asks, putting his hand on mine.

"No," I say honestly.

He squeezes my hand. "It's going to be all right," he says, so confidently I almost believe him.

"I hope so."

"I know so," he whispers, leaning in and kissing me. I'm exhausted even though I slept most of the way here. Pregnancy has that way of doing that to you, and I'm glad for the lack of energy. Because if this baby wasn't stealing all my energy, I wouldn't be able to sleep.

My mind has been racing, and I have to remind myself this isn't a Dungeons and Dragons game. There are no bad guys to fight, and no one to cast spells on or go after in a group attack. Life isn't a storybook. One single day can be an entire chapter, but sometimes a day can be a single page. The point isn't to rush to the ending but to slowly turn each page and keep going.

And I know that's what we're going to do, and we'll do it together.

Dean puts his hand on mine, gently rubbing my fingers as the plane makes it descent. The last hour of the plane ride has been almost totally silent. Everyone returning to the Midwest from a wonderful vacation has the same thing on their mind.

But we're all in this together...aren't we?

Taking a slow breath, I rest my free hand over my stomach, feeling our daughter kick me in the ribs. My eyes fall shut, and I'm thankful for the pain of my baby doing somersaults in my belly.

Because it reminds me that life goes on. That no matter what, we find a way to prevail. Being scared, nervous, or upset isn't a weakness, but a part of human nature. And no matter what, I have my husband by my side, along with a pretty amazing and crazy supportive family.

And if anyone can get through this, it's us. Because we are all in this together.

ABOUT EMILY GOODWIN

Emily Goodwin is the New York Times and USA Today Bestselling author of over a dozen of romantic titles. Emily writes the kind of books she likes to read, and is a sucker for a swoon-worthy bad boy and happily ever afters.

She lives in the midwest with her husband and two daughters. When she's not writing, you can find her riding her horses, hiking, reading, or drinking wine with friends.

www.emilygoodwinbooks.com

PIPER RAYNE

CHAPTER ONE

MAURO

I WALK into the house Maddie and I are renovating next door to my parent's place. The music blares throughout the empty space. I search the first floor, not finding my wife. Since we're in between the stages of destruction and rebuilding, she's here doing measurements.

I climb the stairs. I always crave her more than usual after a twenty-four hour shift. It's like morning wood times ten.

She's on her hands and knees on the bathroom floor when I find her. Her ass is in the air and I lean my shoulder against the doorframe, crossing my arms to admire the view. Time to lecture her on listening to loud music when she's alone in an empty house with the door unlocked. Even if my parents are next door, and it's a rather safe neighborhood, I take no chances of anything bad happening to the girl who owns my heart.

She's measuring the tub and doesn't notice me until she stands and is about to step into the basin of the tub.

"*Ahh*!" She grips her chest and falls against the tiled wall. She's wearing her usual overalls and tight fitted t-shirt with her hair pulled up in a messy ponytail. Adorable and sexy mixed together—that's my Maddie. "Mauro." Her voice holds that tone where she wants to yell at me, but I was on shift all day yesterday, so she missed me too. If it wasn't for the forty-eight hours off, I'd switch careers.

"Hey babe." I step into the small bathroom. "You know the way to measure is if we both get in and see if we fit." I grin and join her in the basin, putting my arms around her. "I thought we were getting rid of this?"

I kiss her and her tongue slides into my mouth instantly. She's never shy about how badly she wants me. I have no complaints. As our kiss draws to a close, she giggles, a clear sign that she's changing plans on me, which happens about twenty times during any renovation we complete.

"I kind of like it. It brings something to the room don't you think?"

I stare down at the porcelain bathtub that'd be a bitch for me to get out of the house but at the same time it's ugly as sin. Not sure I see her vision.

"It's a clawfoot tub. How often do we come across these?" She bats her eyelashes.

I stare blankly and she laughs again, her arms sliding around my waist. She rests her chin on my chest and shoots me that look. The one that's persuaded me to do a lot of things over the years we've been together. She's going to get her wish again this time. I might tell myself that it's because I don't want to carry the monstrosity downstairs and out to the dumpster, but it has more to do with those big eyes and pouty bottom lip of hers.

"Fine."

"Thank you," she says.

"What can I say? You're my biggest weakness."

Her smile grows and my heart warms. How did I ever live without her?

"What do you want to do tonight?"

"You mean other than you?" I ask.

She squeezes me tighter and laughs.

"I'm thinking game night? Want to go to Dice and Spins?" I ask.

"Memory lane, huh?" She unhooks her arms from around me.

"And to what do I owe this special occasion?" She climbs out of the tub and I follow her downstairs.

"You did pay big money for me at the auction."

She swivels around at the bottom of the stairs. "Correction, *Lauren* paid big money for you at the First Responders Auction."

I snatch her up by wrapping my arm around her waist and pulling her against my chest. My face nuzzles into her neck as she squirms to be let free. "Only because you were too shy to bid on me yourself. Where did that timid girl go?"

"You told her to take a hike." She laughs, escaping from my hold. Circling with her arms out to her side, she looks like a little girl who should be wearing a tutu, twirling at her party. "What do you think?"

"I think it's going to be amazing. Like my parent's house without the avocado colored appliances." I walk by her to check out the kitchen to make sure the contractor we hired took down the wall the way we discussed.

"Have you thought about moving in here?" she asks following me through the empty house.

I have, especially since after we have kids, my mom would love to watch them and being neighbors would make it easy. But that means leaving the house we built together. The one we fell in love in.

I walk out of the kitchen to find her looking out the big picture window, out to the park across the street. She's retold me the story of how I kissed her there years before we ever became a thing and though I have no idea what people who suffer amnesia face, it's one memory I'd do anything to remember.

"I love our house."

She glances to me over her shoulder and nods. "Even though you don't remember, that's where I fell in love with you." She nods across to the park. We both know she's talking about the infamous night she had to drive me home drunk from a party in high school.

She pokes me in the chest, and I step back into the kitchen. "Are you confusing lust for love again baby?"

She shakes her head. I open my arms seeing the look on her face and she walks right into them. "I lusted you before that night, but that night I found out you were more than just a dumb jock."

She laughs and I tickle her, her body squirming and wiggling enough that I wish there was a dining table right here so I could lay her down and have my way with her. Having to go without, my hand slides up the back of her neck and I hold her head while I bend down for a kiss, swallowing her laughter and eliciting her moans instead.

My tongue slides in and I turn us around so I can lock her to the wall with my hips. Her fingers dig into the waistband of my jeans, like I'm still too far away. I close the kiss, my lips exploring her jaw and neck. "God, I missed you."

"Me too. Let's hope we never have to go longer than twenty-four hours apart." Her fingers manipulate the button of my jeans and her hand slides down, rubbing my hard length with the palm of her hand.

I capture her lips again, my hands unhooking her overalls and the flap falls forward. It's taken me four months to perfect that move and each time a small gasp falls from her lips. Her nipples poke out of the thin fabric of her t-shirt even though she's wearing a bra. My mouth waters as she arches her back off the wall, begging me to touch her.

Her grip on my dick strengthens as she dips her hand under the waistband of my boxer briefs. I'm aching for more and my mouth attacks her neck, my hands cupping her tits, my thumbs running over her peaked nipples. "I want you so bad," she whispers. "Take me right here."

I look around. There's not even a countertop in the kitchen anymore. The dirty floor is our only option. "You're about to get dirty. In more than one way."

"Good thing I'm not afraid to get dirty."

Don't I know it.

I pick her up and lower her to the ground, standing above her. When I push my jeans down Maddie rises to her knees, hooking her fingers on the elastic band of my boxers and pulling them down.

Fuck.

Our eyes lock as she takes me in her hand, pumping up and down, twirling the small amount of cum around the head of my cock with her thumb. My hand slides to the back of her head, and I grip her strands when she slowly covers my cock with her mouth. Inch by inch, never tearing her eyes off of me.

"Damn." I really wish I was against a wall right now. My head falls back and I relish her hot mouth working me. The euphoria crests and I'm about to go off when the front door opens.

"Yoo-hoo!" Ma says.

My eyes widen looking down at Maddie who hasn't stopped pumping me. Did she not just hear my mom walk in? Her fingertip runs under my balls. She knows that takes me over the edge. I pump into her mouth and she groans, her hand on the base of my dick expertly doing everything I love. My balls grow tight and I explode in her mouth.

"I saw you pull up." Ma's voice grows closer. "Have you heard the news?"

Maddie's panicked expression tells me that she now hears Ma and she scrambles up and rushes to the bathroom, although there's no door on it. I stuff myself back in my pants.

"There you are," Ma comes around the corner. "Where's Maddie?"

"Right here." She comes out, repositioning her ponytail. She did a good job getting presentable. "You didn't have to bring us food."

Maddie breezes by me with a sly smile and takes the dish I would've normally taken out of Ma's hands if my mind wasn't still in la-la land after having Maddie's mouth on me.

"Well Mauro was at the station and I know they don't cook well there."

"They cook fine," I say.

Maddie peels back the cover of the dish and there's my ma's famous meatballs. I snatch one up with my thumb and forefinger.

"Did you two hear the news?" she asks.

"What?" I mumble around a meatball.

"Italy is in lockdown for the spread of the virus."

Maddie glances at me. "Did you get ahold of anyone over there?" Maddie's hand runs down Ma's arm.

"So far everyone is safe, but..." She looks to me and the tears fill her eyes.

Maddie hugs Ma, passing me the dish of meatballs. "I'm sure it will be okay. Everyone will stay safe." She reassures Ma but the disease is growing more and more scary every day. And I can't deny it's about time to come up with a plan in the event that it arrives at our doorstep.

CHAPTER TWO

CRISTIAN

ONE WEEK LATER

"THEY'RE DECLARING a state of emergency and a stay-at-home order for the entire state of Illinois," Luca says.

I blow out a breath.

"They're hoping fifteen days will slow the spread," Mauro adds, standing by his truck.

He called this meeting in the parking lot of my police station because he's worried about Ma and Pa, not to mention the girls.

"I say we put them all together. They'll enjoy that." Luca shrugs.

"Probably, but I'm not sure we should even go to our houses after our shifts." I cross my arms. "Billy got it and he's in the hospital. His wife was having him strip down in the garage and then he'd go shower right away, but now his wife is being tested."

"Fuck. I'd rather be eaten by a crocodile than bring this home to Maddie," Mauro says.

"Then let's decide on whose house," Luca says.

"You have the biggest one," I say to Luca.

He grins over at me. "I've been telling you that all along."

I roll my eyes at reference to his junk.

Luca and Lauren bought one of Maddie's fixer uppers before

Mauro was ever involved and all three of our spouses lived there at one time.

"I don't feel cool about Vanessa being in the apartment right now either," I say.

"Well they all lived there once together. It'll be like a long sleepover for them."

"Lauren's technically essential," Luca says. "She'll still be working."

"Yeah but…" I try to spin it because the last person we want to piss off is Lauren, but technically if we want to keep them all quarantined and safe, Lauren would have to stay with us.

Luca's phone rings and he pulls it out. "Speaking of the girl herself." He steps away.

"I'm scared about Ma and Pa. Will they listen to us and stay in? We can deliver the groceries. They'll both need their medicine." The WHO has been clear about this virus targeting the elderly and those with underlying health conditions.

Luca comes back before Mauro can say anything. "Lauren's been laid off."

"She's essential," I say.

"Yeah but they're lowering the numbers of employees working since business will be slower than normal."

"Then it's settled. They live at your house with Ma and Pa." Mauro puts his hand on Luca's shoulder.

"Am I the only one who feels like a nineteen-fifties husband dictating what our wives are gonna do? Lauren's probably going to kick me in the nuts when I tell her what we've decided for her."

We laugh, but he's right. None of them are going to be happy we had an under-the-radar meeting in a parking lot to dictate their future.

"Then we need to make sure it's their idea," I say.

"You're the police officer so you're better at persuasion." Luca points to me.

"What are you talking about?"

Luca and Mauro share a look between them.

"Persuading people to confess," Luca says. "All you have to do is persuade them into thinking it's their brilliant idea."

I shake my head at Luca and square my eyes at Mauro. "This is your brilliant idea, you tell them."

"Fine. Let's go." He pulls out his phone and types out a message.

A few seconds later Luca and I pull out our phones to see he's messaged our six-person group chat we use when we're talking gifts and parties, or anything that involves all of us. All the dings come in, agreeing to go to Luca and Lauren's tonight but the girls are still in the dark about why.

I hop in my car, driving home to pick up Vanessa and take her to Lauren's.

Twenty minutes later, I open up my apartment door to find Vanessa stark naked on the chair with her legs flung over the side. She's got to be kidding me. She picks today when I'm scared to go within six feet of her. I could've contracted this disease on shift today.

"We're supposed to go to Luca and Lauren's," I say.

She takes her finger and drags it down the valley between her breasts. "We can have a quickie, and no one will be the wiser."

I take off my shoes and place them by the door. "I'm sure you heard the news about the stay-in order."

She pouts and I unbutton my shirt on my way over to her. She's so fucking hot. How did I get this lucky? Although, we've yet to become engaged or get married like my brothers, I still view her as my wife. This woman has ruined me for all others.

"I did and I think you should quit your job so we can do this stay in thing together." She gets up on her knees and reaches for me but I step back.

"You know I wish we could."

She leans back in the chair. "You're denying me? This is a first."

She's right. I never deny her, but an orgasm isn't worth losing her forever either.

"I'm not going to chance me giving you this thing. I deal with people all day long. I told you about Billy."

She nods, frowning. "I hate this thing."

"Me too."

"I've wanted you all day," she says. "You realize we haven't had sex in five days."

I laugh walking to our bedroom. "You should call the Guinness Book of World Records."

Her bare feet pounding on the hardwood floors tell me she's following me. "I guess I should get dressed." She disappears into the closet while I strip down to my boxers. Opening up my drawer to put my watch in, my eyes catch a Planned Parenthood free dental dam sample I took from a safe sex expo I had to talk to last month. It's a thin, flexible piece of latex that protects against mouth-to-genital contact during oral sex.

"I'm going to take a shower," I say.

"Want some company?"

Showering together has always been our thing and I guess if we're killing the germs as we shower than we should be good. "As long as you understand this is a real shower."

I turn on the water, testing it with my hand and shutting the glass door.

She moves to slide her arms around me but stops, jumping into the shower first.

I wash my hands and go in right after her. We wash our bodies down and I wash my hair making sure to get anything off me that might have attached during my shift. It doesn't help that I was a bit of a germaphobe even before this pandemic.

Once we're out and drying off, I grab the dental dam from the drawer. "Since you were such a good girl in the shower, I have a gift for you." I hold up the dental dam pack and Vanessa laughs. "On your back Miss," I say.

"But officer, I didn't do anything wrong," Vanessa imitates her best southern accent.

"I'm rewarding you for being a good citizen." I tear open the package and pull the latex strip out. Then I remember the overzealous woman telling me how to use them—put a little lube on one side, so I open the drawer next to my side of the bed and grab the lube.

"I have been a very good girl." Vanessa continues as I put lube on the one side of the latex and crawl up the bed.

"Open your legs, Miss." She does. "Wider." She bites her lip watching me crawling between her toned and firm legs, one of her best assets by far.

I pull the edges of the dental dam to her pussy she squirms. Running my finger over the latex into her folds I situate my shoulders at the apex of her thighs. She swings one over like she loves to do which gives me more room since I have to keep this damn latex barrier tight in my hands.

The sensation of synthetic strawberry on my tongue instead of the flavor of Vanessa isn't my first choice and it takes a little while before I get into eating her out. Sliding my tongue around, Vanessa's moans start, and her fingers push into my hair. Her eyes close and the more she enjoys it, the more I get into it, though I never truly forget the barrier is between us.

"Oh, Cris," she says, her hands leaving my hair and gripping the comforter tight in her hands. "Harder," she cries. "Faster."

Usually I'd peek my head up and say I know how to get her off but we're in uncharted territory right now. So I follow her directions and peek up to see her back arching off the bed. Her thighs squeeze and not being able to insert my fingers sucks, it's what usually sends her into oblivion.

"Right there. Don't stop." She grinds into my face, riding my tongue and I allow her to get the release she's been dreaming about all day even if it's not the way she thought she'd be getting it.

I'll be dealing with blue balls for weeks to come.

"I'm going to come." Her fingers find my hair again and a minute later she tugs tight and releases me, her shoulder's rising off the bed only to fall back down.

She lays limp on the bed and I sit up, holding the latex in my hand. "I would love to fuck you right now, but you are a talented man Cristian Bianco."

I stand and throw the latex away in the trashcan, wanting to hug and kiss her and crawl under the sheets, never letting her go.

But instead my hard dick points North as I walk into our closet to get my jeans and t-shirt on.

CHAPTER THREE

MADDIE

WE ALL SIT in Lauren's living room. The room that used to my living room once upon a time. My husband stands in front of us all, laying down the rules he'd like us to live by until this pandemic is over. I'm not sure if he thinks because he's the oldest he gets to dictate to everyone or what.

I raise my hand like the child he's treating me as.

Mauro actually points to me to speak.

"I'm sorry, are you asking or telling me to move in here?" I ask.

Lauren laughs. What does she care? She gets to stay at home amongst her things.

"I'm asking."

I look around the room. "Did any of you hear a please or I would prefer or would you be willing?"

Vanessa shakes her head, her arms over her chest like me. Surprisingly, Lauren doesn't have an issue with opening her door for all of us to move in. "I didn't." Vanessa says with her head moving right and left with attitude.

"Maddie, it makes the most sense. We can't very well be out and possibly exposed to it then come home to you guys. So, you stay here, and we'll all stay at our house."

That thought makes me sad. The three Bianco brothers at our house.

"There's three bedrooms. I hooked up that shower in the basement. We'll go downstairs and shower before coming up," Mauro says as if it's the perfect solution.

"Well Mr. Brilliant, what if one of you gives it to the other two?" Lauren asks.

Mauro looks to both of his brothers. "We all work different shifts. We'll barely see one another. You're honestly telling me you guys would rather be in quarantine by yourselves than with one another?"

I shrug. "So what, we won't see you guys until this is over? That's not a normal life."

"Nothing about what's going on is normal," Mauro says and I can't deny what he's saying.

I look to Vanessa and then to Lauren. "We need to converse."

Vanessa shoos her hand at the guys for them to leave. They all huff but disappear into the kitchen.

"So?" I ask.

"I'm in. They're never going to let this go." Vanessa grabs a chip and dips it. "It'll be like the good ole' days. We can watch reality television, pig out on junk food."

"Except that we converted your room into a yoga studio for me." Lauren sheepishly grins. "But there is a futon in there"

"Good enough for me." Vanessa shrugs.

"What about me? What's my room?" I ask.

"Oh, it just has a bunch of Luca's things in it. It'll give me a good excuse to get rid of his stuff without him realizing it anyway."

"Lauren," I say and she laughs.

"I'm kidding. They can put it in the garage or something. I have more than enough room for you guys. There's also the guest bedroom in the basement with its own shower."

Vanessa raises her hand. "I get that one."

The doorbell rings and Lauren stands.

"Who said you get it?" I ask Vanessa.

"I called it first."

"That's not how this works."

"Ma? Pa?" I hear Lauren say.

"What are they doing here?" Vanessa whispers but our question is answered when Ma comes in with a foil-covered plate as usual, Pa trailing behind with two suitcases.

"What kind of cooking pans do you have here?" Ma waves to me and Vanessa and heads straight to the kitchen. We hear all the boys saying hello and foil being ripped off a dish.

"Pa? Did something happen to the house?" Lauren asks.

"Mauro called and said we're all going to quarantine together." He drops the suitcases at the bottom of the stairs and comes to sit down in front of the television, grabbing the remote and changing it to a classic black and white film.

Us three girls all exchange a look.

An oblivious Pa puts his feet up on the coffee table.

"*Mauro*!" Lauren screams and heads to the kitchen, Vanessa and me following her. "Outside." Lauren points and opens up the back door.

We smile at the neighbors, Reed and Victoria Warner. Their daughter is snapping pictures of herself and recording TikTok dances as their other child plays with bubbles. Victoria's stomach is swollen again. Jesus. I wave and they wave back, saying hello over our fence. Looks like I'll have plenty of time to catch up with them once I'm moved in.

"Why are the rents here?" Lauren asks.

Luca's mouth is stuffed full of a homemade cannoli, so he puts his arms up. Lauren's eyes travel around the group and stop on Mauro. I'm ashamed to say my husband's protectiveness over us has reached a whole new level at this point.

"We can't trust them to do what we ask. I told Ma to stay in and she went to the corner bakery telling me it was no big deal. If they're here, you guys can keep an eye on them."

I shake my head but I can't argue with him. Someone has to watch over them and make sure they'll abide by the rules, so they stay safe. But while some couples will probably make a baby this quarantine, I'll be spending mine with two best friends and my in-laws. I'm lucky to have great in-laws but I'm going to come out of this quarantine looking like I'm pregnant with Ma's cooking.

"At least we don't have to cook," Vanessa says.

"Yeah, but she never understands when I tell her that I can't have all that salt." Lauren looks to Luca. He wraps his arm around her waist and lifts her feet off the ground, whispering something in her ear. He sets her down then they make their way down the stairs and have a conversation in the corner of their small yard.

Turning my eyes from them I see Vanessa and Cristian talking by themselves as well.

Leaving me with Mauro.

"Are you mad?" he asks me with his hands stuffed in his pockets.

"No. I know your heart is in a good place. Just stay safe out there. Okay?"

I nuzzle into his chest and he kisses the top of my head. I'd do about anything to ease his mind while he's out there protecting all of us.

"You'll love me with a few extra pounds right?" I ask.

He chuckles. "Is that a real question?" His finger lands under my chin and guides my face up to meet his. "You know I'm an ass man," he says.

I smack his chest. "And here I thought you were going to say something romantic."

He pulls me in tighter. Mauro isn't great with expressing himself with words, but his body says everything I need to know. We stand on the deck in each other's arms hoping this all ends soon.

CHAPTER FOUR

LAUREN

A MONTH LATER

"It's my smoothie," I say to Ma again. We've been over this almost every morning she's caught me in what she now refers to as her kitchen. I love the woman but I cannot eat one more pancake or egg or piece of bacon.

"You're so thin." She pinches my upper arm and I yank it back.

"I'm really not and I have to keep up my strength because they might call me back to work this week."

"Oh no." She pats my hand, taking the smoothie mixer cup away and going to the sink.

Okay, I'll admit I've enjoyed not having to wash one dish since Ma and Pa moved in.

"I have to go back if they call me."

"No. It's too dangerous. They were wrong about it only affecting older people. Young people are getting hospitalized too."

I sit down on the stool, watching her make Pa his breakfast and I thank my lucky stars that Luca doesn't expect me to wait on him like Pa does Ma.

Speak of the devil, Pa walks up the basement stairs and enters the kitchen wearing his boxers, a white t-shirt, black socks and slippers.

"Morning ladies." He accepts the cup of coffee waiting for him. "I'm going to do some yard work today."

"With pants I hope?" I ask.

He shoots me that smirk but shakes his head. "Yes, Lauren. With pants but what do you and Luca do? Those weeds in the patch of grass you have are out of control."

I shrug. "Luca takes care of it."

Which is true but honestly neither of us are much for domestication. If we're both off, you can usually find us either on the couch during the winter or out at the lakefront during the summer.

"I'll take care of it. The neighbors around our house are jealous of our lawn. It's so green."

Ma nods.

"Great. I look forward to it."

"It's so green you could put it one of those drinks you make." He points.

I smile and chuckle.

"Where is Maddie?" Pa asks.

"I think she's still in bed." Although I won't mention I heard her moaning through the thin wall we share. I can't complain, each of us have learned to deal with phone sex over the past month.

"I need to talk to her about that property her and Mauro are fixing up. The grass has to be sod, no seed."

I sip my smoothie and pull out my phone, not really wanting in on this conversation.

"Give them a rest. They're young and have so much going on. They'll do it right." Ma sticks up for them but I hear the tightness in her tone. We're all on edge in this house. I'd like to think Luca and I would be screwing like bunnies if he was here but there's a good chance one of us would be hiding the knives at night.

Luca's messages me his morning text.

Luca: God I woke up with the biggest morning wood. What I wouldn't do to drill it into that sweet pussy of yours.

My entire body heats and I click off the screen like Ma or Pa could actually read it from the other side of the counter, without reading glasses.

"Lauren. You're flushed. You don't have a fever, do you?" Ma walks over and I glance to my phone to make sure it's off and pray that Luca doesn't text me again as she puts her wrist to my forehead like she's a human thermometer. "No temperature," she says. "It feels hot in here though."

"I'll open the door." Pa opens the back door and a cool breeze flows in. It's like opening a mystery box every morning; cold one day and spring-like the next.

"Shut that door," Ma says.

"But Lauren," Pa says.

My phone dings again and all I want to do is cover my ears and tell them to stop bickering with one another.

"I'm good. Promise. Going to get dressed and go for a run."

"Not without a mask," Ma screams after me but I run up the stairs for some reprieve.

Luca messages me again and this time I lay in the middle of my bed, my hand already inches from the waistband of my pajama pants.

Luca: Send me a pic. Tease me like you usually do in the morning. I want to see your hard nipples poking through your shirt.

I giggle and pinch both of my nipples to get them how he likes them and then I snap a picture.

Me: Where's mine?

He sends me a picture of his erection bulging in his boxer briefs. My lady bits go into a frenzy because of the Luca drought they've been living with for the past month.

Luca: You wearing pants or shorts?

Me: Pants.

Luca: How flexible are you still? Can you inch them down so I can see the top of your ass and imagine pulling them all the way off?

He's really getting imaginative here which means he's missing my body as much as I am his.

I snap the picture although I might have to skip yoga today because of the kink I just got in my neck.

Me: Pull the waistband of your boxers down and show me the tip of your hard cock.

Luca: With pleasure and while I'm doing that, inch your shirt up so I can see just the bottom of your tits.

We both send each other pictures.

My phone rings right after I send mine.

"I tried but I need you to speak those filthy words to me. My cock is about to rocket off without the use of my hands I'm so damn horny."

"Me too. My imagination isn't cutting it anymore. Why didn't we make a sex tape?"

He chuckles. "Nothing is going to satisfy me except you. I need to sink into you and pound away."

My hand runs down my chest and it slips under my pajama pants, fingering my clit.

"Keep going," I say.

"Your tits. You'll have to ride me our first time back together because I want both of them in my hands and your nipple in my mouth. I'll grind my pelvic bone right into your clit."

"I'll ride you like the horniest bull in the rodeo."

Oh damn, I'm so wet my orgasm is just dangling there, ready for one last dirty string of words Luca will whisper into the phone.

"You're going to milk my cock so good that my cum is gonna fill you up and in nine months our baby will be born."

With the skill of my fingers I groan as my orgasm comes but it's not nearly as powerful as I need it to be. I haven't been fully satisfied no matter if I masturbate three times a day or only once at night. I get what Luca's saying... wait?

"Luca?"

"Yeah baby?" He's panting, his breathing labored through the receiver.

"Did you just mention a baby?" I sit up in the bed.

"Shit, that picture with your tits teasing me under the thin fabric of your shirt, it's doing the trick."

He ignores my question.

"I'm sliding my hand under the hem of your shirt and your tits are in my hands. I'm gonna come. Shit baby, I'm gonna come so hard."

All I hear are a few swear words and more grunts before it's just him catching his breath.

"God fucking damn it!" He screams.

"What?"

"I'm still fucking hard. Let's break this quarantine shit. I'll sneak into our bedroom."

"Luca," I sigh.

"Fuck. Well you better be prepared because the first day we're free of this hell, I'm coming in hot and I don't plan on letting up until I do put a baby inside of you."

So he did hear me. I smile, my heart warm and fuzzy. Of course he knew what he was saying.

"You want a baby?" I ask.

"Of course I do, and I hope it's a feisty girl just like my rock star of a wife. Just imagine our offspring and the competitive drive they're going to have."

I laugh. "It could go the other way and we have a chill kid."

"I don't really care as long as it's a piece of me and you."

"Yeah me either."

A knock sounds on the door, a key is inserted into the lock and Ma walks in without waiting for me to give permission.

"Ma?"

"I folded your laundry." She sets a laundry basket down and picks up my dirty towel from yesterday. "How is Luca? Wearing his mask?"

I smile at the woman as she sits on my bed, probably not as oblivious as I think about what just happened with that door closed.

"Tell Ma I love her and thanks for taking care of my girl."

I put him on speaker for him to tell her himself and her face lights up when she hears his voice. She tells him about Pa doing the yard work and how I'm too thin. That she fears Maddie's in a depression and Vanessa is shopping too much because of the packages being delivered every day. A tear rolls down her cheek as we hang up with him.

I slide to the edge of the bed and put my arms around her. Vanessa and Maddie both come out of their rooms and walk in and join us. Vanessa kneels on the ground and Maddie sits on the other side. We tell her it will all be good. The boys will return home safe, that's all that matters.

It's then I realize, she can pinch my arm and Pa can walk around in his boxers and slippers. She can have a key to every room for all I care because for her, keeping busy is helping her cope with the fact that her three boys are out there fighting on the frontline so we can all stay safe.

CHAPTER FIVE

LUCA

WHEN THE PANDEMIC IS OVER

I WALK INTO MY HOUSE. Damn did it always smell this much like food?

The past two weeks of quarantine have been the longest fourteen days of my life. I had to stay self-isolated to make sure I wouldn't bring anything home to my wife.

"*Lauren*!" I scream and run up the stairs.

She's laying on the bed in the piece of lingerie I bought her on our first non-real date. I strip off my clothes at the door.

"Damn, I missed you. Ready to make a baby?"

Her eyes well and I leap into the bed, smothering her with my body.

Home sweet home.

ABOUT PIPER RAYNE

Piper Rayne, or Piper and Rayne, whichever you prefer because we're not one author, we're two. Yep, you get two USA Today Bestselling authors for the price of one. Our goal is to bring you romance stories that have "Heartwarming Humor With a Side of Sizzle" (okay...you caught us, that's our tagline).

A little about us... We both have Kindles full of one-clickable books. We're both married to husbands who drive us to drink. We're both chauffeurs to our kids. Most of all, we love hot heroes and quirky heroines that make us laugh, and we hope you do, too.

www.piperrayne.com

QUARANTINED
with Coach

K WEBSTER

CHAPTER ONE

RIVER

"Sea?"

A giggle.

"Ocean?"

Another giggle.

"Pond?"

The squeals that follow mean Daddy has most certainly found our little Brooke and is ready to put her to bed. I'm hiding in the pantry, stealthily eating Oreos, praying like hell they don't find me.

Being nine months pregnant is tough enough.

Add in a stir-crazy husband and an antsy three-year-old?

This quarantine is going to make me go insane.

While I appreciate having the extra time with Everett, who would normally be working at this time of year, he also drives me up a fucking wall.

Breathe, River.

You're just tired and hot and stressed.

And about to freaking pop.

I rub my stomach, wondering when little miss Lake will arrive. She's due next week, but something tells me she's going to make an appearance early.

The house grows strangely quiet. I peek my head out and scan the kitchen for activity. Finding nothing, I waddle my way into the living room. I stop to pick up a few scattered toys, wincing slightly when I get a sharp pain.

Getting too big to do that.

With a frustrated sigh, I continue my trek through our house. As I near Brooke's room, I can hear Everett's voice as he reads a story to her. A smile tugs at my lips as I listen. The book he's chosen is one about the importance of being a big sister.

I peek inside the room, hoping not to get caught. My big, mean, bully of a husband who's a hardass to all his students, has crawled into Brooke's little bed. His long legs hang off the end, but he seems quite content curled up with our sweet girl.

My emotions get the best of me and I tear up. Everett may be gruff to everyone he knows, including me much of the time, but he is a big, cuddly teddy bear for his daughter. I'm looking forward to Lake's arrival. At least then, we won't have time to go crazy trapped at home. We'll have a newborn taking up all of our time.

Another pain has me closing my eyes and clutching my stomach. These Braxton Hicks contractions have been worse and worse the bigger I get. Since I got them with Brooke, I know not to panic and drive to the ER each time I have one. And because of the pandemic, I've been able to video conference my doctor each time I have issues. She assures me I'm fine and the baby is too.

I reopen my eyes to find Everett glaring at me. The same way he used to when he was my teacher and I was his student. Like I was about to get in trouble for just existing. I love that even after all these years, I still madden him in the best possible way. The dark glint in his brown eyes makes me shiver, knowing he's undressing me in his mind.

Most women worry about their bodies while being pregnant.

Most women aren't married to the biggest alpha male on the planet.

I think it turns him on to see me grow with his child inside me.

When I'm pregnant, and he fucks me, there's just a more feral, claiming way about him.

Brooke's eyes are drooping, the rumble of her dad's voice lulling her to sleep. His voice does other things to me. Awakens the female parts. Excites and arouses me. I lick my lips, thinking about letting the bear maul me later. He stutters over the words in the story and then shoots me a hot look that has my nipples hardening to painful peaks.

I leave him to his story and then slowly make my way into our bedroom. The full-length mirror in our room greets me, reminding me I'm huge, as though I didn't already know. I'm no longer able to see my toes. Everett and Brooke painted them, so I'm sure they look frightening, especially since I chose red. I can't trim my bikini area because, again, Lake is so damn big inside my belly. Everett enjoys that task immensely. Walking up to the mirror, I rub my stomach and talk to my little one.

"Almost here, baby girl."

The hairs on my arms stand on end when I hear the soft click of the bedroom door closing behind me. My stupidly hot husband prowls my way. I try not to shiver. He'll think he has the upper hand. I like to make him work for it.

"Talking to yourself, Emo?"

"I'm a great conversationalist," I tease.

His large hands slide over my protruding stomach as he crowds me from behind. I'm fully aware of my effect on him based on the way his cock presses into my backside, thick and hard as steel.

"Why do you still have clothes on?" he rumbles, his nose nuzzling my hair.

"It's too exhausting to have to take them off." Not a lie. Not all truth either. I quite like when he strips me down.

"All I heard was 'wha, wha, wha, I'm a quitter.'"

I stick my tongue out at him.

"You're too big to be getting on your knees," Everett growls. "Don't tease with that tongue unless you intend on using it."

Another pain slices through me, making me wince.

"River." My name is snarled from him, laced with worry.

"I'm fine," I assure him. "Braxton Hicks."

His brown eyes narrow, assessing me. He doesn't seem convinced, but he does continue on his quest to undress and defile me. Far too easily, he pulls off my dress and tosses it away. The clasp on my bra gets undone with little effort which is quite annoying considering it takes me a few tries these days. Once my heavy breasts are freed, he cups them with reverence.

Everett can act like a total ass, but when he's admiring my body, it feels a lot like worship.

For someone like the infamous, mean Coach Long to worship your body, it certainly makes you feel like a queen.

His lips press to the top of my shoulder before he hooks his thumbs in my panties and drags them down my thighs.

I'm naked and waiting.

He steps away, his thunderous expression burning into me in the reflection of the mirror. I watch with glee as he grabs the back of his worn Brown High School T-shirt at his neck and pulls it up over his head. With each inch of skin that is slowly revealed, curls of desire twist up inside me. The man always has and always will have the most lickable abs I've ever seen. The dark trail of hair that disappears into his basketball shorts just begs to be licked and adored. When Miss Lake joins this world, I'll give my man many, many blowjobs because with abs like those, he definitely deserves them. As soon as I can maneuver more easily without a baby in my belly, I'll make sure to reward him properly.

His scowl disappears as a cocky smirk replaces it. In a way meant to tease me, he runs his strong, veiny hand over his tanned torso, drawing my attention to the muscled perfection.

"Like something you see, brat?"

I roll my eyes, feigning disinterest. "Thought I saw a gray hair."

He laughs, rich and dark and tempting. Everett is like a villain you want to get captured by. My villain is my happily ever after.

"Your attempt to lie is hilarious," he deadpans. "And ridiculous."

"You're old, Coach. Sorry to break it to you."

With a dark, lifted eyebrow, he pushes his shorts and boxers down. His heavy, thick cock bounces out, pointing toward me in an accusing way. Even Everett's cock is an asshole.

"Lay down and let me show you all the tricks this old dog can do." His tone is bossy and commanding. It makes me want to fight him on it and make him force me into submission.

Soon.

Right now…

I hurt and I'm tired.

Wincing, I start toward the bed. He pounces on me, his hand gripping my ass.

"If you don't feel well," he rumbles, "we don't have to do this. I'll just jack off on your pretty, big tits instead."

"And they say romance is dead." I turn to look at him, kissing his handsome mouth. "I'd much rather you lick me until I can't see those new gray hairs."

Smack.

I bite back a yelp, glowering at him. "You spanked me."

"Bad girls get spanked. You, of all people, know this."

He grips my hips, turning me before I can toss back a reply. Gently, he eases me down onto the bed. That's my husband for you. One second he's being a dick and smacking my ass, and the next he's treating me like the finest porcelain. The man's got layers.

With his help, I lie back, staring up at the ceiling. My back aches and my eyelids droop, but I'm not missing this for the world. He maneuvers my legs until I've got my feet resting on the edge of the bed and my thighs spread for him.

"Want your pussy licked, my needy wife?" His grin is devious as he kneels in front of the bed.

"Mmmhmm. Hurry so I can go to sleep."

His chuckle is warm and infectious. "You can go to sleep when I say you can."

"Bully," I grumble.

"Just telling you like it is, brat."

I have an insult ready on the tip of my tongue, but then he's using the tip of his against me. A tiny tease as he flicks it at my slick opening. His big thumbs slide along my swollen pussy lips, revealing my throbbing clit to him. I can't see what he's up to over my massive stomach, but I can imagine.

It's filthy and erotic.

Dirty as can be.

His nose rubs against my nub, as he snarls. My only warning before he dives in to devour his treat. Wet. Hot. Demanding. He uses his tongue against my pussy much like he does when we kiss. It's dominating and controlling. All I can do is buckle up for the ride.

And this ride never disappoints.

A moan climbs up my throat, desperate for freedom. I keep it locked away, though, because I'll be damned if I wake up a toddler by being too loud and miss out on this looming orgasm. Instead, I bite on my bottom lip, whimpering against the delicious assault.

His teeth make an appearance, nipping at my clit just hard enough to make me yelp, and then his expert tongue rubs away the sting. Over and over he pushes me closer to the edge but easing back when he senses I'm close. I'm shaking and whimpering, fisting the covers as I pray he'll let me come.

I won't beg because he'll hold off longer.

"Want to come, beautiful?" He bites my thigh. "Beg."

"Please for the love of God, make me come."

His laughter warms me. "Close enough."

This time, he sucks and licks and bites in such a frenzied way, I don't have to worry about being pushed to the edge. No, my entire world bottoms out from below me, the chaos of my explosive orgasm obliterating everything.

I tremble hard, flying high on this wave of bliss. The bed dips beside me and he pulls me up the bed onto the pillows. Gently, he eases me to my side and pulls my hair away from my face.

"Feel good, wife?"

"So good, I feel like going to sleep now."

His hand slides over my large belly and up to my breast. He tweaks my nipple as he nips at my shoulder. "Sorry, but you're going to want to be awake for this."

He grips onto his dick and then pushes the head of it against my pussy. The eager bitch below, sucks him greedily into her warmth. I groan once he's fully impaled me. Pain quivers through me, but I refuse to let him come this far and then make him quit.

My husband can't be fooled though. He must sense my tension because he doesn't move his hips.

"River." The sharpness in his tone is one I know as worry.

"Fuck me, Coach. Just like all those times you did on the bleachers and in the locker room. Fuck me like you're trying to fuck me out of your system," I taunt. "But all you'll be able to do is try. You'll never succeed. I'll always run through your veins and in your soul."

He thrusts hard enough my breasts bounce and I cry out. His teeth sink greedily into my shoulder, just hard enough to hurt but not to break the skin. His cock slides in and out, stretching me and filling me to the point of pain. All the fiery pain is doused, though, when his fingers find my clit. It's still swollen and aching from his tongue. All too easily, he brings me to yet another orgasm.

"Oh God," I whimper.

He grunts, each one more claiming and feral than the last. I hang on as this wild stallion of a man takes me on his ride. Because the man has stamina, he keeps bringing me orgasm after orgasm until I'm nearly in tears, begging for relief as he fucks me. My only warning he's near his own release is when he curses and his body tenses. A hot flood of him bursts inside me, finally signaling his end.

Usually, I love when he stays inside me, but as if he can read my mind and understand my growing discomfort, he slides out of me. Hot cum runs out, soaking my thighs. His palm trails a reverent path over my stomach making my heart leap out of its chest.

"I love you," he murmurs. "You're the best thing that's ever happened to me."

The bully coach is also a sweetheart.

Layers.

The man has layers.

All of them are mine.

"Love you too." I turn to meet him for a kiss that tastes like me. "Always will."

CHAPTER TWO

COACH

"Fuck."

I blink open my eyes, searching the darkness for the source of the cursing. My hand slides over cold, empty sheets. A crack of light can be seen under the bathroom door.

River.

I fly out of the bed, my nerves pulsating with worry. With us being under lockdown, I've been extra stressed. We're not supposed to leave unless there's an emergency, and the threat of illness lurks everywhere. Having a toddler and a pregnant-as-fuck wife only makes the panic a thousand times worse.

The door is locked.

"River," I snap. "Open the damn door."

She groans and then curses again before finally unlocking the door. I push inside to find her doubled over and sweating, my T-shirt she'd thrown on after our shower before we went to bed drenched and clinging to her.

"Are you in labor?" I demand, rushing to her. "What's wrong?"

I fucking knew she was hurting last night when we fucked.

A whine rattles from her, tugging at my heart. "I'm fine. It's just Braxton Hicks."

"Doesn't seem fucking fine to me," I growl out. "You need to lie down."

"In a sec," she wheezes, her nails biting into my bicep. "Until this pain passes."

A snarled sob escapes her, tears pooling in her pale blue eyes.

Fuck this.

I scoop her into my arms, careful not to hurt her, and carry her back to our bed. She moans in pain when I set her down.

It wasn't like this with Brooke.

The doctor induced River and twelve hours later, our daughter arrived.

This is fucking stressful.

"I'm taking you to the emergency room," I tell her as I flick on the light and start throwing on clothes. "Let me run next door and grab Carole."

Thankfully, our neighbor has offered to come watch Brooke if and when River goes into labor, no matter the time of day. Or in this case, night.

"It's just Braxton Hicks—fuck, this hurts," she chokes out. "Fuck."

I finish dressing and bolt out of the house to fetch Carole. By the time I wake her and get back to River, my wife is pale.

"How are you feeling, babe?" I ask, hunting through her drawers for her clothes.

She sobs. "Wet."

I swivel around to face her. Sure enough, the bed beneath her is soaked. "Your water broke. Goddammit, River, your water broke. We need to go."

Her tears are plentiful each time a contraction hits. They're closer and closer which alarms me. It makes dressing her a nightmare, but we finally get her dress pulled on and her flip flops on her feet. Carole sits on the sofa, a worried expression in her eyes. Seeing her in her medical face mask only further manages to stress me the fuck out.

Of course our baby would be due in the middle of the fucking apocalypse.

"I'll call you later," I hiss out, careful not to wake Brooke with my panic.

River stops at the doorway, clutching onto the frame as she suffers through another painful contraction. As soon as it passes, I scoop her up, carrying her out to the car. I manage to get her placed in the passenger seat before I rush in to grab her purse and bag. When I finally sit in the driver's seat, she's having yet another one.

They said to time them.

They acted like this shit would be calm.

Nothing is calm.

I'm freaking the fuck out.

"Hang in there, babe," I grit out as I put the car in reverse. "We'll be there soon."

She wheezes from the passenger seat, drenched in sweat. Each time a contraction hits, she grips the dash and bends forward, letting loose a guttural cry.

Fuck.

My foot is lead on the gas as I tear through our ghost town at three in the morning. I fly through every stop sign, thankful there aren't any other cars out.

"Another few miles and we'll be there," I assure her.

"Hurry," she pleads.

The seconds pass by like hours.

We're almost there.

And then I hear it.

The train.

"So help me, Everett," she growls, "if you try to race a train, I will kill you."

As much as I want to gas the car and fly over the tracks, I'm not stupid. Reluctantly, I hit the brake and grind to a halt in front of the blinking lights. The roar of the train is deafening, but the cries of my wife's pain can be heard over them.

"Oh no," she yelps out. "Oh no."

"What?" I bark. "What's wrong?"

Her head snaps my way, terror gleaming in her pretty blue eyes. "She's coming."

"Of course she's coming—"

"Right fucking now," she chokes out.

I blink at her in shock. We're not at the hospital yet. Lake can't come now.

"I…" She wheezes. "I need you to get my underwear off."

"River—"

"Everett, now!"

I put the car in park and fling open the door. The May air is cool against my sweaty face. I rush over to her side of the car and wrench open her door. She turns, dropping a now bare foot to the asphalt.

"Help me," she pleads, her voice a terrified mewl.

Panic consumes me, but I focus on her instructions. Gently, I push up her dress and then grab onto her underwear. It takes some work, but I get them pulled down her thighs and removed.

"Now what?" I demand.

"I need to…I need to push."

"Now?!"

"Yes, now. Help me out."

I grip her under her arms and ease her out of the car. She spreads her feet apart and then lowers herself to the ground to squat. The train rushes by, long as fuck, like it isn't about to force my wife to give birth on the goddamn road.

"What do I need to do?" I bellow. "Talk to me."

"J-Just hold me up."

I grip her shoulders, kneeling in front of her. "Everything is going to be okay."

She grits her teeth, clenching her eyes, as she bears down. A savage roar competes with the chaotic sounds the train makes. Tears stream down her cheeks and then she's laughing. It's crazed sounding as fuck.

"The head's out. Holy shit." She laughs again. "Look."

I lift her dress and nearly pass out at the sight of seeing the head sticking out of her body. Now's not the time to freak the fuck out.

"You're doing great," I assure her. "Get ready to push her out."

She lets loose a howl that makes my blood run cold. A sob quivers out of her, sounding a lot like defeat.

"She's almost out, babe," I encourage. "Keep pushing until she is."

"I can't do this," she whines.

"You already are doing it. Finish it, Emo."

Her eyes are fiery as she locks me in a furious glare. Another contraction hits and then she's bearing down once more. I cradle our daughter's head with one palm while holding my wife up as she does the impossible. Her fingers brush against mine as she pushes hard enough the weight of our child eventually fills our hands. It's wet and hot as our baby emerges. I don't let go of River as I ease Lake out from beneath her, the umbilical cord slapping the pavement in the process.

An eerie silence fills the long several seconds.

The train is gone.

Our daughter isn't crying.

I pull Lake against my chest as I wrangle River back into her seat. She's sobbing and weak. With a quick smack on Lake's bottom, I bring life into our child's lungs.

She screams like her sister.

Loud, healthy, pissed as fuck.

Thank God.

"Can you hold her, baby?" I ask, my voice shaking. "We still need to get to the hospital."

She nods, tears falling down her cheeks as she takes our now squawking daughter in her arms. I yank off my T-shirt and gently wrap it around our naked baby before closing the door.

In the next second, I'm back inside the car, flying through town. Red and blue lights flip on behind me, but I am not stopping until my family is at the hospital. In another few minutes, we zip into the

ER parking bay, one pissed off cop on our tail. I jump out at the same time Sheriff McMahon exits.

"Man, we just delivered a baby on the side of the road," I bark out. "Get help."

His irritated expression in his eyes melts away. "I'll be right back," he assures me, his surgical face mask muffling his words.

Once again, I'm reminded we had our baby during the fucking apocalypse.

I rush around to her side and open the door. Lake continues to scream her pretty little head off. With our daughter wriggling in her arms, River has never looked more fierce and beautiful. Her dark hair is plastered to her neck and face and her eyes are hooded with exhaustion, but she's a fucking vision.

Several hospital employees all wearing surgical face masks crowd around me.

"We need to take your temperature," a man says.

I snarl at them. "My wife just had a fucking baby in front of a goddamn train. Take your thermometer and shove it up your—"

The man slides the device over my forehead and down my temple. "You're fine, now move, Coach." He shoves me aside to do the same for my wife and daughter. "Dr. Morris," the man who clearly knows me barks out, "the cord is still attached."

I stand aside, equally annoyed and grateful that they've taken over. I'm not qualified to do this shit. They manage to get River onto a stretcher with Lake resting on her stomach. As soon as they push her into the ER, I trot after.

"Dr. Venable," a woman calls out. "He's not supposed to go back there."

The doctor who took my temperature is Dan Venable, someone I have gotten to know over the years. Good guy. One of the best doctors we have at our town's hospital.

"He's fine," he assures her, his green eyes darting my way. "We're going to just put them in room three. I won't let him leave. Bring him a gown or something to throw on."

The woman settles at his words. "Sure thing."

Dr. Venable and Dr. Morris rush River and Lake into the room. I crowd them, unable to sit when I know my family needs me.

"Her obstetrician said, because of the pandemic, I might not be able to watch the birth of my daughter," I grit out. "That's fucked up man. If I would have missed that…" I sigh heavily, frowning.

Dr. Venable's green eyes are hard when he assesses me. "My wife and children are all immunocompromised. Try not being able to physically see the ones you love for weeks. We do what we have to do to protect them but thank God for technology."

I pipe down after that, plopping down in a chair so they can do their jobs. The nurse tosses some scrubs at me. I pull on the shirt over my bare chest but toss the pants into the floor beside me. As much as it sucks having to stay home this whole time and not get to do shit, at least I got to do it with my family. I'd go fucking crazy if I couldn't see my girls.

The two doctors do all the work, including cutting the cord and delivering the placenta, surprising me when no nurses show up to assist. It makes me wonder if the skeleton crew is because of the time of night or if they're off dealing with the sick.

"I'm going to take her to the nursery," Dr. Morris says. "She's looking great, but they'll want to run further tests there." He places little Lake in a plastic bed on wheels. "Tell Mommy and Daddy bye," he says to her.

I stand up to look at my little girl for the first time properly. Dark hair like her parents. Blue eyes like her mother. Same cute as fuck nose and mouth as Brooke.

My heart fucking explodes.

"*Sea* you soon, Lake." My girls love my dad jokes.

She cries out, her fist waving angrily. I brush my knuckle along her brow before stepping aside so Dr. Morris can take her away. Now that there's more room, I can see to my wife as Dr. Venable checks her over.

"We did it," she says, her eyes fluttering closed.

I bend over and kiss her mouth in a worshiping way. My wife is strong and resilient. She's a fucking powerful goddess. I'll never understand why she puts up with my surly ass, but I sure won't complain.

"You did it, Emo. You delivered Lake all by yourself. All I did was coach you through it."

That's how our entire relationship has been.

Me seeing the unlimited potential in this mesmerizing woman and encouraging her—albeit brutally sometimes—to realize every last bit of that potential.

"River. Brooke. Lake." She smiles but doesn't open her eyes. "What's the next one going to be named?"

I chuckle. "Already thinking of the next kid like you didn't do the unthinkable and push out a baby in front of a train."

"I like planning our future."

Smart and sassy, even when tired as fuck.

"Raindrop?" she teases.

"Too emo, Emo."

"Raindrop isn't an emo name," she argues, cracking an eye open.

"Puddle?"

She laughs. "No."

"What if it's a boy? Pond sounds too feminine."

"If we have a boy, we'll make it easier on ourselves and name him Junior."

She's teasing, but I don't exactly hate the idea of having a little me to help look after these girls.

Her eyes are soft and filled with love. "I want to name him after you. The next one. Our boy."

Dr. Venable chuckles. "Unless you adopt like my wife and I do, you don't exactly get to choose the sex."

"How many have you guys adopted now?" River asks.

Dr. Venable nods. "Three boys and a little girl."

River's eyes dart back over to mine. She doesn't have to speak. I can read my wife one hundred percent. I've been able to since the day I met her when she stalked onto the field with more sass and weird ass attitude than Punky Brewster.

She wants more children.

She might even like to adopt.

I clutch her hand and bring it to my lips, kissing her knuckle. "Whatever your heart desires, babe. You know I'm here for the ride until the end, no matter what turns we take."

Dr. Venable excuses himself for a moment, leaving us alone in the room. I take my time stroking her hair from her face and kissing her forehead.

"I love you, Everett." Her eyes water. "So much."

I smirk at her. "I know, brat. Now get some rest. Your heroine quota has been met for the day. Sleep, woman."

"Always a bully." She smiles at me and then closes her eyes.

I press a soft kiss to her lips. "Always yours."

ABOUT K WEBSTER

K Webster is a *USA Today* Bestselling author. Her titles have claimed many bestseller tags in numerous categories, are translated in multiple languages, and have been adapted into audiobooks. She lives in "Tornado Alley" with her husband, two children, and her baby dog named Blue. When she's not writing, she's reading, drinking copious amounts of coffee, and researching aliens.

www.authorkwebster.com

COMING TOGETHER
in the French Quarter
JIFFY KATE

CHAPTER ONE

GEORGETTE

"Good morning to you too," I muse sleepily, relishing in the feel of Finn's naked skin against mine.

He nips at my chin and then dips down further to bury his face in my neck, the new scruff on his jaw tickling as he skims down my body.

I laugh, squirming under him. "You're like a horny teenager," I tease, pretending like I want to get away from him, but really I just love the way his weight feels on top of me when I put up a little resistance.

"You knew me when I was a horny teenager."

Running my hands up his broad shoulders, I can't help the soft grin from forming on my lips. I *did* know him then.

And I loved him then.

"And now," he says, his voice husky and deep, "I'm a horny adult." Popping his head up, he gives me a wicked grin. That combined with his tussled, thick hair, I can't deny him.

Like I'd want to.

"What are we going to do about it?" I ask coyly.

Bracing his arms on either side of me, he pushes up and then his hard cock is pressing into my core, showing me exactly what we're going to do about it.

The same thing we did about it yesterday on the kitchen counter. And last night on the stairs.

If there's one benefit of being in quarantine, it's all this extra time I get to spend with Finley.

I hate that our city is suffering.

I hate that people are sick and dying.

It's a bit all-consuming, which is why we need this time together to lose ourselves and decompress.

Thirty minutes later, we're soaping up in the shower, trying to get clean without getting dirty again. Finn cuts his eyes to me, giving me a knowing smile. "We have to take a rain check," he says reluctantly. "We promised Shaw we'd be by to help take breakfast and lunch over to the Blue Bayou."

Seductively rubbing my boobs under the rouse of washing up, I bite down on my lip.

"Jette."

"Finn," I counter.

He laughs, taking the removable shower head down and spraying me with it.

"You little sex fiend."

I smile to myself, turning into the opposing shower head and rinsing off. He knows he wants me. And I know I'll pay for working him up ... again.

And I'll be ready when he cashes in.

Standing in the foyer, I take a deep breath. Finn and I both have our facemasks in place. We have gloves at the ready and hand sanitizer in our back pockets. Outside of wearing full body cover, we're as prepared as possible.

And this is how we leave the house every time we venture out.

The week of St. Patrick's Day, everything changed. We went from watching the news and feeling like this virus was happening around us to it being in our backyard, literally. Since then, New Orleans, along with the rest of the United States, is on lockdown.

We've been asked to stay home and we do, but we also know there are people in our city hurting and worse off than they normally are. With a shelter-in-place order issued by our government, it left our homeless population more vulnerable than usual.

That need led to a brainstorming session between me, Finley, CeCe, Shep, Carys, Maverick, Shaw, Avery, and Sarah, Shaw's sister. Since none of us are immunocompromised or at-risk, we've band together to take care of people who can't take care of themselves.

We take every precaution and maintain distance, but we've found ways to come together while being apart.

The week after St. Patrick's Day, Carys and Maverick sent Mary and George home for the foreseeable future. Jules decided to shelter-in-place at the hotel because his other places of employment are shut down and he feels more useful at the hotel. After they sanitized every room, they opened them up to people with nowhere else to go.

It's been a little stressful, but also very rewarding.

Shaw and Sarah prepare meals every day for the occupants of Blue Bayou.

Finn and I take turns with CeCe and Shep helping get the meals from the cooking school over to the hotel. Avery stays home with the baby. We're all doing what we can and trying to keep everyone safe and healthy—sheltered and fed.

"I hope Cami knows how much we appreciate her lending us the van from the gallery," Finn says, walking around to the passenger's side to open the door for me.

"She knows and she wishes she could do more," I tell him, hopping into my seat and buckling up. "Although," I continue, when Finn gets in on the other side. "It would've been fun to drive

Shaw's Jeep." Wagging my eyebrows I can't help the mischievous smile.

Finn laughs. "Always conspiring."

"Maybe we should buy a Jeep?" I muse, rolling the window down so I can enjoy what little bit of fresh air we get on our short drive to the cooking school. Glancing over, I see a small, wistful smile on Finn's face. Without looking at me, he reaches over and takes my hand.

"Anything you want," he says quietly, bringing my hand up to his mouth and kissing it. "I'll do the pick-up," he says, holding my hand to his chest. "You stay in the van."

Even though we're all taking precautions and the threat of passing anything between us is extremely low, Finn refuses to take any additional risks. Since I already know arguing with him is futile, I just hum my acknowledgement as we turn down the side road that leads to Come Again and Lizzie's School of Cooking.

When he pulls the van up at the door, Shaw and Sarah have already placed the crates at the front door. Inside the crates are two meals for every occupant of the Blue Bayou, lunch and dinner. They're stored in disposable containers and have individually wrapped plasticware and napkins.

Finn makes quick work of loading them into the back of the van and then walks back over to the front door of the cooking school and gives it a couple knocks, letting Shaw and Sarah know he's been there and is leaving.

A second later, his cell phone dings from the center console and a message from Shaw appears on the screen.

Shaw: Ham and Cheese sandwiches and potato salad for lunch. Gumbo and rice for dinner. We have some extra if they need it, just let us know.

I can already smell the deliciousness from the back of the van and my mouth is watering by the time Finn jumps back into the driver's seat.

"Damn, that smells good," he mutters.

"I know," I groan, feeling my stomach growl as it registers the lack of sustenance. Since we spent so long getting ready, we'd only had time for a quick cup of coffee before heading out. This quarantine has really messed with our schedules. I no longer set the timer on the coffee pot as an alarm, because why? There's no gallery to open. Finn hasn't worked with Lola in the studio in almost a month.

There are no streets to perform on.

There are no clubs to play in.

No restaurants to go to.

Micah sent his entire stock over to the cooking school to contribute to the efforts before closing Lagniappe up for the foreseeable future. CeCe also did the same with what she had on-hand at Neutral Grounds.

To say it's been a group effort is an understatement.

We've literally pulled all of our resources, and thankfully, we have plenty, and done what we can with them. Besides housing and feeding people at the Blue Bayou, we've all donated to any and every cause around the city. Finn and I still try to give business to anyone who still offers services. Being in a city like New Orleans, that thrives off of tourism, it's hard to watch it completely shut down, knowing there are so many people without jobs.

Shep and Maverick are also heading a new foundation that will supplement income for French Quarter businesses and employees. I don't know the ins and outs of it, but I know I'm extremely proud to call them friends.

Family.

That's really what they are—family I've chosen for myself.

As we pull up in front of the Blue Bayou, a similar trade-off happens. Finn puts on his mask and gloves and gets out of the van, unloading the crates onto the front step of the Blue Bayou. When he's back in the van, Maverick and Jules come out and carry them inside.

We're all working together like a well-oiled machine.

CHAPTER TWO

FINLEY

LYING BACK on the green grass in the backyard, I shield my eyes from the bright Louisiana sunshine. It's warm. Scratch that, it's fucking hot, but I welcome it.

I've always loved the heat.

I love the way it feels on my skin, and the contrast between the warmth of the sun beating down and the cool grass at my back is one of my favorite combinations. Georgette's soft, luscious body under mine is my absolute favorite, but I'm trying to not think about it right now. We've been going at it like rabbits over the past few weeks. Part of it is being back together, really together, after so many years apart. But part of it is all this alone time.

Unlike a lot of people, I'm not complaining.

It's like we're getting some weird version of a honeymoon, but we're not married.

Yet.

That's another thing that's burning like the sun—my desire to make Georgette my wife.

But I'm biding my time. There's no rush. And I love this time in our lives. After being apart for five years, not knowing if we'd ever see each other again, this time together feels like a gift from the universe.

"Maggie called," Georgette says from the backdoor. "I told her we'd call her back before we go over to the Blue Bayou later."

I hum my response and get a nice, wet kiss from King who saunters up beside me and practically lays on my head. "Anywhere you like, Buddy," I muse, giving him a solid pat. "Just make yourself comfortable."

"Want something to drink?" Jette asks.

"Nah, I'm good," I tell her, rolling over to nuzzle King. "We'll be back inside soon."

Another thing this quarantine has provided is a chance to slow down and literally smell the flowers. I've spent most of my life hustling—playing gigs and working odd jobs. I've never had less than two jobs. Even now, working with a big name musician in the studio, I still stand on the corners of New Orleans and play for the masses. And from time to time, when we're not in quarantine, I play at Good Times, the jazz club I was playing at when Lola Carradine noticed me and asked my boss to pass on her phone number.

This is the first time in my life someone isn't expecting me to be somewhere or I don't have several hats to wear. Right now, I feel stripped down to my bones. I'm just Finley Lawson. A guy who's in love with Georgette Taylor. A citizen of New Orleans. And someone who's trying to do his part to make it through this trying time.

"Ready to go inside?" I ask King, who raises his head and then lays back down with a groan.

If I had to guess, he's probably weirded out by this whole ordeal too. Normally, he goes to work with Jette a few times a week, hanging out at the art gallery. He's used to being social too.

"I know, dude," I commiserate, rubbing his ears. "Me too."

When I pull myself up into a sitting position and then to my feet, heading back into the house, he follows.

"Finn said to tell you thanks for letting us use the van," I hear Jette say from the kitchen, knowing she's doing her daily video chat with Cami and the baby.

"Thank you," I call out as I walk up behind Jette and rest my head on her shoulder, smiling at Cami who's holding a sleeping June.

Since Georgette moved to New Orleans and took the job at 303 Royal Art Gallery right before Cami went on bedrest, she feels really attached to the baby, which is understandable. She's a really cute baby. And she and Cami hit it off from the start. Their relationship fills a void Georgette had, Cami taking on the role of big sister more than boss.

"Hey, Finn," Cami replies with a smile, gently patting June's back. "And no need to thank me for the van. If y'all weren't using it, it would just be sitting behind the gallery taking up space. I'd rather know it's being put to good use. How is everything there, anyway? Do y'all have enough supplies?"

She's referring to our efforts to keep people around here fed, healthy, and safe. We've all pitched in, some giving more money than time, but it's all working out.

"We're good," I tell her, loving the way Jette leans into me. Wrapping my arms around her waist, I absorb her body into mine. "Shaw said they were able to place another order yesterday. Shep and Maverick told him and Sarah to order whatever they need."

The foundation they've created has really taken off and they've been able to call around, getting support from most of the local business people.

Something Tucker, Cami's brother, told me when I first met him comes back to my mind—Nola might be a big city, but it functions like a small town, where everyone knows everything about everyone else's business. It's true and some might see it as a downfall, but I think it's one of the things that makes this city great. In times of need, everyone pulls together and takes care of each other.

Jette and Cami go on talking about anything and everything and I'm only halfway listening. Before they end the call, Jette reminds her to tell everyone in French Settlement hello. Like us, they're all pulling together to do what they can.

Cami's husband, Deacon, and his brother Micah have been

running a similar operation out of their restaurant in Baton Rouge, offering free meals to the less fortunate and providing staples for those in the area at a low cost.

It feels good knowing we're all in this together, even when we're apart.

CHAPTER THREE

GEORGETTE

AFTER MY ONLINE YOGA CLASS, I went upstairs to find Finley working out in the spare bedroom we've turned into an at-home gym. For a few minutes, I stand at the doorway, watching him work up a sweat and getting worked up in return.

When he grunts as he pulls himself up on a bar, his muscles flexing and pulling his skin taught, I clench my thighs.

Yeah, that's my cue to shower.

We're supposed to be at the Blue Bayou at eight o'clock and it's already seven.

And having some simulation of a schedule is what's helped keep us all sane during the past few weeks. So, even though no one would be mad if we weren't there on time, it's nice to be expected at a certain time. We have people depending on us and that's a good feeling.

As soon as I step into the shower, I feel Finley's presence.

"What are you doing?" I ask, giving him my back as I step into the stream of water.

His husky laugh fills the steamy space. "Getting clean," he murmurs, his lips finding my neck.

We've all joked that it will be a miracle if all of us escape this quarantine without getting pregnant. Even Avery and Shaw, who have a baby, have been overly active. She was saying the other day she's even thought about telling Shaw to wrap it up because she doesn't want to be pregnant when they get married, to which we all had a good laugh.

Carys was telling us that some people are predicting a baby boom in nine months. Unlike our grandparents, who waited until after the Great Depression was over to have children, we're all taking advantage of our predicaments and occupying ourselves with sex. Lots and lots of sex.

Others are speculating the quarantine will have the opposite effect and people will hold off having babies due to the state of the world.

I've always been of the belief that a baby is never a bad thing.

Having a baby with Finley has been on my mind a lot, even before the quarantine. It's no secret I want a family, sooner rather than later. We've given it a lot of thought and Finn's on the same page. Neither of us are afraid of the idea, but we're not actively trying.

But, damn, practicing is fun.

"That's just going to get you dirty," I mumble, my eyes fluttering closed as Finn's lips nibble my skin and his hand slips down my belly to the sensitive nub begging for attention. When my body turns to jello under his ministrations, Finn holds me up and brings me to orgasm.

"Now look who's dirty," Finn teases. Turning to face him, I wrap my arms around his neck and my legs around his waist, putting myself in the perfect position for him to slip inside. My head lulls back, resting against the wall of the shower as Finley thrusts. "Oh, God."

"Finley is fine," he says on an exhale. "Or baby…" His words drift off, replaced with carnal grunts of pleasure. When he chuckles, I feel it in every inch of my body.

I love this.

I love Finley.

I love being with him like this.

When we're satiated, for the time being, we dry off and get dressed.

Before we leave, I grab a bottle of wine out of the fridge and two plastic cups while Finley gets his saxophone. As we head out the front door, masks in place, we repeat the same procedure as when we make our runs to the cooking school and Blue Bayou for food deliveries. Except this time, we're going for our new nightly ritual— socially distant drinks and conversation in the courtyard of the Blue Bayou while Finley serenades us and the rest of the neighborhood with his music.

The first night, we didn't think anyone would even notice. It felt like the entire city was asleep. With the streets bare and every restaurant and bar closed up, it doesn't even feel real. To go from something so vibrant and alive to quiet and sedated, it's a bit unsettling. But when Finley started playing, people opened their windows and a couple across the street set their chairs out on the sidewalk.

Now, every night around eight o'clock, Finley plays and we all regain a small piece of the city we love. If I close my eyes, which I often do, it feels like nothing has changed.

Once we make the short drive, Finley parks the van on the side of the road and once again, I'm reminded of everything that is different.

No cars.

No people.

No noise filtering down the street.

Inside the courtyard, Carys has chairs spread out six feet apart in groups of two. There's enough room back here for quite a few people to sit spaced out like this, but usually, it's just the eight of us—Carys and Maverick, Shaw and Avery, CeCe and Shep, me and Finley. Occasionally we have extras. Jules joins us when he's not catching up on his class work. And sometimes Sarah and Paulie walk over from the cooking school once they prep whatever food is being served the next day.

It's weird not hugging everyone when we walk into the

courtyard lit up by twinkling lights, but we're fortunate to have this space to safely gather and we know it's not forever.

I have to believe that.

I have to believe at some point in the future, we'll find a new normal that includes hugging our friends and sitting down for a meal together.

CHAPTER FOUR

FINLEY

"Y'ALL CHECK UNDER YOUR CHAIRS," Carys says to the group as she walks over to where Maverick is already sitting. "Looks like someone left some surprises."

I glance around the courtyard to see everyone following her orders, so I do the same. Sure enough, there's a six pack of locally-brewed beer and a bag containing macarons made by Carys, some hand sanitizer, and a couple of what look to be handmade masks.

Excitement and laughter fills the muggy air around us as we all take out our goodies and admire them. Typically, we wouldn't get too worked up about a few scraps of fabric and some alcohol, but these are unusual circumstances.

Now, the macarons. We're always excited for those.

"Sarah found a bunch of fabric at a local store last week and we thought they'd make great masks. We've made quite a few to donate but, of course, we saved some for all of us," Avery explains.

Looking down at my masks and then at Jette's, I can't stop the huge grin that covers my face. The design on the fabric is a bunch of New Orleans' specialties like beignets, Hurricane drinks, fleur de lis, and Mardi Gras beads and they're very colorful. There won't be any blending in when we wear these, but that's okay with me.

"These are amazing, Avery. Thank you," Jette gushes.

"Yeah, they're perfect. Thanks," I say.

Avery smiles as Shaw pulls her to him. The baby is home with Sarah, who decided to quarantine with Shaw and Avery when all of this started. So, at night, when we all gather here in the courtyard, they get a little adult time. Sometimes they switch off and Sarah and Paulie come in their place.

"I hate that we can't hug each other," CeCe whines. "And I know we see each other every day but I still miss y'all. Is that weird?"

Shep scoffs. "There is no way in hell you're missing out on physical contact." He's wearing one of his new masks but there's no mistaking the quirk of his eyebrows or how his eyes crinkle above the fabric when he looks at CeCe.

Jette and I share a knowing look.

Apparently, we're not the only people fucking like bunnies these days.

"You're incorrigible," CeCe replies. Her laughter turns into a squeal when Shep grabs her and places her on his lap.

"I agree, CeCe. I can't wait for this social distancing to be over with so I can hug every fucking one of you."

The courtyard goes quiet as we all stop what we're doing and gape at the big, burly man who just spoke. Shaw O'Sullivan is a man of few words and does not make a habit of PDA. To say we're all in shock is putting it mildly.

"What are y'all staring at?" he bristles. "You know I love and appreciate everyone here and it's been an honor serving our great city with you. We're more than friends, we're family."

Still, no one moves or speaks.

"Fuck all of you. Is that better?" Shaw asks with a growl. "Now, drink up."

As he reaches for the beer still under his chair, I hear him mumble about this being the last time he talks about his feelings. I'm pretty sure he calls us "assholes", too. Avery tries to soothe him, calling him her "squishy teddy bear" and covering his face with kisses. Eventually, he relaxes and kisses her back and the rest of the group continues with what we were doing before—enjoying each other's company and making the best of things.

After the conversation settles down and each couple is in their own little bubble, I decide it's time for some music. Standing, I grab my sax and lean over to kiss Jette before making my way to the center of the courtyard. Warming up with a few soft notes, I know exactly what I want to play.

The notes to *What a Wonderful World* by Louis Armstrong begin filling the air, and when I close my eyes, it's easy to forget everything. For a moment, nothing's changed. This could be any random night in New Orleans—the muggy air acts like a balm to my soul.

I've always been a musician who feeds off my audience and right now, all I can feel is love and gratitude. Shaw's right; we're a family and I'm so thankful I get to do life with these people.

I'm also thankful to be here in New Orleans, a city with such strength and resilience.

I know we'll overcome this.

Music will flood these streets again.

Bars and restaurants will thrive.

Hotels will be bursting at the seams with people here to experience our vibrant city.

Art will be made.

Life will happen.

Until then, we'll continue to take care of each other in the best way we know how.

ABOUT JIFFY KATE

Jiffy Kate is the joint pen name for Jiff Simpson and Jenny Kate Altman. They're co-writing besties who share a brain. They also share a love of cute boys, stiff drinks, and fun times.

Together, they've written over twenty stories. Their first published book, Finding Focus, was released in November 2015. Since then, they've continued to write what they know—southern settings full of swoony heroes and strong heroines.

www.jiffykate.com

ADRIANA LOCKE

CHAPTER ONE

LINCOLN

"I'm not getting any younger!" I shout.

"You getting younger isn't what I'm worried about."

I roll my eyes at my wife even though she can't see me. "You should be worried that I'll fall asleep. You've been in there for fifty minutes already."

"Try fifteen. Maybe," Dani says from the bathroom.

"I don't wanna wait anymore."

Her head pokes around the corner. *Just her head.* Not a glimpse of the curve of her shoulder or the tops of her breasts.

It's like she enjoys torturing me.

"Dani ..." I whine. "Come on."

"Patience, Landry."

I fall back against the pillows and sigh. Loudly.

It's her turn to roll her eyes as she disappears once again into the depths of the bathroom.

It's funny how life works. Being stuck inside a house with my gorgeous wife has been a dream of mine since the day I spotted her outside that elevator. I envisioned a lot of nakedness and sweat. Late nights and even later mornings. Movies that only got half-watched because we couldn't keep our hands to each other.

That's not what I got.

At all.

Instead, I got a national quarantine that's making things hard—and not in a good way.

Still, I'm not really mad about it. Why? Because I still have her. Even if she is being a little shit right now.

"Dani ..." I whine again.

"I swear, Lincoln. If you don't give me a few minutes ..."

"You'll want more than a few minutes in a little bit," I point out.

Her head pokes around the corner again. Pieces of her hair have been curled into big, sexy waves that makes me even harder.

"I'm going to tell you what I tell Ryan when he's begging for cake after dinner. The more you bother Mommy, the longer it's going to take to get dessert," she says.

"You get five minutes, and I'm coming in there to get you."

"Deal."

I settle back in the pillows and try to think of something besides Dani. But with no sports, a sleeping baby, and a host of movie platforms that I've already depleted, I don't have anything. I'm ready to go to the kitchen to get a drink when my phone buzzes on the nightstand.

An incoming text from my mom lights up the chat she started for me and my siblings like we're still little kids. It's kind of cute, though, in a very Mom kind of way.

Mom: How is everyone?

I peek at the doorway. Still no Dani. Her shadow drifts across the threshold as she moves about.

My fingers slide against the phone.

Me: I'm as handsome as ever.

Mom: I bet you are, and I miss that handsome face.

Ford: Just got done doing a hundred push-ups. How many have you done today, Linc? Love you, Mom.

I roll my eyes at my brother. Out of all my siblings, Ford irritates me the most. It used to be Graham with his stick-in-the-mud persona, but he loosened up over the years. Barrett's gotten funnier as he's gotten older. Ford, though—still a chump.

A chump who would give me a run for my money, but I'll never tell him that.

Me: Did a hundred before breakfast.

Mom: Love you, Ford.

Barrett: Linc and Ford? Here we go …

I look up again at the bathroom but still no Dani. Instead of harassing her—and delaying dessert—I go back to my phone.

Mom: You are going nowhere, Barrett Landry!

Ford: Want to Zoom a push-up contest, Linc?

Fucker.

I bite my lip and get situated against the pillows.

Barrett: I'm not, Mom. Don't do this, Ford. Please.

Me: You're on, Ford. Are we counting who does the most in a certain timeframe or just who can go the longest?

Barrett: I'm not taking part, but I bet I'd win that last challenge.

Ford: Don't humiliate yourself, Linc.

Me: I was a professional athlete. Pretty sure I can take out a retired solider.

Ford: You're retired too, genius.

I start to respond when my attention is redirected. Dani walks into the room dressed in one of my old Tennessee Arrows shirts that hangs just above her knees. Her hair is poufy and wild—like she's already been fucked.

Dear lord.

I toss my phone onto the floor.

"Get over here, woman," I growl as I reach for my wife.

CHAPTER TWO

FORD

I STARE AT THE PHONE. And wait.

One. Two. Three seconds pass and still no comeback from Lincoln. Nothing. No upping the ante on my challenge, no self-aggrandizing behavior.

What?

I type out a text to the family.

Me: Someone should check on Lincoln.

Barrett: I was just thinking that.

My wife, Ellie, distracts me from my brother's behavior. A plate of whipped cream looking cookies is set down in front of me. I keep my eyes glued to them. And not her.

I've never been afraid to look at my wife before.

Lifting my eyes warily, I take her in. She's standing on the other side of the island with a warning written all over her pretty face. It's a caution shot, a deterrent—a message not to say anything negative about another baking project.

Every day, Ellie bakes. It was awesome at first. The house smelled like cinnamon and vanilla from the stacks of cookies piled onto plates every night. There were muffins for breakfast, homemade bread for sandwiches for lunch, and a variety of carb-loaded items for dinner.

Then we hit another level. It became an obsession so deep that even I know now that a Brookie is part chocolate chip cookie and part brownie. That's a fact I'll never admit to anyone just as I'll never admit to her that I'm so sick of baked goods.

"That looks delicious," I say, infusing the words with as much sincerity as I can.

"They're meringues." She shoves the plate toward me. It scrapes against the counter. "Try one."

The little fluffs look like spun sugar. I wonder vaguely whether ingesting that much sugar at one time could put you into a diabetic coma. But it's as if Ellie knows I'm waffling because she narrows her eyes.

I take a deep breath and ignore my stomach's complaint. I also ignore the fact that a woman I outweigh by at least a hundred pounds is bossing me around as I lift a meringue to my lips.

The meringue breaks in half as my teeth break the sugar barrier. It literally dissolves on my tongue.

"Wow," I say as I pop the rest of it into my mouth. "This is amazing, Ellie."

She looks relieved. "I was worried it was too humid outside, and they wouldn't be right. The recipe said that humidity can screw it up."

"They're perfect."

She grins happily and heads toward the refrigerator. I consider eating another meringue when my phone chirps.

Mom: Guess what your father is doing.

Me: First guess—golf.

Barrett: Did someone say golf?

146

Me: Be glad Linc is missing in action, or you'd never hear the end of it.

Barrett: Why does he think that all I do is golf?

I type out a reply. As soon as I hit send, Mom's text pops up just beneath mine.

Me: Because it's true?

Mom: Well, Honey, you do golf a lot with your father.

Graham: Because the file I emailed you four days ago has never been opened. Suffice to say, Lincoln might be right this time.

Me: No one texts "sufficing to say", G.

I laugh at Graham. I imagine he's irritated that none of us are working at the moment and complaining under his breath that he's the only one keeping things afloat. He's probably sitting in his office, wearing a button-up shirt, and surrounded by files and calculators.

I almost feel guilty.

Almost.

Ellie clears her throat. I look up before I can think twice about it. This time, she's holding a plate with a four-tiered cake in front of her. Each tier hosts a different color of icing and what I think are flowers piped on the top.

She worries her bottom lip between her teeth as she studies me.

"I'm ready to admit it. I might have a problem," she says as she sets the cake on the counter. "I can't stop, Ford. I can't freaking stop baking. It's ... I don't know what it is, but I need help. And I just keep doing it almost out of defiance."

I laugh.

She slumps against the cabinets. "Don't laugh. Help me. Stage an intervention."

"Do they make those for bakers?"

"I don't know."

"Well, there's only one thing I can think of to do for you right now."

I get to my feet. The barstool squeaks on the tile as I scoot it back. I keep my eyes on her as I walk around the corner of the island.

"What you need," I say, standing directly in front of her, "in my expert opinion, is to keep your hands occupied."

She lifts her chin as I lean down and plant a kiss against her lips.

"And your mouth," I say. "And your mind."

"Ooh. I like the sound of this."

"Do you?"

She stares into my eyes as I rub my nose against hers.

"Every time you want to bake," I whisper, "I want you to come find me."

I place my palms against her hips. She shimmies against my touch.

"And I'll occupy you until the urge is fulfilled," I say, my lips brushing against hers.

"Well, just so you know—I was planning on baking a red velvet cake today."

The tone says she's teasing, but I'm not. In one quick motion, I sweep her off her feet and head toward the bedroom. Her squeal drowns out the sound of my phone buzzing again. Thank God I left it on the counter.

CHAPTER THREE

GRAHAM

I LOOK at my phone again. My last text sits at the bottom of the screen with no response.

Me: Intelligent people do, thank you.

They're all probably off shopping online or watching movies. It's like they don't know that stocks are down. It's as if they don't care that our family business still needs to operate, to expand because none of them have been responding to my emails or taking my calls seriously.

Not even Barrett.

Such a disappointment.

My brain starts to formulate a game plan on how to close the deal we have hanging out there with Holt Mason when my attention is redirected to the doorway. Mallory is standing there in the same sweatpants and tee shirt she's worn for the past three days. She's not changed, except to sleep, and that's only because I peel them off her every single night.

"Kids are asleep," she says with a grin. "I was going to do some yoga, if you wanna join me."

I stare blankly at her. "I think you should give your employees at the yoga center a raise right now. It's the right thing to do."

She rolls her eyes as she walks toward me. Her hands find my shoulders. As much as I want to stay rigid, I can't. I'm putty in her hands.

"We did that last week," she says.

I bend my head to the side as she works her magic. "I knew we talked about it. I didn't know you did it."

"Don't I always do what you say?" She bursts out laughing. "Never mind. Don't answer that."

She finds the knot in the base of my skull, the one that seemed to form in the middle of the night. It became so uncomfortable about two hours after I was sure Mallory was asleep that I got up and went to my desk downstairs.

Over and over, she works the area like she knows how bad I need it. Like she knows the exact area that's irritated and tight.

She probably does. Not much gets by her.

I bend my neck again but this time to see her.

Her face is free of makeup, her hair a wild mess that's been piled on the top of her head. She's beautiful … and mine.

My chest tightens as I let that fact wash over me. It's the same feeling I get every day when I look at her and want her so badly and then realize I already have her.

This thing between us is something I never thought I'd find. It's not even something I realized I wanted. What I thought would be a burden—to take care of someone—has turned out to be the most important and best thing of my entire life.

Even if she has made working at home difficult.

She peers down at me with a pensive look. I know it well. She's wondering how to give me the space she knows I need to run our businesses but to ask for what she needs at the same time. It's painted on her face.

And that's all it takes. Because workload or no workload, the answer is the same.

Mallory comes first.

"Why don't you pour us a glass of wine and run us a bath?" I ask.

Her eyes light up. "Are you sure?"

"Do I ever say something before I think it through?"

She runs her hands through my hair. Her fingers lace through the strands as she gently tugs on them so I have to tilt my chin toward her. The humor in her eyes pales as she searches mine.

"Aren't you in the middle of something?" she asks.

"About fourteen somethings."

"Then we can do it later."

I grip the backs of her thighs and pull her to me. She presses my face against her abdomen as I rest my cheek against the soft cotton shirt.

"Go run us a bath," I say again.

"But you're busy."

"True. But you come first."

She grins the one I love most—the playful one. The one she gave me the day she ended up in my arms on her first day of work.

"Promise?" she teases.

"Don't you always?"

She laughs and kisses the top of my head. "So, no yoga?"

I run my hands under the hem of her shirt. She leans ever so slightly into my touch.

"You want to yoga over bath?" I ask.

"I like you hot and sweaty."

I grin. "I like you wet and wild."

She laughs again before pressing a kiss to the top of my head and then heading toward the door. "I probably need to do a quick workout first. I've been eating all the stuff Ellie has been leaving on the porch ..."

She pauses in the doorway and looks at me over her shoulder. There's something buried in her eyes. It sends a fire through my body as I try to decipher what it is.

If there is an ounce of uncertainty in this woman, I'll spend all night replacing it with fact about just how gorgeous she is. And it really has very little to do with what she actually looks like.

I narrow my gaze. "Bath. Clothes off. I'll be there in ten or less."

"Make it twenty."

"You want to play this game with me?" I ask.

"Maybe." She sends me a flirty grin. "But I won't. If you're not there in ten, though, I'll start without you." She tosses me a wink before disappearing around the corner.

My cock now hard, I shuffle the papers I've been poring over into a pile. Before I get to my feet, I see my screen full of texts.

Mom: The delivery guy just dropped off golfing clubs. For me. Your father bought me golf clubs. What is happening here?

Barrett: It'll get you some fresh air and quality time with Dad. Think about it.

Mom: Maybe he'll meet me halfway and spend some quality time with me doing dishes.

Barrett: Likely not.

Lincoln: He might repay you in other ways, though. *winks*

I pick up my phone and type out a response.

Me: That's our mother, Lincoln.

Mom: Well, I have been wanting that new bag in Ellie's shop.

I shake my head at Mom's naivete.

Barrett: That's exactly what he meant, Mother.

I turn off my phone and leave Barrett to deal with Lincoln. Flipping off the light, I head toward the bathroom and my hopefully naked, or soon-to-be naked, wife.

CHAPTER FOUR

BARRETT

Mom: I might buy Alison one of those bags too for her birthday. Do you think she'd like blue or green?

I KICK back in my chair and type my answer.

Me: Whatever you think.

Mom: She's your wife. You should choose.

Me: Blue then.

Mom: Is that because you like blue or because she does?

I sigh.

Me: Green then.

Mom: Your dad is calling. I'll be right back or BRB as Huxley would say.

I grin at her attempt at being cool. Huxley, my son, has been trying to teach her new lingo. I have no idea why Mom is so interested in learning the language of the kids these days, but she is. It's kind of adorable. Huxley thinks it's hilarious. My youngest siblings, Camilla and Sienna, find it ridiculous.

I take a drink of my beer and wait to see if one of my brothers or sisters pops on again. By the time the bottle is empty, I'm still alone.

It's been three weeks since I saw any of them. Graham and I had a meeting over a land deal with Holt and Oliver Mason. Lincoln came in to talk to them about making a charitable donation to Dani's organization. And that was it. I haven't seen any of them since.

I miss them. A lot. Despite the fact that they make me half-crazy most days and that I lived for a few years in Atlanta when I was governor, I've gotten used to seeing them on an almost daily basis.

I didn't realize how much I liked or maybe even needed that.

The older I get, the more I value our relationship. They're built-in best friends and partners in crime because they don't have a choice but do have loyalty. We have dinners almost every week at the Farm with Mom and Dad. My brothers and Camilla's boyfriend head to a bar at least once a month for some drinks. It's a part of who I am. It balances the roles of husband and dad. It makes me a better man. Period.

Stretching my arms overhead, I gaze across the lawn. The sun is setting and painting the sky vivid purples and bright pinks. A gentle breeze kicks over the treetops, whistling through the branches and leaves, and I take in the moment and savor it.

After being in politics and the hassle of getting back into a normal life again, moments like this mean everything to me. They're slow. Deliberate. They're what life is all about.

Moments like this give me time to think. To feel. To listen. And while I have a full, loud, robust life, I've also discovered some holes that I'd like to fill.

I'd like to be more involved in our family's charities going forward. I'd like to take time away from Graham's spreadsheets and golf more with Dad. I'd also like to fill this six-bedroom house with lots of babies with Alison.

Just the thought makes my balls ache.

It's not just a sexual thing either—although Alison is fucking hot. It comes from a different, deeper place. It's about creating something that Huxley can fall back on. It's become so important to me that Huxley has siblings to fight with, to lean on, to share inside jokes.

I want that. And I want to give that to Alison, if she wants it.

As if on cue, she shows up in the doorway.

"What are you doing out here?" she asks.

"Thinking."

She smiles slowly. It's only now that I see her hands are behind her back.

"What are you up to?" I ask.

"Thinking."

I stand in front of her. Sweeping my gaze down her body, I forbid myself to reach out. Yet. I make myself wait until I hear what she's thinking because if I touch her, I'll lose all thought processes.

"What are you thinking about?" I ask.

She bites her lip as a bowl full of grapes comes from behind her back and is pressed into my abdomen. The bowl is cold and damp and the grapes bright purple.

My entire body fires. My core pulses with anticipation because this means one thing: game time.

"Hungry?" she asks with a twinkle in her eye.

"Always."

She pulls on the hem of my shirt. "Come on, then."

"Lead the way."

We round the corner into the house when my phone buzzes in my hand. I look down.

Mom: Your dad is hungry. Guess I'm making dinner. Again.

Me: I'm about to go eat too. Alison just delivered a big bowl of grapes to me.

I chuckle at the reactions my brothers will undoubtedly have to that message and shove my phone in my pocket.

CHAPTER FIVE

VIVIAN "MOM"

I PAUSE at the kitchen counter and read my oldest son's text. My face parts into a smile as I sit my phone next to the cutting board.

"That's my boy," I say aloud. "He always did love fruit."

ABOUT ADRIANA LOCKE

USA Today and Washington Post bestselling author Adriana Locke lives and breathes books. After years of slightly obsessive relationships with the flawed bad boys created by other authors, Adriana has created her own.

She resides in the Midwest with her husband, sons, and two dogs. She spends a large amount of time playing with her kids, drinking coffee, and cooking. You can find her outside if the weather's nice and there's always a piece of candy in her pocket.

www.adrianalocke.com

RACHEL BROOKES

CHAPTER ONE

EDEN

"Pretty girl, where the fuck are you?"

With my phone resting precariously between my shoulder and cheek, I tugged the zipper on my camera bag to ensure one of my most prized possessions was secure and away from harm's reach.

"I'm packing up from a shoot. What's up?" I asked Josh, my brother-in-law and the man who decided it was his God-given right to call me pretty girl from the moment we met.

"You need to get your ass home. Ky is freaking the fuck out because he can't get in contact with you. There's some crazy weather heading your way, and my big brother wants you home."

Standing tall, I hitched my camera bag over my shoulder, and for the first time all day, I looked outside through the floor-to-ceiling windows. Holy shit, yep, sure enough, the snow had begun to fall.

"I'm locking up now. I'll call Ky on my way home." I locked up the warehouse and headed for the elevator. "How's Monroe? How are Ash and Aria? Christmas wasn't the same without you guys."

Josh, his girlfriend Ashlyn, and baby girl, Aria, had been in Monroe, Ashlyn's hometown, for the past two weeks, and I was becoming needy, and the daily FaceTime chats didn't suffice. Especially since I couldn't love on my niece and spoil her with endless Christmas candy.

"Monroe is good. We are spending a lot of time with Ashy's brother, Austin, and his girlfriend, Marnie, and that's always a good time. We miss you guys too. I sure as fuck missed your gingerbread."

My phone beeped with an incoming call, and when I glanced at the screen, Ky's handsome face stared back at me. He'd been mine for years. There was no doubt he was my soul mate and love of my life, but still to this day, staring at his face and getting lost in his soulful eyes, kissable lips, and scruffy jaw unleashed a billion of butterflies to flutter in my stomach.

"Your brother is calling me. We will try and FaceTime you guys tonight."

"Okay, answer his call and get your ass home so he stops calling me!"

I rolled my eyes even though he couldn't see me. "Yes, Dad," I teased.

"It still blows my mind that I'm a dad," he muttered, and I could picture him shaking his head in disbelief. "Who would have thought?"

"Joshy, your brother." I chuckled as I beeped the lock on my car when I'd made it to underground garage.

"Shit, yes, go! Talk soon!"

As soon as he hung up, I connected with Ky, and as soon as I did, he spoke.

"Where are you?" he asked, worry curling around every word.

After I settled into the driver's seat, I connected his call through my Bluetooth. "I'm on my way home now." I replied softly, trying to soothe his panic.

"Babe, the weather's turning to shit. You need to get your ass home so I can lock you inside and protect you from the shitstorm heading our way."

Warmth flooded me, erasing any cold that had penetrated the car windows, and of course, I smiled at my husband's ability to make me swoon even when he was being bossy and sounding irritated.

"I'm on the road now, and I'll be home in thirty minutes. Do you need me to pick up anything from the store? Do we need snacks? Beer? Chocolate cake?"

He huffed loudly. "Eden, babe, I just want my wife home safely. Do not stop on the way home. Not even for chocolate fucking cake."

The night we met, we shared the most amazing slice of chocolate cake, so it was kind of our thing now. And eating chocolate cake always led to a marathon sex session or a mind-blowing orgasm brought on my Ky's mouth or fingers, so yes, I suggested chocolate cake every chance I got, and he never refused… until now!

"Okay, okay, I won't stop. See you soon. Love you."

"Eden, get your ass home."

"Ky, did you forget something?"

"I love you too."

I hung up with a smile on my face and new determination to get home safely to my man. Never in my wildest dreams could I have predicted I'd find a love like the one I shared with Ky, and every day, I thanked my lucky stars that the universe gave us one another. For as long as I was breathing, I'd thank Ky for asking me to be his December because the reality was, he ended up being my everything.

As I headed out of the city and made my way home, I switched on the radio, desperate to hear the latest news on the crazy weather Ky mentioned. Every station was talking about record-breaking snow fall, freezing temperatures and life-threatening wind gusts. *Great. Freaking great.* It had even been given a name; The Big Freeze. I'd never experienced anything like this. The predictions were petrifying. Sure, I'd experienced large snowfalls, but not to this extent. The more I listened, the higher my freak out levels soared and the urgency to get home and locked away with Ky took precedence over everything.

Forty minutes later, I pulled into the driveway. *Home.* The tension in my shoulders and the painful grip I had on the steering wheel eased and I released a massive sigh of relief. Outside, the sky had switched to an ominous gray, and the wind squealed in warning as snow fell heavily, covering everything in a blanket of white as far as the eye could see. After parking next to Ky, I climbed out of my car, grabbed my camera gear, and then headed inside through the door that connected the garage to the main house. Warmth and low light caressed the air, cocooning me with comfort as I shrugged off my jacket and hung it over the back of one of the barstools in the kitchen. I scanned the space for any sign of Ky and then heard his deep voice bouncing off the walls from the direction of his home office.

It wasn't a secret that my husband was a workaholic. He loved what he did, and he'd worked his ass off to become CEO. To be honest, his work ethic was a major turn-on, so I had no complaints. Plus, I knew, and he made it very clear that I always came first.

I busied myself with making us both a drink – whiskey for him, vodka for me – then headed down the hall toward his home office. His voice grew louder with every step I took. When I stepped through the door, his head snapped up, and his eyes came to me. He scanned me from head to toe, twice, taking me in, in the way I knew was him making sure I was okay, safe, and whole. I smiled softly and placed our drinks on his desk while he continued talking on the phone. Through all of this, his eyes never left mine.

"Yeah, it's going to be a shitty couple of days. I'm closing the office until next week. I don't want anyone going out in this weather. Yeah, work from home, and deadlines are still deadlines."

Three steps took me to Ky. My smile twisted into a smirk, and I pushed his chair away from the desk, making sure it allowed me enough room to climb onto his lap and straddle his thighs. His brown eyes flashed with heat, deepening into the color of rich, dark melted chocolate as they burned back at me. I knew that look and everything it promised. My husband was thinking wicked thoughts that included me, him, and a hell of a lot of pleasure. I dropped my mouth to his neck and sucked gently, using my teeth to nip at the sensitive spot below his ear. He buried his free hand in my hair at the nape of my neck and his thick fingers tangling around my dark locks. Throughout this, he continued talking on his phone. His voice remained cool, calm and collected. Classic Ky Crawford. My lips left a trail of kisses from one side of his neck, along his jaw and down the other side. His grip tightened and tugged on my hair, and it took everything not to moan.

"Office is closed until next week. Eden's home, and I need to see my wife. Call me if there are any issues and stay safe."

I sucked harder on his neck and pushed myself flush against his body when he referred to me as his wife.

Ky ended the call, threw his phone onto the desk, and yanked my hair. "Give me your mouth, baby."

Obliging, I lifted my face from his neck and smiled before dropping my lips to his. He wrapped his arms around me, hauling me closer and causing the chair to creak beneath us. Our kiss deepened, our tongues tangled in desperation, and our teeth clinked together as we reclaimed each other's mouth and stole one another's breath.

"I made it home," I said, breathlessly, after pulling away from our kiss. "Nothing would stop me from getting to you."

"I was so fucking worried about you."

My gaze softened. "I was on the phone with Josh when you called. He made me aware of your worry."

He cupped my cheeks, and his eyes held mine. "I'm a little protective of you. Always have. Always will be."

Truer words had never been spoken. Ky had a front row seat to every horrific and terrifying moment of my life, and they'd left deep scars we both had to live with. Ky wasn't secretive of his need to protect me. He cared for me in a way no one else had ever done before, and he'd made it abundantly clear that he'd put his life on the line for me. He was and forever would be my safe place.

Leaning in, I brushed my lips against his. "I'm aware of that and it's one of the many reasons I love you."

"I'm going to keep reminding you for the rest of your life."

"Is that a promise?" I flirted, kissing the corner of his mouth as my fingers ran through his hair.

He moved his mouth until it covered mine, and when he spoke, his lips caressed mine. "I promised myself to you for life, baby.

You've got me forever, even when I piss you off and become too bossy and overprotective."

I pulled away slightly and rolled my eyes dramatically as a smile tugged on my lips. "It's such a hardship being married to you. You're always protecting me from getting hurt, making sure I'm safe, and giving me endless orgasms. Wow, how do I survive?"

"Whoa, whoa, whoa, hold up a minute. I didn't mention anything about orgasms."

"Are you refusing me, Mr. Crawford?" My brow rose in question. "Because I can also—"

Outside, the wind let out an ear-piercing squeal, then something crashed, and the sound of glass breaking stabbed the silence of Ky's office.

"Holy shit!" I screeched. Jumping in Ky's arms, I tumbled off his lap and landed on the floor with a thud. "Ow! What the hell was that?"

I blinked up at Ky, hoping for all the answers. Instead, I found him wearing a huge smile and biting his lip to stop himself from laughing.

"Babe," he choked out before throwing his head back and laughing deep. And when I say deep, I mean loud, unrestrained, down in the pits of your stomach kind of laughter. The kind where his eyes were shut tight, his chest rumbled, and the sound bounced between squeaks and roars. "Are. You. Okay?"

I glared up at him, trying to rein in my own giggles. My ass cheeks throbbed, and my cheeks flamed, and I still had no freaking idea what was going on outside and what had shattered into a million pieces. I opened my mouth to faux blast him but was interrupted by another ear-piercing squeal, and this time, the lights flickered before darkness filled the room and I lost sight of everything.

Shit!

CHAPTER TWO

KY

THE WEATHER HAD TURNED to shit a lot quicker than expected. I'd been watching the weather predictions closely all week, and I was aware it was going to be a bad one. However, all news outlets and the weather reports had forecast it to hit us in a few days, which is why I didn't attempt to stop Eden from going to her photo shoot this morning.

"Oh, my god! Oh, my god! Ky!" Eden stammered with fear etched in her words.

Leaning down, I placed my hands under her arms and lifted her off the floor and back onto the safety of my lap. My girl was shaking like a fucking leaf, and my protective instincts kicked in. We had some shitty weather over the years, but this would be the first superstorm she experienced and it seemed like it was going to be one for the books.

With Eden secure on my lap, I wrapped my arms around her and rested one of my hands on the back of her head. "It's okay, baby. I've got you."

"You laughed at me," she grumbled although there was no malice in her voice. "I hurt my ass, and you laughed. Worst husband ever." I tightened my arms around her as my body began to shake again. "And you're laughing again!"

"Eden, come on, you know that shit was funny."

She buried her face in my neck, and her body began to shake with laughter, and the faint sound of her giggles hit the air.

"How about we find some candles and camp out in the living room. It looks like we'll be hanging out by candlelight and the fire tonight."

She lifted her face from the confines of my neck, and I felt her eyes on me even though I couldn't see her. "Stop trying to seduce me when I'm trying to be annoyed at you."

From the moment I met Eden, she'd shown me time and time again how funny she was, but over the years, I'd come to realize just how fucking hilarious she was.

"You are so fucking cute." I chuckled.

"Uh, I wasn't trying to be cute." She said, and I could visualize the cute fake pout she'd be wearing.

With my hands on her waist, I stood us both up and kicked my chair back. One of her hands encased my wrist, and with my free hand, I patted my desk and searched for my phone. After knocking off a pile of paperwork and sending it falling to the floor, I grabbed my phone and switched on the torch app, and a dim light blanketed my office.

"Okay, Pouty McPout Pout, let's go," I teased, calling her the name I always did when she was pretending to be pissed at me or whenever I wanted to get a rise out of her. I linked my fingers with hers and pulled her out of my office and down the hall toward the living room. As we got closer, the space around us began to glow orange from the fire I'd started earlier in the day.

"You're annoying," she teased, her fingers squeezing mine gently. When she glanced up at me, her eyes shimmered with amusement.

"Annoyingly awesome and handsome, and let's not forget, brilliant at delivering orgasms."

"Don't forget to add cocky and mediocre in the humor department to the list."

Another loud bang sailed in from outside, causing Eden to shriek and press herself up against me. Resting her hands flat on my chest, she buried her face into the fleece of my hoodie. The wind continued to howl, showing no signs of stopping its taunting and menacing ways. I didn't even want to imagine how much snow was getting dumped outside. News anchors had warned we'd be housebound for days, and cities would close down because of this storm. I have to say, though, I had no problems with being locked up with Eden because I knew there'd be plenty of things we could do to do to occupy our time, both clothed and naked.

"You okay?" I whispered as Eden dropped her hands from my chest.

She nodded. "Yeah. It just scares me and catches me off guard. You know I freak out at the littlest things, so something crashing outside and then the wind sounding like a stampede of ghosts are ohhhhhhhing outside cause a girl to become a little uneasy." See, told you she was fucking hilarious. "I'll be okay, though. Let me go and see what I can put together for dinner. I didn't get a chance to eat much today, and I'm starved."

I let her go and handed her my phone to use as a torch. When she disappeared into the kitchen, I opened drawers and cupboards in the living room and found the random candles Eden had accumulated over the years and spread them around. With a flick of a lighter, more light filled the space, and in about thirty minutes, the house would be filled with a combination of lavender, vanilla, and strawberry scents.

With Eden banging around in the kitchen and making who knows what for dinner, I grabbed a few logs out of the basket next to the fire and placed them onto the simmering coals and watched them ignite. The crackling fire and dancing flames held my attention until Eden's soft voice broke the silence.

"Here we go." She announced, stepping into the living room carrying a wooden board filled with a variety of cheese, meats, dips, crackers, fruit, and veggies. "I'm calling it the locked in charcuterie board a la Eden."

With a smile, I tugged Eden's favourite throw rug from the couch and laid it out on the floor in front of the fire, then scattered some cushions around before grabbing a few magazines from the coffee table and placed them in the center of the rug. When I glanced over at her, I found her face soft and a gorgeous smile on her lips as she watched me.

"What?" I asked before quickly walking to the kitchen to grab a bottle of her favorite wine and then returning with the wine and two glasses. I placed them on the magazines, which would be used as a makeshift table.

"We're having a picnic?" she whispered, her eyes bouncing between the rug, wine and fireplace before locking back onto me.

"Let's call this the locked-in picnic a la Ky." I winked, holding out my hand to her. "I've gotta keep romancing my girl. Rain, hail, shine, or in this case, a lockdown-causing blizzard."

In the orange haze radiating from the fire and in the middle of the living room in the home I'd created with the love of my life, Eden gifted me with soft, revealing eyes, and all I saw shining back at me was pure happiness. And for a man obsessively in love with his wife, that's all I ever wanted to see.

After Eden placed the overflowing charcuterie board on the rug, we both took a seat and collapsed onto the cushions. We sat opposite one another, our eyes locked, a smile tugging at her pouty pink colored lips. I reveled in all that she was as I picked at the grapes and the strawberries. Eden Rivers, now Eden Crawford, was my life, the air in my lungs, and the beat in my heart, and I made sure she knew that, every chance I got. I would die for her. It was a simple as that. She made me a happy man when she agreed to be my December, but she made me the luckiest man in the fucking world when she said yes to becoming mine for eternity.

We ate in silence, the only noise coming from the crackling fire inside, and the wind screaming outside. Occasionally, something would crash outside, and Eden would jump.

"Shit," she whispered when what I expected was the neighbor's bins tumbled over outside and landed with a loud crash. "It's getting scarier out there."

"We are safe in here."

She nodded before an even louder crash pierced the air and rattled the window right behind her. "Fuck!"

"Baby, come here," I whispered, moving the food and drinks to the side and pulling her toward me until she scrambled onto my lap. "You're safe. We're inside. We're warm. We've got each other. I promise you nothing is going to happen," I whispered, kissing her softly, desperate to ease her fear. "We're probably going to be locked in here for a few days. It might get scarier, or it could ease. But we have each other, right?"

She stared at me with wide blue eyes and lips slightly open. But I didn't stop talking.

"Let's grab some blankets, pillows, drag a mattress out here, and we'll camp out in front of the fire tonight. We'll find my iPad, watch one of the hundred Netflix movies you've already got downloaded, and just chill out." I tucked her hair behind her ear, and as I did, the wind picked up its aggression outside and howled, roared, and squealed all at once. But Eden didn't jump; she didn't even flinch.

"You're my comfort," she whispered, tracing my bottom lip with her thumb. "Not just my love and protection. You're my comfort."

I placed my mouth against hers and stole her breath and worries. She opened for me, and my tongue found hers. Together, they danced in a silent promise of never-ending commitment and a forever kind of love you read about in books.

"Keep eating. You've barely touched the cheese and I know my girl is a huge fan of cheese. I'll go and grab something for us to sleep on," I said after breaking our kiss. I tapped her nose lightly, grabbed another grape from the board and popped it in my mouth and climbed to my feet. After grabbing one of the candles, I headed toward the dark hall but stopped when Eden called out my name.

"I love you, Ky Crawford. More than you'll ever know. I became the luckiest girl in the world when you asked me to be yours."

She was so wrong. So, so wrong.

I smiled and shook my head. "When you said yes to me, I became the luckiest man in the entire fucking universe, Eden. Nothing compares to you, baby. Nothing."

CHAPTER THREE

EDEN

"I think it's time."

I tore my attention away from a dancing flame I'd been staring at and shifted my head slightly from its position on Ky's chest to gaze up at him. "Time for what?"

He'd done exactly what he said and dragged out blankets, pillows, and the mattress off the futon in my photography studio, and we'd created the comfiest locked away from the world bed in existence. We'd demolished the charcuterie board and polished off the bottle of wine and were now both in a food coma slash tipsy haze. Even with Mother Nature still screaming at the top of her lungs outside, I couldn't deny that Ky had made me felt safer than I'd ever had before. *My comfort.*

He ran his thumb down my cheek, his eyes locking with mine. "For us to bring a little Crawford into the world."

With my heart pounding louder than the howling wind, I twisted in Ky's arms until my chest partially covered his. He tucked my hair behind my ears and gave me a sweet yet knowing smile that had my insides instantly run to mush. "A baby?" I whispered, my words catching in my throat.

Starting a family together was something we both wanted. We'd spoken about it in the past, but we'd decided to enjoy married life before we brought a mini Ky or Eden into the world. We'd spent the time since we got married renovating and creating our dream home, traveling, working our asses off, and most importantly, falling even crazier in love with each other.

I never hid the fact that I wanted it all with Ky. The whole shebang. And that included babies and a lot of them.

He nodded, and a smile that had the potential to light up the world transformed his handsome face. "Yes, babies. I want nothing more than to start a family with you. The thought of you with a tiny little person we created snuggled against your chest does things to me. Fuck, Eden, you have no idea how much I want to see you become a Mom."

"Yes," I replied eagerly while I immediately started visualizing Ky cradling our child and talking baby gibberish. My ovaries could not handle images like this but I never wanted to stop imagining it.

"Yeah? We're going to do this?"

Wetness filled my eyes, and I nodded. Suddenly, the blizzard, snow, wind, superstorm, or whatever it was called that was battering our home was forgotten because nothing else mattered other than the idea of Ky and me starting a family.

"Yes, I want that more than anything." I whispered and curled my body around his and hung on tightly. "Girl or boy?"

He answered without hesitation. "Boy."

"Why a boy first?" Lifting my head, I rested my chin on his chest and gazed up at him. His eyes flashed down to mine.

"Because I'm going to need my princess to have a big brother to look out for her when I'm not around to make sure little punks stay away from her. I have no doubt that she's going to look like you, so the idea of a mini you walking around gives me cause for concern. So that's why I want my boy coming first."

I stared for him for a beat and then burst out laughing. My entire body shook against him, and I was doing my crazy laugh where no noise came out, just an occasional squeak here and there. He smirked down at me, lifted his brows, and I lost control of my laughter all over again.

"Eden, this is a serious issue. I've got a cock, my reformed manwhore of a brother has a cock, and I have very vivid memories of what we were like around pretty girls. I refuse to let my daughter be around that debauchery." He shook his head and sliced one of his hands roughly through his hair. "Jesus, I'm already thinking of my unborn daughter dating. Fuck me dead, it's going to be a long thirty years until she's allowed to start dating."

I buried my face in his chest as I tried desperately to get control of my laughter. It was funny because that is exactly how I could imagine Ky being as a dad. Overprotective wasn't the word for it but the love he'd have for our kids would overshadow everything else. Even the fact that he had plans of not allowing any future daughter to date until she was thirty.

Ky's phone beeped with an incoming text message, and he removed one of his arms that was wrapped around me to reach out for it. He tucked me back in close to his side and held up his phone.

Josh: How are things going over there? I'm guessing by the lack of calls that Eden got home.

With one hand, Ky tapped in a reply.

Ky: Yeah, she made it home. Weather is worse than predicted, and it's arrived quicker. We lost power, and the wind's howling. Snow is falling thick and fast.

Josh: Shit! Well, stay safe. We were due to fly home the day after next, but our flight was canceled due to the weather. I'll keep you posted about when we get a new flight. Give Eden a big, sloppy kiss for me.

Ky: You're an asshole. Give Ashlyn a boob grab, ass slap, and kiss from me too.

Josh: Touché, big brother.

I woke with a start when Ky moved slightly to put his phone back on the table. I hadn't even known I'd fallen asleep. Ky tightened the blankets around us and curled me in even closer. I sighed contentedly and snuggled into his warmth.

"How long do you think we'll be stuck inside for?" I asked softly as my eyes began to grow heavier.

"Probably a few days but we are well stocked, so we will be fine. However, I wouldn't mind if the weather stayed shit for a long time. Even forever if it means being with you like this."

I sighed with happiness and swooned at my husband's way with words. "You don't need a blizzard to keep me forever."

His arms tightened around me, and his lips pressed firmly against my forehead, and the last thing I heard before I drifted off to sleep was my husband whisper, "Forever, baby. You and me forever."

ABOUT RACHEL BROOKES

Rachel Brookes is from the east coast of Australia and writes irresistible romances that guarantees epic happily-ever-afters. With countless story ideas circling around in her head and an obsession for writing alpha heroes and the sassy women who bring them to their knees, she has no plans of stopping. An avid reader, Rachel can often be found getting lost in a fictional town she wishes was real and claiming book boyfriends as her own. As well as writing and reading, she possesses an unhealthy obsession with cupcakes, the Walking Dead, and social media, and loves hearing from readers.

www.rachelbrookes.net

A BRIE-A-LICIOUS
Hideaway

RED PHOENIX

CHAPTER ONE

"WHAT SHOULD WE DO, SIR?" I ask in concern, cradling Hope close to my chest.

Sir wraps his arm around my waist as he looks down at our baby girl. "Based on everything the CDC is telling us, I think there is only one prudent thing we can do."

Glancing around the rustic cabin, he tells me, "It looks like we'll be calling this home for a while."

Rytsar Durov lets out a loud whoop beside me. "I say this calls for a toast!"

I giggle as I watch the sexy Russian head into the kitchen to get out three shot glasses.

Looking at Hope, I hug her tighter, my mothering instincts to protect my child kicking in full force.

"I can certainly think of worse places to isolate." Sir lifts my chin to kiss me tenderly on the lips.

Rytsar walks up with three glasses balanced in his hands. "And to think you were too busy to stay another day." He chuckles with amusement. "Now, you get to spend four weeks in Russia, if not more!"

Even though I have a huge deadline looming with my film, a part of me likes the idea of being forced to isolate here—far from the pressures of everyday life.

The excitement in Rytsar's blue eyes is charming as he hands me a shot glass. "We will make good use of this time."

I nod, cherishing the memories I've made in this cabin and I look forward to adding more while we shelter here…

Rytsar holds up his glass to us. "Here's to spending time with my favorite people."

I raise my glass to both men. "There is no one else I'd rather isolate with."

Hope raises her hand, opening and closing it repeatedly, babbling as if adding her own little toast.

"Hear, hear, little angel," Sir says, gazing down at our daughter with such intense love it brings tears to my eyes.

The three of us clink glasses and down the vodka together.

Before I can ask for a pickle, Maxim appears with a jar of them. I pull one out and lick the salty brine before biting into the dill goodness. There is nothing like the combination of fine vodka and a good pickle.

Knowing Hope loves pickles as much as I do, I let her take a bite using her new teeth, which have just come in.

Hope screws up her little face after tasting the salty brine, then smiles at me and chews her bite. I swear there is nothing cuter!

Both men take a pickle from the jar and chew in silence. I feel a sense of harmony between us as the vodka begins to soothe my worried heart.

Sir suddenly furrows his brow. "What about supplies?"

Rytsar snaps his fingers. "I'm on it."

Turning to Maxim, he orders, "Tell the men we're heading out."

"I'm coming with you," Sir offers, following behind him.

"*Nyet*. Stay with your woman and the babe. This is bound to take a while."

Sir looks uncertain but answers, "If you insist."

"I do, *moy droog*."

When Sir pulls out his wallet, Rytsar looks at him with amusement. "Your money is no good here, comrade."

Sir shakes his head. "If I'm not going with you, the least I can do is pay for my family's food."

The Russian laughs. "They are my family too, brother."

Looking at me affectionately, Rytsar asks, "Is there anything that you want me to get, *radost moya*?"

"Maybe some coconut water, if you can find it."

He frowns. "You're not serious."

I shrug, bouncing Hope in my arms. "She really loves the stuff."

He looks at Hope as if she has betrayed him. "How can this be, *moye solntse*?" Closing his eyes, he takes a deep breath. "Fine. If I find some, I will buy it."

Luckily, Hope has a very devoted *dyadya*. I know the sacrifice he's making, considering his recent experiences with coconut milk and how much he despises the substance.

I glance at Sir, who is smirking.

Rytsar gives me a quick peck on the cheek and leans down to kiss Hope before leaving. "I'll be back."

Once they're gone, I find myself alone with Sir.

Feeling a bit shocked, I tell him, "This is certainly an unexpected turn of events."

He reaches out and pulls me close, grazing his hand against Hope's cheek. "I will do whatever it takes to protect you both. There is no reason to worry."

I look up at him and smile.

"However," he adds, "it does mean we need to reschedule several things. I'll make the call now to change our flight."

I nod, realizing our cat won't be seeing us tomorrow as we'd planned. "I'll see if I can find someone willing to watch Shadow for us. An automatic feeder isn't going to cut it for such an extended amount of time."

"I agree."

"Hopefully, Lea is willing since he doesn't get along with very many people. Even though he's shy around her, at least Shadow tolerates her."

"We still have a large supply of Rytsar's caviar at home. If Lea bribes him with that, they should become friends in record time."

I grin, liking his suggestion. "Shadow definitely likes his caviar…"

"A very discerning cat," Sir chuckles.

I set Hope on the floor and watch as she crawls over to the giant stuffed Kodiak bear that Rytsar gave her. Grabbing my cell phone while she plays, I call my best friend.

"Hey, Lea. How are you doing with all this craziness?"

"Girl, they're locking us down here. It's nuts to think I'm going to be stuck in my apartment for weeks."

"I can't believe it, either, because we're still here in Russia."

I hear Lea cry in disbelief, "No way! You're so dang lucky, Stinky Cheese."

"I can't believe it myself. Rytsar's off getting supplies while Sir and I try to get things arranged in LA for this unexpected delay."

Lea makes a cute pouting sound. "How is it fair that I'm stuck here by myself while you're partying with two sexy Doms?"

"It's not fair, girl, I know. I do have a proposition for you, however. Rather than stay at your apartment, how would you feel about hanging at our beach house during lockdown?"

"What! Are you kidding me?"

"No, girlfriend. I'm hoping you don't mind taking care of Shadow, though."

"Not at all. I welcome the companionship, although he still seems unsure of me."

"You don't have to worry. We still have that stash of caviar that Rytsar gave Shadow. You can use it to make friends with him, and feel free to partake as well. No reason Shadow should get all the good stuff."

"Caviar, too? This sounds too good to be true. Instead of looking at these dreary walls, I'll be enjoying the ocean view while I munch on expensive caviar and tell Shadow jokes all day long."

I giggle. "You might want to restrain yourself with the jokes."

"But I have a ton of animal jokes! He'll love them."

"Proceed at your own risk, my friend. He's famous for bringing down trained assassins."

"Don't worry, Stinky Cheese. I'll have that pussy eating out of my hand and purring at my jokes." Lea suddenly lets out a happy squeal. "I can't thank you enough, Brie! I've been dreading this lockdown up until now."

"I'm just grateful you're willing to help us out."

She tsks. "I still can't believe you're lucky enough to be in Russia with Sir and Rytsar."

"At the cabin," I add.

"Girl, I officially hate you now."

I laugh. "Talk to you later. Be sure to call me if you need anything."

"Wait! Before you go…"

"What?"

"I've got the perfect joke for this moment."

"Oh, boy…" I groan in anticipation of another one of her bad jokes.

"You ready?"

"Yes," I whimper.

"Due to self-isolation, I will only be telling inside jokes."

"Well, dang. That's actually funny, Lea," I chuckle as I hang up the phone. I look over at Hope, who is lying on the stuffed bear, her eyes at half-mast.

When I pick her up, she lets out a big yawn. "Looks like someone is ready for a nap."

After putting her to bed, I walk out of her room and Sir beckons me to him. I smile as l kneel on the floor beside him, laying my head against his thigh.

Sir begins to stroke my hair and I purr softly.

"Were you successful in finding someone to watch Shadow?"

"Yes, Lea is super excited about it. How about you, Sir? Were you able to get our flights changed?"

"It took a bit of negotiating, but the Russian airline is allowing us to reschedule at our convenience. Since no one can see into the future, I refuse to select a date for our return flight." He cups my chin, lifting my head to meet his gaze. "Until then, we must find ways to entertain ourselves."

I grin, still as much in love with the man as I was the first time we scened together at the Training Center. He is incredibly handsome, with a head of thick, dark brown hair, a chiseled face, and those sexy eyes I can lose myself in.

With time, I've come to appreciate so much more than his good looks. I know the tragedies he has suffered, the depth of his love, and the skill of his talented hands…and mouth. Thane Davis is everything to me.

And our daughter, Hope?

She is a beautiful combination of both of us.

I lightly stroke the collar around my neck, knowing I am the luckiest submissive in the world.

"Now that we have unlimited time, what do you want to do with it?" he asks, grazing my cheek with his thumb.

I let out a long sigh. "I regret not bringing my computer on this trip. I feel lost without it, knowing how much needs to get done with the film."

"I didn't ask what you still have left to do," he says with a gentle smile. "What do you *want* to do?"

Letting my breath out slowly, I feel uncertain. I haven't had time to think about having spare time in years—what with my film documentaries and raising our little girl.

"Anything I want?"

He nods. "Within reason, of course."

"Maybe I could learn how to sew."

He looked amused. "Is that something you're passionate about?"

"Not exactly…" I laugh at myself. "But it would be a practical use of my time."

Sir pulls me onto his lap. "This isn't about being practical. I'm asking you to be true to yourself. Without any other distractions, including your work, what would you want to do with this time?"

I look at him with a half-smile. "Honestly?"

"Yes."

"If I could do anything, I'd choose to spend more time with you."

"I feel the same way." He chuckles lightly. "In a world run by appointments, deadlines, and averting the next crisis, this may be a gift."

I nod in agreement.

"So, I propose we take this rare opportunity to just be."

"Just be…" I repeat wistfully. "What a lovely concept."

I look up at him and moan when his lips touch mine, struck by the electricity that passes between us. "I love how secluded this cabin is…" I murmur.

"I agree, babygirl," he says with a low growl. His kiss deepens as he explores my mouth with his tongue. Lifting me in his arms, he starts carrying me toward the door.

"Where are you taking me?" I ask breathlessly.

"I'm going to follow the urge to stake my claim in the great outdoors."

"Oh, yes…" I feel the butterflies start. "Take me."

He looks down at me with a sexy smirk. "Oh, I will. Repeatedly."

The coolness of the mountain air is a refreshing contrast to the fire that burns inside me. Sir carries me into the woods like a man on a mission. He navigates the rough terrain effortlessly, heading north of the cabin. He doesn't stop until he comes to a large white boulder surrounded by an outcropping of smaller rocks.

I look at the large rock, noting its length and the sexy curve of it. It reminds me of our tantra chair back home.

When he sets me down, his lustful stare causes pleasant shivers down my spine. "How would you like me, Sir?"

His smile gives me butterflies. "Stand facing the rock with your pelvis pressed against the upper curve of it."

Turned on by his command, I stand with my legs slightly spread and slowly lower myself against the curve of the rock, pressing my cheek against the hard surface. It causes my ass to be nicely displayed for his pleasure.

I hold my breath as he runs his hands up my thighs and under my skirt. Grabbing the material of my lace thong, he rips it apart and tosses it to the ground.

I purr, loving his rough treatment.

Lifting my skirt, he exposes my naked ass to the mountain air and tenderly caresses it. "I can tell this excites you, babygirl," he murmurs huskily.

It's true. My pussy is already wet.

I moan softly when he slaps my right ass cheek. Even though I'm a girl who doesn't like pain, I love when he spanks me. Under his talented hands, his spankings only serve to increase my sexual desire.

I close my eyes as his hand caresses my ass soothingly. When he lifts it to spank me again, I bite my bottom lip in anticipation. His hand comes down forcefully, the contact causing jolts of erotic pleasure in my nether regions.

The woods echo with the sexy sound of his palm making contact with my ass. Sir's swats are slow, solid, and controlled, meant to build my arousal.

His caress has the power to possess me, body and soul—and he knows it.

Slipping his finger into my pussy, he teases my G-spot. I grind against his hand, desperate for him.

Fisting my hair, he pulls my head back and asks in a gruff voice, "Is my goddess ready to be fucked like a slut?"

"Yes…" I beg, the openness of the outdoors making me feel feral and free.

Goosebumps rise on my skin when I hear the sound of him unbuckling his belt. He slowly unzips his pants before placing his hands on my hips.

I whimper softly, desperate for his claiming.

Sir rubs the head of his shaft against my opening several times, covering it in my wet excitement before thrusting inside me. I moan in satisfaction as I take his full length.

Grabbing my waist with both hands, he begins ramming his cock into me.

God, I love the challenge of his shaft! With no need to be silent, I cry out, letting the world know how wildly turned on I am.

Sir's manly grunts mingle with my cries of passion as he pounds me, relentless in his claiming.

We both give in to the primal connection. To feel such freedom in this open terrain, pressed hard against the rock as my Master takes out his carnal passion on my willing body, is pure submissive bliss.

"Oh, God, yes. Yes!" I cry out.

Wanting more than my cries of pleasure, he reaches between my legs and starts rubbing my clit with his cock still buried inside me. Having pounded me so hard, it doesn't take him long to bring me to the edge.

I whimper in excitement as my pussy starts pulsing with an impending orgasm.

"Come for me, babygirl."

I moan loudly as the intensity becomes unbearable just before I climax, and my pussy starts pulsing hard against his finger.

"Good girl..." he murmurs gruffly.

It's obvious he is as turned on as I am. Sir suddenly grabs my waist and starts thrusting with even deeper strokes. I cry out in pleasure as I take his sexy onslaught.

Sir lets out a ravenous yell that echoes through the woods and I feel him pump his seed inside me.

In that moment, we become one in spirit.

But, my body is greedy. As soon as his thrusts stop, my pussy begins pulsing with a second orgasm. I close my eyes as it takes over, my inner muscles contracting powerfully around his shaft as I climax again. This orgasm is even more intense than the first.

I whimper softly afterward.

Sir buries his hand in my hair and pulls my head back to give me a sweaty kiss. "Consider yourself claimed."

CHAPTER TWO

Rᴙᴛꜱᴀʀ ᴅᴏᴇꜱɴ'ᴛ ʀᴇᴛᴜʀɴ until late that afternoon, and it takes his men almost an hour to unload the vehicles and find places for everything he has purchased—including several chickens and a small coop.

I giggle as I watch several of his men set down the coop and start building a fence around it. Little Hope is fascinated by the birds, and points to them babbling excitedly.

"Why chickens?" I ask.

"Fresh eggs, *radost moya!*"

Sir gives Rytsar a side-glance, stating sarcastically, "How incredibly thoughtful of you."

Rytsar slaps him on the back. "You will thank me, *moy droog.*"

"I highly doubt that."

"Just wait, comrade. You *will* thank me."

Knowing how much Sir hates eggs, I can't help but wonder if Rytsar is up to something. However, I am totally distracted by the numerous cases of vodka and pickles he's brought. "You'd think we were preparing for a year, not a few months."

"We will lack for nothing," Rytsar assures me with a wink.

After his men are done unloading the supplies and the fence has been built, Rytsar gets out his wallet and hands each man several large bills. "Go in good health and keep your families safe."

I can tell by the expressions on their faces that his men are not only surprised by his gesture, but also touched by it. Only one man remains once he's dismissed them all.

Putting his hand on Maxim's shoulder, Rytsar asks, "You are certain you want to stay?"

"*Da, gospodin.* My parents are safe with my sister, and you need me."

Rytsar nods. "I am grateful to have your service."

Maxim nods stiffly.

Rytsar claps him on the back. "You may retire for now. It's been a long day for all of us." He hands Maxim a bottle of vodka and a jar of pickles before dismissing him.

The Russian's gaze rests on me after Maxim leaves. Raising an eyebrow, he pulls a pine needle from my hair. "I see you went for a walk while I was gone."

I blush slightly, glancing at Sir. "We did."

Rytsar grins, nodding at us both. "Nothing like fresh mountain air to get the blood pumping."

"Among other things," Sir replies with a smirk.

Rytsar chuckles knowingly. Taking Hope from my arms, he smiles as he lifts her into the air. "With you three here and the pantry stocked, I shall want for nothing—no matter how long this self-isolation lasts."

"Thank you for your hospitality, old friend," Sir tells him solemnly.

"What hospitality?" Rytsar scoffs. He looks at me and grins. "This is *radost moya*'s cabin, after all. I am grateful to be invited."

I purse my lips in a smile. "Best birthday present ever."

"I couldn't agree more," Rytsar growls, wrapping his free arm around me to pull me close. "A gift that keeps on giving…"

"I'm grateful we can spend so much time here together," I confess.

He squeezes me tight against his muscular body. "Let's make memories together."

Bouncing Hope in his arm, he surprises me when he announces, "First on the list is feeding the chickens with *moye solntse*."

I smile as I follow him outside with Sir. The beautiful thing about Rytsar is that he is highly unpredictable but unfailingly passionate about the people he loves.

Taking a small handful of grain from the container, he tosses it into the pen. The moment the three chickens run up and start pecking at the ground, Hope bursts out in a string of giggles.

As they peck away, Rytsar points to each one and names them. "I think that black and brown one should be called Sir Clucks-A-Lot, in honor of you, *moy droog*. The pretty white-crested hen reminds me of *radost moya,* so I'm calling her Mother Clucker."

I giggle, amused by his name choice.

"And the majestic golden bird is the Grand Pecker."

Sir snorts. "Named after you, of course."

"Naturally."

Rytsar grabs some more grain and puts it in Hope's tiny hand so she can feed them. Being a curious child, she opens her mouth and tries to taste it, but Rytsar gently stops her. "*Nyet, moye solntse*."

Guiding her hand over the fence, he helps her spread the grain on the ground. The chickens make happy clucking sounds as they gobble it up. Hope squeals with joy and holds her hand out for more.

Sir smiles tenderly at his daughter. "I may have questioned your purchase of the chickens, but they have entertainment value I can appreciate."

Rytsar smirks. "I knew you'd come around to my way of thinking, comrade."

194

I wake up the next morning with a feeling of such profound joy that I feel I might burst. As the first rays of light announce the new dawn, I sneak out of bed, careful not to wake Sir.

Wrapping myself in a fluffy robe, I slip my cold feet into my slippers, and walk outside. The birds are already chirping in the trees above me, welcoming the new day.

I stand, holding my breath in awe, waiting for the sun to breach the top of the mountain and fill the valley with its warm light.

Mesmerized by the miracle and majesty of a new day, I sigh in contentment.

"Beautiful, isn't it?" Rytsar says, walking up from behind me.

"It is. Funny to think that this happens every day, but I rarely have time to enjoy it."

He nods. "There is a lot we miss each day."

"So true…"

I turn my head when I hear Sir approaching. "Good morning, Sir."

"I figured I might find you out here," he says, wrapping his arm around me.

"I couldn't miss this," I tell him, looking up at the sky painted with pink, purple, and orange.

He lifts my chin and kisses me on the lips. "We would be getting ready to fly this morning if the lockdown hadn't taken place."

I shake my head. "It's crazy to think about."

Sir takes something out of his pocket. In his palm is the piece of glass jewelry he had me wear once when I was under Tono's care. "I wanted you to wear this during the plane ride home, but I prefer to have you wear it here." He leans down and whispers in my ear. "I want you to anticipate what I have planned for today."

My eyes widen. "What's that, Sir?"

In answer, he glances at Rytsar and smiles. Just thinking about being taken by both men makes my pussy contract in pleasure.

He places the erotic jewelry in my hand. "Go put it on and get dressed. I have already picked out what I want you to wear for today."

"Yes, Sir," I answer excitedly. Standing on tiptoe, I give him a quick kiss before going back into the cabin. The butterflies start as I head down the hallway knowing that those two men are talking about the scene they will be playing out with me.

I look down at the blue glass accented by gold attached to a thin black thong and purr inwardly. I remember how important this piece of jewelry was while Sir and I were separated. I'd spent many happy hours in the gym thinking about him with it inside me.

After taking a quick shower, I slip the longer glass end into my pussy while the other end rests snuggly against my clit. This particular jewelry has a dual purpose. It adorns my clit with gold but also stimulates my inner muscles with the smooth portion of the glass. The hard material ensures that I will feel its pressure as I move about my day.

I look in the mirror and turn from side to side, enjoying how it covers my clit in shiny gold. The jewelry gives my pussy a sexy and exotic look.

I put on the white dress that Sir has laid out for me. It has a silky texture that caresses my skin as I slip it on.

I look again at my reflection. The dress has a deep V-neck that frames my breasts nicely, and the cinched waist accentuates my hips. The material not only excites my nipples, but the sheerness of it allows them to be seen clearly.

When I turn to look at my back, I can see the outline of the black thong through the dress. It adds another sexy element that I'm certain both men will enjoy.

I appreciate Sir's thoughtful choice in clothing and want to complement his look by taking extra time with my hair, adding a few playful curls to my long, brown hair. I choose to keep my makeup simple, only emphasizing my eyes and lips.

I return to Sir and he greets me with a low whistle of appreciation.

I blush in pleasure when Sir tells me to turn around slowly for him and I bask in his lustful gaze.

"She looks good enough to eat, *moy droog*," Rytsar growls.

"That she does, old friend."

Sir takes my hand and pulls me to him. Leaning down for a kiss, he hesitates for a moment before pressing his lips against mine. My heart starts to race as he runs his hands down my body and grasps my butt before giving me a quick swat.

My pussy contracts around the jewelry inside me, causing pleasurable tingles of excitement.

He smiles with a wicked glint in his eyes. "I plan to tease you mercilessly today."

I shiver with anticipation. "I look forward to it, Sir."

The morning becomes a pleasurable game of "torture the submissive" as Sir touches and kisses me whenever I pass him as I go about my day. By the afternoon, I am a quivering ball of need.

Rytsar, watching with interest since the beginning, suddenly declares, "I'm taking *moye solntse* to play on the swing set." He picks her up and starts toward the door.

"I'll join you. It's such a beautiful day outside," I exclaim as I go to follow him.

Sir takes me by the arm, lightly brushing my lips with his finger before commanding, "Stay for a moment, téa."

Hearing my pet name gives me goosebumps because it lets me know that the scene has officially begun and I answer dutifully, "It would be my pleasure, Master."

After Rytsar leaves with Hope, Sir kisses me. At first, his kiss is tender as he presses his lips firmly against mine. Then his tongue parts my mouth…

My entire body aches to be possessed by him as the kiss deepens and becomes more passionate. I'm left breathless when he ends the sensual embrace.

"I want you to kiss Durov in the same way," he commands. "Let it be a surprise. Don't even hint that you are going to do it."

Sir's kiss has left me trembling—but his command makes me weak. "If it pleases you, Master."

"It does." Sir kisses me again, pressing my body against his before releasing me.

I feel a little lightheaded as I leave the cabin to join Rytsar by the swing set. I have never taken the initiative when interacting with the Russian, and I am uncertain how the sexy sadist will react.

As soon as I hear Hope's giggles as he pushes her higher, I break into a smile.

"Your little one is a daredevil," he comments with pride.

I look at her lovingly. "She does have an adventurous soul."

Rytsar glances at me, raising an eyebrow. "Much like her mother."

My heart starts racing, knowing what Sir has commanded me to do, but I try to hide it by nonchalantly giving Hope a push myself.

She lets out another peal of laughter that tickles my heart.

After several minutes of innocent fun, I decide it's time to go for it. Taking a deep breath, I turn to face Rytsar.

Standing on my tiptoes, I grab his face in my hands and kiss him. Before he can react, I slip my tongue in his mouth and hear his low groan.

He suddenly fists my hair, pulling my head back as he claims my mouth. I lose myself in his kiss, a captive of the Russian's possessive hold. He lets out another groan before breaking the embrace.

We stare at each other for several seconds before Rytsar goes back to pushing Hope.

My body aches with desire as I stand there, literally shaking.

Maxim walks out of the cabin and nods to me before telling Rytsar. "I have come to push the baby."

Rytsar smirks. "Did Davis send you?"

"He did, *gospodin*."

Rytsar stops the swing and kisses Hope on the top of her head. "You are in good hands, *moye solntse*."

Turning to Maxim, he orders, "After the swing, take her to feed the chickens."

Maxim gives him a curt nod.

Rytsar breaks out in laughter. "I bet you never thought this is what you would be doing when you vowed to protect me."

"As long as I don't have to touch a diaper, I won't complain," Maxim states somberly.

Rytsar takes me by the wrist and leads me to the cabin. When I see the ravenous look in his eyes and the large bulge straining his pants, my heart skips a beat.

My unexpected kiss seems to have awakened the beast in him.

CHAPTER THREE

"*Moy droog!*" Rytsar calls out as soon as we enter the cabin.

"What?" Sir answers from the back.

With his hand squeezing my wrist even tighter, Rytsar leads me to the back bedroom. Sir is standing beside the bed with a length of rope dangling in his hand.

My eyes go straight to the jute and pleasant chills course down my spine. Sir knows how much I adore bondage...

"Did you order your submissive to assault me with a kiss?" Rytsar demands.

Sir looks amused when he answers, "I did, and it appears you enjoyed it." He throws the rope to Rytsar. "Bind her wrists behind her back."

Rytsar looks down at me hungrily. "First, you must be punished for being so forward with me, *radost moya.*"

Knowing he's a sadist, my heart starts racing again. Instead of a hard swat like I expect, he lifts the skirt of my dress and grasps my ass cheeks in his hands as his lips descend on my throat.

He bites just hard enough to bruise my tender skin and a chill courses through me. The possessive nature of the bite calls to my submissive side. That's when the room echoes with the sound of his palm making contact with my bare ass. I squeak from the intense sting of it.

"Now that you've been punished, you shall be rewarded for obeying your Master," Rytsar murmurs huskily. He wraps his hand around my throat and kisses me. The ardent passion behind his kiss has my pussy clenching the toy inside me.

After the Russian releases his hold, he turns me to face my Master as he takes off my dress before binding my wrists with the jute. I look at Sir as Rytsar finishes binding me, marveling at the fact that he knows my deepest desires and is honoring them in this scene.

After my wrists are securely bound, Rytsar leads me to the bed. I follow, a willing captive to their kinky desires.

Sir gazes at me intently as he slowly undresses before me, the hardness of his shaft announcing his state of arousal. Sir then removes the jewelry from my pussy. It drips with my obvious arousal. Looking at me with a pleased expression, he lays it on the side table.

"Come to me, téa."

I melt into his open arms, my nipples aching with desire when they brush against his bare chest.

But Sir isn't the only one who wants me.

Rytsar quickly discards his clothes, growling like a Kodiak bear once he's shed them. He approaches us, his raw need easy to see.

"I want you, *radost moya.*"

I can barely breathe as he rolls my nipples between his fingers before lying on the bed. "Grind yourself on my cock."

I join Rytsar on the bed and position myself above his hard shaft, pressing my wet pussy against it. Grabbing my waist, he pushes me down onto his cock. I cry out in satisfaction as he guides me up and down on his shaft with his powerful hands.

I completely lose myself in the intimate connection until I feel Sir caress my bare ass. The sensual feel of his touch travels straight to my loins, causing my inner muscles to contract around Rystar's shaft.

The Russian groans in pleasure. "*Radost moya…*"

I feel a jolt of electricity when Sir presses the head of his lubricated cock against my tight opening.

"Your ass begs for my attention," he growls as he slowly presses it into me.

I moan as my body accepts the challenge of taking both men at the same time.

Rytsar stops moving as Sir penetrates my ass slowly so my body can adjust to having two cocks inside me. When I eventually take his entire length, I am gratified to hear Sir's low grunt of pleasure.

I savor this moment, enjoying the feeling of both men buried deep inside my body.

When Sir begins thrusting, I open my eyes and gaze down at Rytsar.

"You like it this way," he growls knowingly.

"Yes…" I purr, unable to deny it.

Sir grasps my bound wrists while he caresses my ass with his long strokes, expressing his love for me through this intimate connection.

I moan in pure ecstasy.

My cries of passion spur Rytsar to grab my waist as he matches Sir's strokes, and I take both men equally. Chills course through my body as I open myself to their deeper thrusts.

My desire to please both Doms tests my body, but the sub-high their double penetration creates is like nothing else I've experienced, and I beg for more.

Sir responds by moving subtly, the new angle of his strokes causing the sensation to become more intense. I throw my head back, crying out in pleasure.

When my orgasm hits, it is so intense that tears prick my eyes.

"Oh. My. God!"

My passionate screams fill the air as I come. It seems to break the control of both Doms and they respond by coming inside me at the same time, joining me in my climax.

I moan as my inner muscles milk both cocks, contracting with intense pleasure. After the last pulse subsides, Sir grunts in satisfaction as he pulls out and lies down on the bed beside me.

Rytsar unbinds my wrists before rolling me toward Sir as he disengages, so I am lying between both men.

We lay there panting together in unified silence.

I stare up at the ceiling—my heart full and my body completely satisfied.

After several minutes, Sir breaks the silence by telling me, "This is only the beginning, babygirl."

I turn to him and smile weakly, still flying on the sub-high he's created with this scene.

Oh, how I love being his submissive…

ABOUT RED PHOENIX

USA Today Bestselling Author Red Phoenix is an award-winning romance author who gained popularity with her series, Brie's Submission.

A submissive in real life, Red enjoys sharing the joy and fun of BDSM through Brie's encounters at the Submissive Training Center.

www.redphoenixauthor.com

WINE CELLAR
Rendezvous
D. KELLY

CHAPTER ONE

WYATT

"Why did you offer to drop me off? Mac was ready to go," I ask Sawyer as he punches in the gate code for the sprawling estate in front of us.

"It was either go for a drive and drop you off, go to a bar and find a rando to fuck, or stay on the bus and annoy Princess and Noah. Figured this was my best option."

Sawyer is trying to be sincere, I can tell, but he's got so many issues that taking a drive isn't going to solve them all. "Why do you push them? Especially her? You could try being nice for a change, Sawyer."

The house is lit up as we turn off the long entrance road to the circular drive in front of the estate. "I'm just trying to get to know her—see where her boundaries lie and what I can get away with. Don't let her sweet smile fool you. We've only known her a few weeks, and she has more access to our lives than we've ever given anyone. She could still screw us over."

Sometimes, Sawyer's skeptical nature gets the best of him. I wish he had more of an optimistic personality like his twin, Noah. "Tonight is a good night, and I'm not going to let you get me down. When you go back, try to be nice, if for no other reason, do it for Noah."

"We'll see… it's fun watching her blush," he replies with a smirk. "Don't forget you've only got three hours, Wyatt, so make them count. And hey," he says as I reach for the door handle, "tell Bethie Happy Anniversary from me."

"Will do, but don't forget while you're making her blush that she's off-limits. Mel works for us, remember?"

"Doesn't mean I can't have a little fun. Later, Wyatt."

I close the door and bound up the stairs to the entrance. My wife, Anna Beth, is Anna to everyone except Sawyer, who calls her Bethie. They've been best friends since we were in junior high, and I know it's killing him not to see her tonight. But I figure on today, of all days, husband trumps best friend status. He'll see her soon enough.

Our band Bastards and Dangerous, aka BAD, has only been back on the road for a few weeks. This is our last tour, and as much as I'll miss performing, I can't handle constantly being away from my wife. We agreed early on she would focus on her career and that means staying behind while I'm touring. I'm immensely proud of her for rising through the ranks of her publishing company, but only seeing each other once a month blows. For years, she's sacrificed for me, so now, it's my turn.

Today is our anniversary, not of our wedding but from when we first started dating. It's been fifteen years, and as much as I wish we could have more time, our bus leaves in a few hours, and this was all we could make work. This house belongs to an executive from our label, and he graciously offered it up to us while his family is out of the country. Really, he did it for Anna—they hit it off years ago, and he's had a soft spot for her ever since.

I pull out the key and open the door, locking it behind me. We can never know for sure when we've been followed by a fan, and since I managed to get our security team to let me come alone, the last thing we need is trouble.

"Anna, are you here yet?" My words echo as I walk through the empty house. All the lights are on, and as I enter the kitchen, I see her phone on the counter and her suitcase next to the island. I bet I know exactly where she is.

We've stayed here a few times over the years for networking events, and Stan isn't the least bit stingy with his wine collection. Anna was extremely excited when he said we could help ourselves because we've never actually seen the inside of his prized cellar. As I pass the library, I notice the door to the stairs leading down to the wine cellar is ajar.

After descending the stairs, I open the massive door to the cellar. The lights are on, but they're dim, and I don't see her right away. "Anna, are you down here?"

"Oh, Wyatt, thank God! Don't let the door–" The door slams shut behind me as she rounds the corner. "Close," she adds with a sigh.

"What's going on? I thought you'd look happier to see me."

She flashes me a soft smile, "Baby, I'm always happy to see you, but something is wrong with the door. I don't know how long I've been down here, but it's been a while."

I turn back to the door and try opening it, but it's no use. It's stuck. The door is solid oak, and the hinges are on the outside.

"No problem. I'll just call and tell Sawyer to turn back around."

"Oh good, you have your phone. I left mine upstairs in the kitchen."

The first thing I see when I pull my phone out of my pocket is the flashing no signal warning. Shit. I show Anna my phone, and her face falls slightly as she takes my hand and leads me deeper into the cellar.

"The impressive thing about this house is that Stan thought of everything. There's a small kitchen down here, and it's fully stocked with glasses, meats, cheeses, crackers, and there is even a bathroom. Don't be mad, but I started without you."

Stan is a foodie and a bit of a lush, so when we round the corner and come upon a plush extra bedroom with a nice sitting area, I'm not surprised. An uncorked bottle of wine and a nearly empty glass of Cabernet are on the table. Anna leads me through the bedroom and into the bathroom, which is equivalent to five-star hotel suite accommodations.

I wrap my arms around her and kiss the top of her head. "Well, we won't starve, and we won't be dirty. Everything else will work itself out."

She leans against my body and sighs. "What about your show?"

"I'll make it."

"How do you know?" she asks, turning in my arms to face me.

"Warren talks a good game, but we've never left anyone behind before. Mac will drive up here and find us when I don't show up. Even if the rest of them head out, Mac will have a backup plan."

Warren is our manager, and Mac is our head of security—they'll be more worried than anything. Disappearing is a Sawyer or a Darren thing. Noah and I are the reliable ones, and since they know I'm with Anna, once either of us don't answer our phones, they'll come straight here.

"I'm sorry, Wyatt. This isn't exactly how I thought this would go."

I take a few steps forward, backing her into a wall, and her eyes widen. "I'm not. There is no one I'd rather be locked up with than you."

She inhales audibly, and the connection between us zaps with electricity. I trace her lips with my finger. "It's been far too long since these lips were on mine."

"It has… but first any truths?"

Anna and I have a system. We've found that the key to a successful relationship is to have complete and total honesty. Between overzealous fans, meet and greets, hotel ambushes, and the way the media can take a photo completely out of context, we had to find something that worked for us. Before we lose ourselves in our desire, if something is bothering either of us, we pause and ask for the truth.

"Nothing, Anna. My heart, my love, and my body are only for you."

"Promise?" she asks softly, and I know she saw something that's put her on edge.

"Cross my heart. Do you want to talk about it?"

She shakes her head. "Not now."

That's not how this is supposed to work, but we have such little time together tonight that I let it go.

"Can I kiss you?"

"I hope you'll do more than that."

My lips graze hers, and she wraps her arms around my neck. Damn, I've missed the feeling of her body against mine. The scent of her perfume lights my senses on fire. It's times like these that I know I made the right decision to stop touring. Anna is my entire fucking world.

Our lips meet, and her mouth opens to me. As our tongues collide, I taste a hint of wine as she slides her leg against mine. I lower my hands to her ass and lift her. Anna wraps her legs around my waist and whimpers as my cock presses against her. I lower my mouth to her neck and bite down as I pull her hair, and she cries out.

"God, I've missed you. I want to feel you for days Wyatt."

"Is that so?"

"Mm-hmm."

Anna tosses her head back, allowing me to nip her neck and jaw with my teeth. She holds me tight and writhes against me. I slip my hand up her skirt and groan… "You're not wearing any panties."

"We have limited time, and they'd just get in the way. I love you, Wyatt."

"I love you, too."

"Good, now fuck me like you don't."

I love that my wife tells me exactly what she wants. I carry her over to the bathroom counter and set her down.

"You're feisty tonight." I step back and take off my shirt before kicking off my shoes and unzipping my pants.

"Maybe it's the wine… or maybe I'm just tired of getting myself off."

I try not to let that last part get to me.

"Whatever the case may be, I like it when you're riled up. It makes fucking you into submission all the more fun."

She bites her bottom lip and nods. "Take the boxers off, Wyatt. I want to watch you stroke yourself."

Anna scoots back on the counter, putting her feet up on the edge, and spreads her legs wide. As I reach for my dick, she slides her finger through her wetness and then holds it out to me. "Want to taste?"

My cock leaks, providing the added lubrication I need. She watches mesmerized at I step closer and lower my mouth to her outstretched finger. As my tongue circles her essence, she whimpers, never taking her eyes off me.

"You're sure you want to feel it for days?"

"Weeks." Her voice cracks. "But I figured that was too big of an ask."

Reaching for her legs, I slide her to the edge of the counter. "Good choice with the flowy skirt."

"I thought so, too," she whispers as I pull her from the counter and face her toward the mirror.

"Bend over."

She does as I tell her, and I flip her skirt up, giving me a perfect view of her ass. As I run soft circles over the globes of her ass, her eyes meet mine in the mirror. "Please, Wyatt."

When I lower my hand to her ass, the sound echoes through the room. Her eyes light up in the mirror, and she smiles. "Harder, babe. Make it bruise."

Anna has one big kink; she loves being spanked. Even more, she loves seeing the imprint of my hand on her ass. Turning my wife on is my number one goal. When she's turned on, I am too, but sometimes, I have a hard time with the idea of bruising her.

"Wyatt, look at me." Our gazes meet in the mirror. "Don't freak out on me. We're two consenting adults, and this makes me happy. You're visibly turned on, so stop overanalyzing and feel how wet I am for you already."

I lean over her and kiss her neck as I slip my finger inside her. She's extremely wet, and it's been way too long since we've had sex. As I slide my finger to her clit, I spank her again and again. Her pleasureful cries fill the room, and when her ass is bright red, I thrust into her.

"Yes, Wyatt, yes!" she screams as I fill her completely. Nothing feels as good as being inside my wife. Knowing I won't last long, I reach around and squeeze her clit, and she comes fast, bucking back against me as she screams my name. With one last thrust, I come inside her before gently lying on top of her.

Anna giggles, and I kiss her cheek before pulling out of her and standing up. "What's so funny?"

She moves over to the massive oversize bathtub and turns on the water. "Take a bath with me?" I nod, and she moves around the bathroom, opening cabinets until she finds towels and brings them back to the counter. "I was just thinking that most people locked in a room would be freaked the fuck out, but we just jump right into sex."

I step into the tub and hold out my hand to her. I'm so much taller than she is, so she waits until I'm settled and then tucks herself between my legs.

"Well, I'm perfectly happy to be locked up with you in our own private sex dungeon. We've got enough stuff down here to live happily for at least a week."

She giggles, "There's enough food for about six months. I think Stan hides from his wife down here for weeks at a time."

"Even better. We'll be well-fed, happily buzzed, and we can fuck like rabbits. What more could we want?"

Anna leans against my chest and sighs contentedly. "Nothing. It sounds nearly perfect."

We relax in a comfortable silence for a few minutes before Anna laces our fingers together. "Do you realize that's the first time we've had sex since I went off the pill?"

Recently, we decided we're ready to start the next phase in our lives. Since it can take a while to get pregnant, and we only see each other once a month, Anna went off the pill. I couldn't be happier—I'm so ready for this next step.

"I didn't even think about it, but that's cool. Are you okay with your choice still?"

"Totally. With how much we see each other, I'm sure it won't happen right away, anyway. Knowing that we're trying after all these years makes me undeniably happy."

I squeeze her hand and kiss her head, "It's incredible. Now, do you want to tell me what was bothering you earlier?"

"Nope, I want to enjoy my buzz and my post-orgasm high. We'll talk later. Right now, I just want to relax and relish our time together."

Sounds good to me.

CHAPTER TWO

ANNA

AFTER OUR BATH, I found two big fluffy robes in the closet for Wyatt and me. While he looks for a couple of bottles of wine for us to try, I'm making us a tray of snacks. He's giving me space, but I know he's worried about what's bothering me. Hell, I'm worried too. We have debriefing rules in place for a reason. When you spend a lot of time away from your uber-famous spouse, things can fester quickly if you let them. We are not a couple who typically lets anything fester.

I'm honestly more angry with myself right now. Ever since I stopped taking the pill a little over a month ago, my hormones are all over the place. I know my husband is faithful, but for the first time, I can't shake the feeling something happened he isn't telling me about.

"Earth to Anna… you've got enough food there to feed an army."

I look down at the summer sausage I was slicing and chuckle. "Oops, I got lost in my thoughts. We'll pack up any leftovers once we're sprung from our jail, and you can take them on the bus."

"Jail? Hell, baby, this is paradise. I'm going to ask Stan if I can send him on vacation just so we can do this again for an entire weekend next time."

Wyatt grabs some wine glasses and a super fancy corkscrew

while I put the finishing touches on our food before following him to the little sitting area in the bedroom.

"Just be sure you clear the destination with Stan's wife," I caution, Lydia is a force to be reckoned with, and no one wants to end up on her bad side.

Wyatt nods as he pours our wine. "Noted." He passes me a glass and lifts his in a toast. "I know we don't get much time together, but I love that we make the best of the time we have. You are my best friend and the love of my life. Happy Anniversary, Anna."

"Happy Anniversary, my love." As our glasses touch, I blink back my tears, and Wyatt sets down his glass.

"Okay, enough. You aren't an emotional person normally. What's going on?"

I shake my head and sniff. "Nothing big, I swear. I think it's birth control hormone withdrawal or something."

He looks at me, and his brow furrows. "The doctor said that could happen right?"

"Yes, she said some women have hormonal shifts as their bodies reset, and it should be temporary."

Wyatt leans back in his chair, and I gulp my wine. It's really good and meant to be savored, but I need some liquid courage and fast.

"Well, that's good, but if you keep feeling off, promise me you'll make an appointment."

"I promise."

We snack a little and sip our wine, but the whole time, he keeps glancing at me as if he doesn't know what to say.

"Oh, this is ridiculous!" I throw my hands in the air before blurting out what's been bothering me. "There was a photo in a tabloid of you hugging Eliza Waterstone." His eyes widen, and it's not a good look. My stomach lurches as more tears spring to my eyes.

"Anna, it's not what you think."

"Then tell me what I think, Wyatt, because we had an agreement that you'd *never* hang out with her again. I know pictures can be misleading, but your hands were around her waist and resting on her lower back. The two of you looked awfully cozy with smiles and all."

With an exaggerated sigh, I reach for my wine. I hate being this person, but the only time Wyatt and I have ever fought over other women has been when Eliza is around. She's one of the executive's daughters, and she gets whatever she wants. Eliza has the world's biggest crush on Wyatt and even went as far as getting him drunk before kissing him at a party. What hurts the most is that he kissed her back. It was early in their career, and she's the reason we tell each other everything now, even if it hurts. So the fact that he didn't even mention that he saw her screams betrayal.

"I'm sorry, Anna. I know I screwed up." Wyatt places his wine on the table and gets down on his knees in front of me.

"Why didn't you tell me you saw her?"

He pulls my hand to his mouth and kisses it. "Because I wanted to avoid arguing. I took care of it, and it will never happen again."

"You were hugging her, intimately!"

Wyatt releases an exhausted sigh. "No, I was hugging you. Fuck… just listen for a minute and believe in us, okay?"

"Okay," I answer wearily.

"Some executives showed up the second week of the tour. Eliza is working at the label now, so she was with them. She thought it would be a 'hoot'—her words, to make me think you were there. She told a brand new intern she was my wife, and she wanted to surprise me. Long story short, I closed my eyes, and when I opened them, I was hugging her, not you."

"You couldn't tell?"

He runs his hands through his hair. "Of course, I could., I knew I wasn't hugging you immediately, and that's when I opened my eyes. Rapid-fire flashes blinded me the second I did, and I instinctively smiled because that's the job. It lasted less than a minute, but that's all it took."

I believe him, but I'm also furious with him and with the guys. "God, she's such a bitch! Why didn't anyone tell me?"

"They didn't tell you because I asked them not to. I handled it.

We were in a meeting, and the intern pulled me out—said there was something important I needed to take care of and then filled me in on my surprise. As soon as I could, I pulled Eliza from the room, back into the meeting, and threatened to leave the label. They fired Eliza, security got the reporters to delete the images in exchange for interviews, and that was it."

Wyatt stands and pulls me from my chair. "I planned on telling you. I just wanted to find the right time. I didn't want to hurt you or piss you off, and it was important to me I do it in person. Baby, I couldn't stand knowing I disappointed you again, but I promise you, it was nothing but a nightmare. You're my world, Anna, and I will quit the band right now if it makes you feel better. Nothing is more important to me than you."

He pulls me into his arms, and my worries melt away. "You had to know the photo leaked."

Wyatt sighs. "Yeah, but you don't read tabloids, and everyone knows you don't enjoy hearing tour gossip. I thought if you saw it before I could tell you, you'd talk to me about it. Sawyer told me I was being stupid, but he's not exactly a relationship expert, you know?"

"He's my best friend. He should've told me."

Wyatt tips my chin up so our eyes meet, "No, I'm your husband, so I should have told you. He respected that boundary, even if he didn't like it. He also wanted me to tell you Happy Anniversary."

"You should've asked Mel for her advice."

He cracks a half-smile, and I melt a little more because Wyatt has the best smile. "I barely know Mel, but since she's a romance author, I'm supposed to assume her advice would be good?"

I reach up on my tiptoes and kiss him briefly. "No, you're supposed to ask her advice because she'd give you a woman's point of view."

"And let me guess, women are always right?"

Wyatt pulls me close and spins me around before tossing me on the bed. I can't help but laugh as he lands on top of me. "Not all women, but Mel's a smart cookie. I trust her. Hopefully, we'll become friends."

"That would be nice," he murmurs against my neck as he peppers a trail of kisses along my skin. "Forgive me, Anna?"

"Always, as long as you never break my heart."

He unties my robe and sits up on his knees and takes his off. Naked Wyatt has always been my favorite view. He doesn't give me long to enjoy it before he lies down next to me.

"Take your robe off, Anna," he says before stroking his cock.

I follow his instructions while watching him play with himself.

"Are you just going to stare?"

"What would you like me to do?" I'm torn between sucking him off and riding him until we both come.

"Ride me, baby. Give me something to think about when I'm alone on the bus."

I climb on top and position him at my entrance before slowly sliding down his length. When he's fully seated inside me, I gasp. I'll never tire of the way it feels when Wyatt fills me.

His hands move to my hips, and he squeezes me tightly, just the way I like. We find our rhythm easily, and when I lean down to kiss him, he moves his hands up my back, pulling me flush to him.

Losing myself in Wyatt's love is what I was made for. As we kiss, our bodies move in a seductive dance. We make love until we're breathless, and just when I feel like I'm about to levitate out of my body, he brings me back to earth with a soul-shattering orgasm. My screams are loud enough to rival one of his shows, but thankfully, no one is around to hear me. Wyatt comes with me, and when we're both spent, I collapse on his chest.

"I miss this so much." I gasp, heart still racing from our sexcapades.

He runs his fingers through my hair and kisses the top of my head. "One more year, Anna, and then we're going to have so much sex you'll wish you could send me back out on tour."

"Hm, never, the sex is far too good. Besides, your new job as a stay-at-home dad will probably tire you out."

I'm having a hard time keeping my eyes open. The sex, the wine, all the emotional turmoil—I'm ready for a nap.

"Oh, I remember, and I can't wait."

Bam, bam, bam!

I jump up, still half asleep. "What was that?"

Wyatt is off the bed in a flash and grabs his robe off the floor as the banging starts again. Scurrying out of bed, I toss on my robe so I can follow him. When I reach the outer room, I'm not surprised to see our friends.

"What's with all the banging?" I ask through a yawn, and notice that the door is now propped open with a cinderblock. I vaguely remember seeing it out in the entryway, guess I know why now.

Sawyer smirks and motions toward me, clutching my robe. "Thought we'd give you a chance to get decent. You're welcome, Bethie."

Darren, the band's drummer and our other best friend, laughs. "Personally, I think we deserved a show since we had to come all the way out here to rescue you two."

"Sorry, guys, I got excited about the wine and got locked in. Then Wyatt came looking for me, and I didn't catch him in time, so the door closed before I could warn him. I feel awful."

"Likely story." Sawyer smiles and shrugs at the same time. "Well, get dressed. Noah and Mel went ahead to the next venue on our bus. The four of us and Mac are flying, which means you two lovebirds get your own room tonight after all."

"Uh, not me. I'm supposed to stay here and fly out in the morning." I'm tired, but I'm not delusional.

Darren snorts. "It's funny she thinks she has any say about this. Anna, you know us well enough by now to know that this is already a done deal."

"Don't be a dick," Sawyer snaps back. "Look, Stan feels bad. Mac called to see if he had camera access to the house, and that's when he remembered he didn't fix the cellar door. Stan said he'd prefer if you wouldn't stay here alone since the wine lures people in or some shit like that. Warren called Sam, told him what happened, and Sam said you deserve an extended trip, and he'll pick you up at the airport when your flight lands tomorrow night."

My boss, Sam, is married to the band's manager, Warren. Sam is a hopeless romantic and would do anything in the name of love.

"Okay, well, not to burst your bubble but chop-chop. I have a Skype sex session set up, and the two of you are seriously cock blocking me. The sooner we're on the plane, the sooner I'm in my hotel room and can get rid of my blue balls. I'll be in the car with Mac." Darren takes off, and we all burst out laughing.

I head toward the bathroom to get dressed, but curiosity gets the best of me, and I turn around. "Who is he Skyping?"

"Belle," Wyatt and Sawyer answer in unison.

"That's still going on?" I'm shocked. Darren is usually a one and done, fuck 'em and leave 'em kind of guy.

"Yup, I think our boy is whipped," Wyatt replies.

"That's two tonight," I warn him. "Better not make it three."

"Two?" Sawyer asks curiously.

"I told her about Eliza. She saw the photo."

Sawyer whacks Wyatt on the shoulder. "Told you, dumbass. Bethie, it was no big deal. She's a bitch, but if you want to figure out if Wyatt forgot to fill you in on anything else, you can sit by me on the plane."

"Not happening," Wyatt growls.

"Whatever offer stands if she wants it. Seriously, though, you two need to get dressed. The jet is waiting for us."

Sawyer leaves, and Wyatt and I quickly get dressed. I find some Ziploc bags in the kitchen and bag up the snacks while Wyatt washes the glasses. The least we can do is leave the place almost as clean as we found it.

I take one last look around, and Wyatt wraps his arms around me from behind. "This was fun," he says. "But I am sorry for keeping that secret. I know I broke our rules, and I will never do it again."

"I know you won't, and you're right. This was fun. If we hurry and get on the plane, we can have some more fun before I go home tomorrow. Happy Anniversary, Wyatt."

He spins me around and kisses me deeply. "Happy Anniversary, Anna."

ABOUT D. KELLY

D. Kelly, author of The Acceptance Series, The Illusion Series, and standalone companion novels Chasing Cassidy and Sharing Rylee, was born and raised in Southern California. She's a wife, mom, dog lover, taxi, problem fixer, and extreme multi-tasker. She married her high school sweetheart and is her kids' biggest fan. Kelly has been writing since she was young and took joy in spinning stories to her childhood friends. Margaritas and sarcasm make her smile, she loves the beach but hates the sand, and she believes Starbucks makes any day better.

A contemporary romance writer, D. Kelly's stories revolve around friendship and the bond it creates, strengthening the love of the people who share it.

www.dkellyauthor.com

UNDENIABLE
Love

REBECCA SHEA

CHAPTER ONE

I HOLD my breath as Landon and I stand shoulder-to-shoulder in the cramped elevator.

"Stuck." That's what the security guard told us. Until further notice no one is entering or leaving the hospital due to a "situation" outside the emergency room. Of course, Landon would think this was the perfect opportunity to head to the cafeteria to get coffee and catch up.

My stomach flip-flops as we stare straight ahead while people filter in and out at floors as we descend. It's been just under two years since I've been alone with him, and while I love Gabe, my heart still flutters in my chest for Landon, just like it did the night I met him. Landon was my safety net when I was falling apart, and selfless in his love for me by leading me back to Gabe knowing that he was who I needed—loved. And I do love Gabe. My heart and soul also loved Landon.

This is the first time I've admitted that to myself. I *loved* Landon. I still do. In a non-romantic way, but I loved him nonetheless. Unexpectedly, he shifts, sliding his hand into mine and squeezing it gently. It's exactly as I remember it—rough yet soft. Firm, yet caring. Warm and loving, just like him.

I exhale, releasing all the anxiety I've been holding back since finding Lindsay last night. Tears fill my eyes as the memories of the last twelve hours flash through my head like an old slide projector. How did this happen? How did Lindsay get to this point and none of us intervened earlier? The elevator slows to a stop and everyone exits—except for us. Landon glances at me and tightens his grip on my hand again as the doors slowly close. I squeeze his hand back just before he pulls me into his arms. It's a comforting embrace—familiar. The smell of his musky skin is exactly as I remember it. I inhale deeply, breathing him in. Calm settles in and my heart rate begins evens out.

"I'm sorry," he mumbles against my head. I fist his shirt in my hands, holding onto him like I have so many times before. He was always a safe space for me to land, and I relish that while we've moved on he still knows exactly what I need.

I swallow hard against my dry throat. "It's not your fault."

He hugs me harder. "I should have been here for her."

"You've always been there for her. You can't save everyone, Lan." But he does. He saved me and he'll save Lindsay, because that's what he does—that's who he is.

He shakes his head and clears his throat. "I don't know what I'd do if something happened to her."

I pull out of his embrace and look up at him. "Stop. She's going to be fine. She's going to make it through this. She's a fighter. Just like you."

His eyes mist over and he takes a deep breath as he reaches out and cups both sides of my face with his hands. His thumbs stroke my cheeks as his eyes search mine. "Just like you," he whispers. "I've missed you, Jess. I didn't realize how much until I saw you." His eyes fall from mine to my lips, just like they used too, only this time he won't kiss me, I won't let him.

"I've missed you too." We stand holding each other for I don't know how long, all I know is it feels good. "Come on. Let's grab coffee and catch up." I shrug out of his embrace as the elevator stops. I find a quiet corner table tucked away in the back of the cafeteria while Landon grabs two coffees from the barista.

I can't help but smile at him as he saunters across the white tile floor toward me. His worn blue jeans fit him perfectly in all the right places and his black shirt, rolled up at the sleeves, show off a new tattoo on his muscular forearm. Everyone in the cafeteria watches him; his presence fills the space. Women stare and he doesn't even notice—that's who he is, confident, sexy, and unaware.

He sets the coffees on the table and discards creamers and sugar packets from the palm of his hand.

"So talk to me," he says, settling into his chair. "It feels like it's been forever since we talked." His blue eyes find mine and his gaze is sincere. It has been forever, because talking to him is dangerous. It brings back feelings I shouldn't have since I'm engaged to Gabe. His lip curls into a half smile, and I can't help the butterflies in my stomach. That face. Everything about him still ignites something inside me.

"I'm doing really well. I went back to school and got a degree in psychology."

He cocks an eyebrow at me while dumping two sugar packets into his black coffee. "I've been doing some outreach and public speaking on sexual assault. I feel like I've found my voice—for that I have to thank you." He purses his lips like he's going to say something but offers me a tight smile instead.

"I'm proud of you, Jess. I really am." He pauses. "And everything is good with, Gabe?" I see his jaw muscles tighten when he says Gabe's name, and I bite my inner cheek to keep from smiling. I know he's with Reagan. Lindsay told me all about her, but it's cute to see that he still has that jealous flare in him.

"Everything is great. We're…" I hold up my left hand and flash my ring. "We've been engaged for a while, but decided to wait to get married until I finished my degree. Not rushing into anything, you know?" I look down at the cardboard cup of coffee in my hands and spin it around nervously. I didn't exactly expect to get into relationship details with Landon, except this is the first time we've talked since I left Wilmington.

"Congratulations," he says quietly.

I nod in awkward acknowledgment. "Lindsay told me you're getting married too." I shift the conversation to him. He nods his head.

"I am."

"Tell me about her." I sip on the hot coffee and focus on the burning liquid that settles on my tongue.

"Her name is Reagan. She's a doctor…." He sighs and looks across the table at me. "She reminds me so much of you, Jess. She's tall, and beautiful, and strong." His voice is strained and trails off. I smile at him.

"I know I already said this, but seeing you again—" There's a long pause and his gaze holds mine. I didn't realize just how much I missed you."

"I miss you too," I admit. "But you have Reagan, and she sounds amazing." He looks away from me and out the window of the cafeteria that overlooks a courtyard full of small shrubs, trees, and beautiful flowers. It's such a tranquil place in the middle of a huge hospital. Silence fills the space around us as we settle into each other's presence. It's not uncomfortable, but peaceful. It's not awkward, it's comforting. It's how we always were. Sometimes short of words, but at peace in each other's presence. His face twists into a look I've never seen before, and it's enough for me to pause and question him.

"Lan, are you happy?" Our eyes lock and something passes between us. Unsaid words bubble at the surface. He swallows hard and nods. Not necessarily a lie, but also not convincing either.

He takes a sip of his coffee and asks me. "Are you?"

Am I? I am. I have the best man on the face of the earth. The love of my life. The person I am going to commit my life to. But within arm's reach, across the table, lies the other part of my heart. The other best man on the earth. The other best man in my life. The man who brought me back to life. I can't deny that or the feelings I once had for him.

"I am," I whisper. My eyes drop to my hands that rest on the table and they're trembling. One of his large hands moves in to cover mine, squeezing them gently. A silent gesture of knowing that we'll always have those feelings for each other, the ones we have to leave unspoken.

"Do you ever wonder…what if…" he stops himself.

"I can't—" I start before stopping abruptly.

"Why?" His voice is strained with emotion. His hand grip mine again and my throat tightens.

I let out a long exhale before speaking. "Because you're happy, Lan. And I'm happy. What if's will strangle that happiness and eat us alive. We have to leave the past in the past and live in the present."

"But are we really happy?" he asks. "I mean are we, or are we lying to each other? To ourselves?" We sit staring at each other across the small table. Minutes pass and the cafeteria starts coming to life with people who are taking a break from the friends and family they're here to see or hospital staff on their breaks. Noise fills the once quiet space and I don't answer Landon's question, because I can't.

There will always be a sense of the unknown between us. We will never know what could have been, and that's how we have to move forward. We have to put faith in the fact that everything happened the way it was supposed to. Landon's cellphone vibrates on the table and he glances at the screen.

He clears his throat then takes a deep breath. "We should probably head back up." He knows I can't answer his question, and even if I did, what good would it do? Would I leave Gabe and would he leave Reagan? Would he move to California or would I move back to North Carolina? The answer is no to all of those questions. Fate brought him into my life when I needed him, he showed up in the way he was supposed to, and he let me go exactly when I needed him to.

I slide my chair back from the table and stand up. "Thanks for the coffee and the talk." As I turn to walk away, Landon catches my elbow, stopping me.

"I have to say this or it'll always be something I regret," he says, his voice breaking. I cock my head to the side and wait for him. It's unusual to see Landon so serious, so full of emotion. My stomach tightens with unease.

"Okay," I drawl.

"There was something I should have told you before you left North Carolina…but I chickened out. With everything you revealed, I panicked and didn't want you to feel I was feeding you a line of bullshit just for the sake of saying it."

"What is it?" I ask him, knowing damn well what he's about to say. I hold my breath and wait.

"Jess, I know it doesn't matter now. But it mattered then." He swallows hard and takes a deep breath.

I have to stop him. "Landon. Remember…you're happy and I'm happy, right?"

He nods.

"Once you say something, those words can't be taken back. It may have mattered then, but maybe that's where it needs to stay. In the past."

He steps in closer and brushes his knuckles across my cheek. His thumb stops, resting on my cheekbone. "You're happy and I'm happy," he whispers, his eyes searching mine as they soften before he nods. "Right. Let's get upstairs."

I turn quickly and walk in the direction of the elevators but there's no mistaking what he mumbles behind me.

"I've always loved you."

My feet become cement blocks and I stop suddenly, digesting his words again. I turn to look back at him, and he quickly catches up, stopping when we're toe-to-toe.

"Jess—" He pauses, looking away from me.

"I heard what you—" I begin before his hands grasp my face and pull me to him. His warm lips press against mine, stopping my words. My mind takes me back to Wilmington where he last kissed me. He tastes like mint and coffee, and he's everything I remember him to be. Safe, comforting, and controlling, and I let him kiss me. I bask in the memory of everything he was for me before he breaks our kiss and pulls away, his hands falling from my face to my upper arms.

"I'm sorry…I shouldn't have done that—"

I simply nod, accepting his apology. Only I'm not sorry he did it. It was the closure we both needed, the finality of what we never allowed to happen when I left North Carolina.

"Friends forever, okay?" I tell him. He nods.

"You're happy and I'm happy, and that's what we focus on from here on out." He reaches for my hand and slides his fingers into mine again. He pulls me gently toward the elevator and presses the button while we wait for the doors to open.

He holds my hand tightly before releasing it as we step into the elevator, the doors closing behind us symbolic of our past. We've closed the doors on what we were, and I've never been more content with where we are now.

ABOUT REBECCA SHEA

Rebecca Shea is the USA Today Bestselling author of the Unbreakable series, including: Unbreakable, Undone, and Unforgiven, and the Bound and Broken series, including: Broken by Lies, Bound by Lies & Betrayed by Lies. As well as standalone novels, Dare Me, Fault Lines, and Unexpectedly Yours. She lives in Phoenix, Arizona with her family. From the time Rebecca could read she has had a passion for books. Rebecca spends her days working and her nights writing, bringing stories to life. Born and raised in Minnesota, Rebecca moved to Arizona in 1999 to escape the bitter winters. When not working or writing, she can be found on the sidelines of her sons football games, or watching her daughter at ballet class. Rebecca is fueled by insane amounts of coffee, margaritas, Laffy Taffy (except the banana ones), and happily ever afters.

www.rebeccasheaauthor.com

WILLOW WINTERS

CHAPTER ONE

ARIA

THE SNOW FALLS SLOWLY, drifting in the wind along the once-dark tree line. With the blankets of snow covering every inch that I can see from the large kitchen window, everything shines brightly.

Parting my lips, I close my eyes and down the last bit of sweet red in the stemless wine glass. I've never been fond of the cold, but this ache in my chest today… it's not from the feet of snow that keep us locked inside the house.

"He's out there," I whisper, feeling the brooding shadow of the man I call my husband behind me.

"Yes, songbird, our son is out there and just fine."

With my long hair falling from my shoulder I turn around to face Carter. "When are they going to be home?"

With all of his hard features and dark gaze, Carter still manages a smirk that lights a fire in the pit of my stomach. It rages for him to deny the fact that our son is still young and last night was the first night he spent away from us. And now it's snowing… feet of snow.

"Chloe said he's having fun."

A sigh leaves me and a part of me knows that ache in my chest is because my little baby boy is growing up. He's on the move and wanting to play.

I miss the late-night cuddles and the way Anthony used to wrap his chubby little fingers around my pointer.

"I just wish I could see him…" I comment, making my way to the large polished counter where, upon inspection, the wine bottle I was going to get is now empty.

"You didn't want to go. Miss 'I don't love the cold.'"

I stare down at my glass as if it's a traitor and somehow it swallowed up my wine before I was able to drink it.

Two large hands grip my shoulders tenderly. Carter's thumbs rub soothing circles along the blades of my upper back and then higher, where they dig in deeper, soothing my sore muscles.

With his lips at the shell of my ear, he whispers, "You're stressed."

I swallow thickly and admit, "I know."

"You're a good mother and he's in very capable hands."

"The house is empty…" I stress. Everyone else left to enjoy the snow. This house, typically filled with the sound of so many family members, is now silent.

"Yes," Carter's voice deepens. Moving his lips to the crook of my neck, he lets them fall and lays a kiss right there, sending a pulsing wave of desire through me. My back to his chest, he pulls me in closer and I drop the empty glass to the counter, bringing my hand up to run my fingers up the nape of his neck as he kisses me again and then says, not hiding the lust, in the shell of my ear, "We have the house to ourselves. We should take advantage of that."

CHAPTER TWO

CARTER

MY WORRYING WIFE IS BEAUTIFUL. She's always radiant and poised. When that soft smile hits her lips, life itself seems to melt away into nothing but peace. That's what this woman gives me: a life I never thought I'd have, let alone deserve. One I want to share with her forever. I'll give her everything to keep that smile that lingers on her wine stained lips in place, right where it belongs.

"Let's get you another bottle…" As I take a step back, my songbird places her small hand in mine, letting me lead the way. After three years together, there's no fight for power, no resentment at the way we came to be. I led her away from a pain and darkness that kept her trapped and she did the same for me. There is only love that remains and from me, a gratitude I'll forever be in debt to her for giving to me.

In a dark blue, silk to the touch nightgown she glides to the wine cellar door, opening it with a soft creak, but only inches before turning on her heel in her bare feet to look up at me.

"Cross," her voice turns tempting, with a hint of sin that dances from her tongue. "Are you trying to get me drunk?"

A deep chuckle rises from my chest and the hint of a smile lingers on her lips… "Mrs. Cross," I emphasize her name and remember a time when the idea of me responding in that way would have been an impossibility. A time when she called me 'Cross' out of pure resentment for who I was. "That goal is a little too easy to achieve for a man like me," I tease her back, watching the simper on her beautiful face grow as the blush rises from her chest to her cheeks and she shyly looks away.

With a swat of her hand against my broad chest, Aria shakes her head. "Well if he's not coming home tonight and we're making the most of this," she speaks as she peeks up at me through her thick lashes, "I think I'll have one more glass."

My hand splays along her back and I pull her in close to me, feeling her warmth and softness curve around me. She gasps when I nip her exposed shoulder, "Well go get it then."

CHAPTER THREE

ARIA

THE CELLAR DOOR closes with a click and with only the dim illumination, Carter's brooding frame takes up too much of the light.

"I can manage to grab a bottle," I tease him and make my way to the back of the cellar and to the right. The wine cellar is far too much, with four rows of wine lining the aisles from floor to ceiling and a bricked floor made to look worn, hints of brown matching the dark wood and iron accents in the space that's much larger than most bedrooms. I love it though.

"You could," Carter starts as I round the back corner, aiming for a section of Cabernet that Addison and I are both fond of. My breathing halts when I see the cream throw blanket laid out on the floor. Two glasses of red are already poured, waiting next to the blanket and chocolate covered strawberries are piled in a balanced stack on a silver tray. "Or we could make the most of tonight."

Carter's whispered answer forces me to turn from the scene and stare up at the man I love so dearly.

Taking one step closer to me, he asks, "Do you remember that spot? When you were first here and what you told me, drunkenly as you stared up at me wanting things to change?"

Tears prick my eyes and I shake my head. I try not to remember those times if I'm honest. I don't tell Carter that, I only shake my head. It's not often my Beast turns into a Prince. This is so unexpected, so sweet and it takes me by complete surprise.

"I don't."

An asymmetric smile picks his lips up, "It doesn't matter, really, what matters most is that I never wanted you to leave. And now I have you forever."

Shaking off the wave of emotions, I gaze into his dark eyes watching the flecks of gold that brighten when I smile up at him. "Forever and always," I whisper as I get on my tiptoes to plant a kiss on his lips.

There's a groan that escapes when I lean back just slightly. A deep sound of approval but also of want.

"Lay on your back and close your eyes," he gives the command with his own eyes closed. Restraint showing in the way he lets go of me and his body goes still, waiting for me to obey.

I don't hesitate, quickly finding my spot on the already smoothed out throw blanket. With a slight chill in the air, my nipples are already hardening. I'm careful not to knock the glasses or tray as I lay down, and wait.

Anticipation rolls through me, from my toes up to my neck and then higher, forcing my breathing to come in faster.

"Dessert tonight is going to be exquisite," Carter comments as he pulls the button-down shirt over his head, only unbuttoning the first few. He's eager. In past times he's made me watch as he's undone every button, showing off his taught skin and muscles that coil beneath the expensive fabrics of his shirts and suits. Not tonight.

Tossing the shirt behind him carelessly, he comes closer, taking his time to round my body but never taking his eyes off of me, as if I'm his prey. He takes more time undoing his pants and letting them fall along with his boxers. Towering above me, naked and with a deep hunger etched in his expression, my heart picks up its pace, no longer wanting to stay where it should. The *thump, thump, thump* heats my entire body.

He kneels at first, letting his deft fingers linger on my collar and then slipping down the strap to my nightgown. He exposes one breast, groaning once again that deep primitive sound, before sliding the remainder of my nightgown down to my hips. He pauses then, dipping his head between my breasts and letting his tongue run hot circles along my tender skin. He bites down ever so gently around my nipple and my back arches involuntarily.

"Still, songbird," he commands, not lifting his head and only pausing in the torturously pleasurable act enough to remind me that I'm to stay still.

I already know, but my body doesn't obey. It takes focus to ignore the need to writhe under him as he plays with my body. His fingers just barely touching my skin as he glides his hands down my curves and removes the garment completely.

Still on his knees he rakes his gaze along my body, balling the silk fabric and then dropping it to be nothing more than a puddle on the floor behind him. Naked beneath him, I should be cold with the chill of the cellar, but I'm hot and greedy for more.

He takes his time, leaning over me, but not touching a single inch of skin to mine to take the first chocolate covered strawberry.

"One small bite," he demands, tracing the tip of it along my bottom lip. The chocolate is sweet and decadent as I bite into it and the strawberry even sweeter. It's heaven on my tongue.

But what Carter does next is even more delightful. Letting the bitten part of the berry travel down my skin to leave a trail of juice in its wake, he licks behind it. Starting at the tender under-side of my chin and working his way down my neck and chest, the cool touch of the berry is quickly followed by his hot tongue. When he gets to my breast, he pauses placing the strawberry at my lips again and once again I take a small bite, but he commands me to take a larger one and so I do. As I swallow, he finishes off the fruit and takes another, repeating the act over and over, half a dozen times, causing every nerve ending in my body to spark.

He works me up, but never finishes me, never touches the one place I ache the most for his mouth to linger.

"Tell me what you want songbird," he commands, the last strawberry in his hand as he stares down at me.

"I want you," I beg him and even to my own ears I sound as if I'll die if he doesn't enter me right this second. My hands clench at my sides, hating that I can't simply take from him, but knowing it's so much better if I'm patient.

"Don't bite it," he tells me, sliding the strawberry halfway into my mouth. I keep my gaze on him as his broad shoulders travel lower, his strong hands gripping my inner thighs to part them. He settles between my legs, his shoulders propping up my thighs until the balls of my feet are on the floor. His warm breath trailing along my most sensitive area.

He takes one languid lick of my pussy and my head falls back from the wave of pleasure.

"That sound," he groans at my heat, "I fucking love it when you make that sound." With the statement still in the air, my sex-driven mind slowly comprehending his words, Carter sucks on my clit, massaging his tongue against it and I disobey him, biting into the berry and pushing myself into his face.

He grips my ass, pinning me down and continues to suck and lick and dive his tongue inside of me as the waves build and the pressure mounts and then finally, all at once and so much faster than I expect it to, pleasure erupts inside of me. Rolling from the tips of my fingers down my body and back up again.

With my heavy breathing making my chest rise and fall, I stare up at Carter, ready to apologize for biting into the berry. But he doesn't give me the chance.

My beast of a husband parts my legs wider and thrusts himself inside of me without warning, to the hilt. My palms hit the ground as my back bows and the orgasm I thought had subdued rages inside of me, growing hotter with every pounding thrust of his hips.

"Carter!" I scream out, feeling the overwhelming loss of control as he pistons himself inside of me.

"Yes," the word falls from his lips as a hiss and he drops his body to lay across mine, although his forearm, braced above my head, supports his weight. "Cry out for me, Aria. Scream my name."

Losing all sense of control, my heels dig into his ass and my hips tilt, letting him fuck me deeper and harder as I scream out his name like he told me to and like everything inside of me wants to do.

He's ruthless and relentless as he takes me, fucking me until we find our release together.

Lying beside him, I wince when I turn over, still feeling him inside of me. "I bit the strawberry." I whisper and the small admission awards me a chuckle from the spent man beside me. Deep and masculine and everything Carter is.

With a wicked smile he stares down at me, "I'll prepare for your punishment tonight."

I can only smile back, so aware that it would be impossible not to keep the strawberry where it was while he did what he did to me. He can play these games, he can lead me wherever he deems fit, and I will follow loving every step of the way.

"I love you Carter Cross."

"And I love you, my songbird."

ABOUT WILLOW WINTERS

I'm just an avid reader and mama turned writer. This passion of mine has grown to something I never could have imagined and I'm so grateful to share my words with you!

www.willowiwnterswrites.com

Checkmate

SKYE WARREN

CHAPTER ONE

AVERY

I'M SUBMERGED in the dark waters of exhaustion. Something reaches down to shake me, and I fight it off. Sleep. I need sleep. An invisible hand on my shoulder, and I groan softly.

My eyelids weigh a thousand pounds. I force them open. The room is dark, only the faintest moonlight coming through the window. Everything is quiet and cool.

What woke me?

The other side of the bed is empty.

The bathroom door is cracked open, darkness within—empty.

The armchairs surrounding the fireplace—empty. Shadows stretch across the chessboard, the pieces poised and ready in the middle of a game. We've been playing the same game since before I went into labor, before the hospital. Before our child was born.

Tiredness weighs heavy on my head. The clock glows 3 am. I was up only an hour ago feeding little Geoffrey. I force myself out of bed again, dropping my feet onto the plush carpet. I take the familiar path, well worn in only the two months he's been with us, to find his little apple-shaped lamp casting a pale warmth.

Gabriel carries him against his shoulder, murmuring words I can barely make out. He wears only a thin sleep shirt and pajama pants, which highlight his broad shoulders and lean hips. "I know you're hungry, sweet boy, but it hasn't been so very long. The doctor says you don't need to snack. A good meal is what you need, and more sleep for your tired mother."

My heart squeezes at the sight of him bargaining with our fussy baby. The infant makes a sound of discomfort. From the beginning he's wanted to snack. Schedules we found online of three hours, four hours, even five hours between feedings are impossible dreams.

At first he slept in the same bed with us, nursing almost constantly, fussing if he was pulled away from me for a diaper change. I reached a point of tiredness where I was stumbling over nothing and running into walls, so Gabriel put his foot down.

Geoffrey would sleep in his crib, even if Gabriel had to watch over him there.

How many times has he paced back and forth with the infant on his shoulder? How many nights has he bargained with a baby for even a single hour of sleep for me?

Love for them both wells inside me. Little Geoffrey doesn't understand this bright world, he doesn't understand the schedules grown-ups want. Snacks seem totally reasonable to the two-month-old. And Gabriel—my husband, my love. My champion in these exhausting times.

"He's hungry," I say softly.

Gabriel turns to face me, seeming unsurprised to find me there. "He could have waited another hour. We were having a discussion on the subject of patience, man to man."

That makes me smile. "I don't mind."

"So demanding," Gabriel murmurs, "the men in your life."

I give him a sideways glance. Gabriel has demanded nothing of me since I got home.

Geoffrey, however, fusses. Having heard my voice he knows that food is nearby. "Come, darling," I whisper to him. His eyes are a pale golden fire, like his father's.

I settle us both onto the large rocking chair, unstrapping my nightgown so he can nurse at my breast. Gabriel leans against the wall, his eyes ablaze as he watches me. It's not the first time I've noticed that nursing affects him in some primal way. My stomach tightens in both apprehension and excitement.

We haven't made love since the birth.

Geoffrey nurses hungrily, and I bite my lip at the pressure of the milk bearing down. Then he suckles contentedly, his eyes closed as if in bliss. I sing to him softly, rocking him in my arms, taking advantage of the moment to cuddle him close, this child I nurtured inside me.

When the song ends, Gabriel crosses to the window.

Without looking I know the view will be barren. From his mansion we have a view of the rolling hills and the winding lane that leads into Tanglewood. There are no cars. Haven't been any cars for the two months we've been home with the baby. The pandemic hit while we were still in the hospital, and we drove home, faintly panicked, wondering if the infant had contracted something. But he's been healthy. Our friend and doctor Anders returned from his honeymoon when quarantine started, and he's been stopping by for almost daily checkups.

"What a time," Gabriel says. In his voice is the weight of every worry of every parent, wondering what kind of world they're giving to their children.

"He'll be fine," I say, my tone insistent. As if I can will it to be true.

The opposite is too horrible to imagine. Thinking of my small baby coughing, sick with fever. Thinking of him in a world of masks and gloves and sterility. It makes my heart seize.

Gabriel sits in the other rocking chair. There's another chess board between us. We have games going in a few different rooms of the house. In the bedroom game, I'm losing. Here in the nursery, where I play and nurse at the same time, I'm winning. It makes me wonder if he lets me win in here. Or maybe I'm more deeply in a place of power when I'm nursing.

It's his turn and he moves his knight forward.

I'm usually a more careful player than him, more aware of risk, more cautious. Except with this baby at my breast I feel like one of those warriors who rode into battle with their babies on their backs. I move my queen forward to capture him.

His lips quirk. "You look very pleased with yourself."

"I am."

He takes a bishop in retribution, but it does not bother me, not when I have both my rooks and he has none. In a game of trading pieces, victory goes to the one who's ahead.

Geoffrey's suckling slows, and his eyes flutter closed. He falls asleep when he's fed. In only an hour or two he'll be awake again. My darling boy. "Sweet dreams," I whisper to him, pressing my lips to his velvet-soft crown, to the wisp of his golden hair.

Gabriel takes the baby gently from my arms and settles him in the crib. Plush chess pieces circle above him. The baby camera emits a pale blue light, showing that it's on.

I snap my nightgown back into place, but I still feel exposed when Gabriel turns his golden eyes on me. He looks darker somehow, more certain. Determined. I feel the determination in his hand when he leads me from the room.

He's a fierce man, thick with muscle and stubbornness and pride.

But he's gentle as he tucks me back into bed. He enters the bed behind me, curling his body around my back, resting one arm over my stomach.

I know I should go to sleep. I should use my time wisely. Every single book and blog on new motherhood says that, but I can't help but remember that golden gaze on my bare breasts. They squeeze now, as if they have a mind of their own, the milk and arousal combining in strange alchemy. "Gabriel," I whisper.

His voice is the merest sound. "Go to sleep."

It occurs to me that he might not have sex with me out of—concern? Worry? Maybe even fear, though it seems almost ludicrous to use that word with this man. Labor had been an excruciating experience, for both of us. Did he think it had broken me?

Did he imagine I was that fragile?

I press my hips back, and the iron-hot brand of his cock pushes against my ass.

He groans against my neck. "Don't tease me, little virgin."

That makes me press again, and he responds in a delicious way, grasping my hip so hard it might bruise, his grip brutal and terribly masculine. Something sharp on the back of my neck. *He's biting me.* I shiver in his grip, feeling primal and fully captured.

He reaches around and runs a thumb across my nipples. I gasp, and he does it again. They're sensitive from nursing around the clock. He's gentle but insistent as he presses down. I feel a little milk spill onto his fingers, and my cheeks flame. It's bad enough being wet between my legs for him. Another thing entirely to produce milk on his hand.

I shrink back, which only serves to push me deeper against his body. He must feel my squirming. He palms my breast with soft possession. "Does it hurt?"

"No," I say, feeling breathless and shy. "It's tender, but it doesn't hurt."

"Then why are you shivering?"

"I'm—I'm leaking."

His thumb and forefinger surround my nipple. He squeezes, and more milk slides onto his fingers. "This milk you use to nourish our son. This milk you make is beautiful."

"Yes, b-but not during sex."

Another bite to the back of my neck. "Yes, during sex. I want to lick the milk from your nipples. I want to watch you leak in the shower. I own every part of you, little virgin—even this."

My sex clenches at his words. I'm his, and he's mine. "Gabriel."

He reaches down between my legs, as if he can feel the clench. His fingers are knowing and sure as he slides two inside me. His thumb plays with my clit. He's bringing me to orgasm with quiet determination, almost grim about the way he forces me to the edge. I go over in a rush of liquid and spasms of pleasure that make me cry out.

When I fall back down to earth, Gabriel still has his hand at my sex. He slides his fingers lazily through the wetness, back and forth, back and forth, drawing it onto him.

Then he leans back, and I hear the sounds of clothing rustling. I turn to see what he's doing—and I'm greeted by the sight of his large, proud cock, standing upright from above his pushed-down pajama pants. His shirt is pulled up only enough to reveal the ridges of his abs. And his wet hand, the one that had been inside me only seconds earlier, slides up and down his cock, his fingers slick, spreading my arousal over his velvet-iron flesh.

For a moment I watch him, reveling in the way his cock glistens, the way his whole body strains against his fist. And then I realize he's going to come this way.

He's going to come outside of me.

"No," I whisper.

Such a small protest, but he stops immediately. "What?"

I need to do more than ask for his cock. I need to show him what I want. The certainty sinks into my skin, even as a flush spreads across my cheeks. My nightgown is still on, so I take it off and toss it over the side of the bed. If he isn't ashamed of my breasts leaking milk, if he likes them, then let him look. Then I slide one leg over him, straddling his hips.

He sucks in a breath. "Avery."

"I need you." I take his cock in my hand, almost flinching at the heavy heat of him. "I need this. Inside me, Gabriel. Not only your fingers. You."

"You're still hurting. You're raw." He makes a choked sound. "You *tore*."

Yes, I tore. Yes, I had to be sewn up. But I'm healed now. I suppose it's up to me to prove that to him. I nod toward the wooden bars of the headboard. I've held those carved spindles in my hands many times while he made love to me in inventive ways. "Hold them."

His golden eyes promise vengeance in the most sensual manner, but he obeys, reaching muscular arms up to hold the headboard. He's made himself my prisoner. And with that I sink down onto his cock. There's a twinge, a stretch, enough to make me wonder if I really *have* healed enough. Then after a moment it passes, and I feel only the sweet fullness.

He makes a growling sound. "Move."

I press my palms against his chest and lift up, and then push back down. It's a little awkward for me. This isn't a usual position for us. Gabriel usually likes to hold me down, but now I see the power that I have here. I'm the one setting the pace. And I'm doing it slow.

His arms tremble, shaking the entire bed. Restraint does not come easy to Gabriel Miller. I lift up slowly, relishing every centimeter that slides against me, that delicious friction. And then I sink down onto him again. My eyes roll back, and I drop my chin to my chest. "God."

"Little virgin." The words are a warning.

"I could do this forever," I moan as I lift myself and fall once more.

There's no time to even register that he's released the bedframe. His hands are on my hips, holding me down as he thrusts up into me. How did I think I had the power? Even above him I'm powerless to do anything but hold on, grasping his shoulders as he fucks me from beneath. "Forever," he says between gritted teeth. "I'm going to hold you to that. You're mine, Avery Miller. Mine forever."

He shifts the angle, finding a new place inside me, and an orgasm slams into me from between my legs, radiating out in a surge of pain and pleasure, keeping me on the knife's edge. I clamp down onto him, and he comes with a roar.

I collapse onto his chest, and he cradles me close.

For a moment there's only the sound of our breathing.

A sated warmth has taken over my body. I prop myself up to look at him. He stares at me from beneath heavy golden lashes. "I'm surprised you didn't wake the baby."

He glances at the baby monitor, which shows a sleeping baby in grayscale. "I'll have to learn how to be quiet," he admits. Then he grins. "I suppose I'll need lots of practice."

That makes me laugh, a soft and tired sound.

He frowns and tips me gently to the side. I tumble onto the

pillows, my eyes already closing. "Sleep," he whispers to me, pressing a kiss to my forehead. "Sleep, my queen."

True to form, the baby wakes up in an hour and a half. I nurse him again, moving another chess piece when he sits across from me. He already knows he's lost when he moves the bishop to block my check. I push my queen forward, and he tips his king over. It's a forfeit.

"That's checkmate," I whisper to the sleeping baby in my arms.

Gabriel takes him gently, and sets him down beneath the circling chess pieces.

Then he leads me to the bedroom, where he makes me hold the headboard.

He takes his revenge in slow and aching certainty, using my body in the way that makes me moan. I writhe against him, fighting, fighting, fighting—which makes the surrender even more sweet. After coming three times, I collapse into a dreamless sleep.

When I wake I find Gabriel thrusting inside me, using me, ruthless in his need. He captures me, piece by piece, but as I look into his golden eyes, I know that I have won.

ABOUT SKYE WARREN

Skye Warren is the New York Times bestselling author of dangerous romance. Her books have sold over one million copies. She makes her home in Texas with her loving family, sweet dogs, and evil cat.

www.skyewarren.com

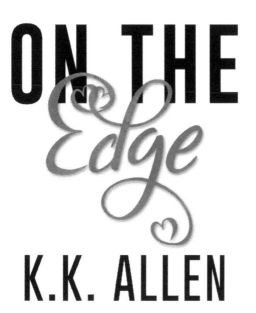

ON THE
Edge

K.K. ALLEN

CHAPTER ONE

I WAS slow and quiet as I carefully tiptoed into the small private studio in the east wing of Gravity Dance Complex where I worked and danced. It was the only studio in the entire building that was no longer used due to its gradual transformation into a storage room. Dusty crates, old set designs, antique furniture, and broken chairs filled the room, among other forms of chaos. After searching the studio for the past thirty minutes for my boyfriend, Theodore Noska, someone finally gave me a tip that I'd find him here.

An Imagine Dragons song, "Natural," was blaring from the surrounding speakers, and loud grunts could be heard from the man twisting and pulling his body all over the floor. He was partnerless, but the way his arms were locked as if he was in hold, made me think there should have been someone with him.

I watched him glide and whisk himself in circles, heels up and posture sticking with every quickly timed movement. It was clear he was executing the steps of a passionate Latin dance I recognized immediately as a Paso Doble. Dancing usually made Theo happy. That didn't seem to be the case today. Today, he wore frown lines with the depth of a pug, and eyes so sharply narrowed, I swore they might wield razors at any moment.

The last time Theo looked this angry was the day he caught me spying on him in the theater when he had been choreographing. He had thought that he was alone, but I was glued to one of the theater seats in adoration for a man I'd only known from online videos. There he was, my idol, in the flesh—and completely in the zone.

Just like now.

Sweat was pouring off his skin while his rapid breathing sounded off the walls of the room. I continued watching him, half-tempted to step further into the dim light to reveal myself, while the other part of me was frozen in place. Curiosity coursed through my veins as the pounding in my chest thumped through my ears. The intensity of his movements did that to me always, but there was something different about what was happening now. Theo's anger wasn't just a play on the music. He looked genuinely frustrated.

As if he could hear my thoughts, he broke out of step and started stomping toward the stereo. Then he smashed his finger on the power button, cutting the music and letting out a low growl. He swiped at a stack of papers that had been resting on the stereo and sent them flying from the surface until they floated around him like confetti.

"What the—" I clapped a hand over my mouth, knowing my shock got the better of me, but still not wanting to be seen. I contemplated tiptoeing right back out of the room and leaving Theo to whatever demons were invading his thoughts.

There were no sounds, other than my voice, but Theo still hadn't picked up on my presence. He was too in his head. Too angry—probably at himself. I knew this, because we'd been dating for two years. I knew him better than I knew myself, and when Theo got stressed, he felt it in his entire body. And while dancing was like therapy for the both of us, Theo's stress came from the responsibility of whatever he was choreographing. The man put more pressure on himself than anyone I'd ever met. It was what made him brilliant. And it was one of the many reasons I loved him.

Theo started to pace, his eyes turned down, and it was as if nothing existed around him. It was at that moment I made the decision to step forward into a solid stream of late afternoon light pouring in from the large box-paned window and cleared my throat. He looked up with a snap of his eyes, his wild blue-green gaze a burst of shock and confusion mixed with fury with no hope of being stifled.

"Lex." He said my name, almost confused.

I stepped forward with a smile, but he was still too far away. "I'd ask if you're ready to go home, but you look kind of busy."

He cursed and pulled up his wrist to glance at his watch. "Shit." He jammed his fingers through his hair and dropped his hands to his waist before blowing out a breath. "I lost track of time."

I stepped forward again, never losing my smile. There was something about seeing him all worked up that had my heart beating fast—just like in our first real encounter. Only this time, I'm more turned on than I am afraid. I approached him and settled my palm on his chest. "What's wrong?"

He released a heavy sigh. "It's this routine that I agreed to choreograph for a concept video. I'm just not feeling it, and I'm ready to throw in the towel even though the damn shoot is tomorrow."

A concept video. So, that was why he was feeling the pressure. Concept videos are like music videos without the singing. Just lyrics and dancing. Even worse, Theo was more of a contemporary and hip-hop dancer than a ballroom dancer. Why anyone would task him with the choreography of a Paso Doble was beyond my understanding. Unless…

I scrunched my brows together and tilted my head. "Let me guess. Janelle put you up to this?"

"Yup." His lips popped on the word, causing me to laugh. "Well, an investor nudged her to ask me, so you know she was extra convincing."

I nodded, knowing all too well how the most well-known choreographer in all of LA could convince a dancer to do anything she pleased. It was her specialty. I wrapped my arms around his waist and tilted my head to peer up at him, a smile still teasing my lips. "I'm sorry to be the bearer of bad news, but Theodore Noska doesn't break promises."

He narrowed his eyes at me in warning, but I wasn't done.

"Luckily—" I added with emphasis on the word. "There's someone in his life who's willing to help him out." I wiggled my brows. "And she happens to dance a mean Paso Doble."

Despite the anger still pulsing off his body, he flashed me a smile and slipped his arms around my waist. "Is that so? Is this the same dancer who just flew in after being away for a week and pulled an eight-hour day of rehearsals for her first award-show appearance?"

I shrugged like it was no big deal, but Theo knew as well as I did what an achievement it was to even be asked to choreograph something for the Grammys. "Maybe, but she's also the same dancer who happens to be madly in love with a hot choreographer. And she's here to help."

Something about the intensity radiating off Theo changed. What was once a man rippling with anger was now cupping my neck and pressing his lips to mine in a kiss that spoke down deep to my soul.

Theo lived his life full-out—with dancing, with his mentorship programs, and with me. Never once did he leave me to question the depth of his love, because he showed me in every way possible. And this kiss was no different.

His hand moved to my arch as he bent me backward, all the while supporting every inch of my body, my soul, my heart. When he righted me again, my head was spinning, and my stupid grin wouldn't leave my face.

"What are you waiting for, Noska," I teased as I finally regained my breath. "Show me what you've got so far."

I could feel a wave of tension roll off his body and dissolve just at my offer, but the focus in his eyes remained. I couldn't imagine the pressure Theo endured on a daily basis just from having such a high-profile career. I also knew he wouldn't have it any other way.

"Start with your back to me, like this." He places me a few inches away from him. "I'll reach for you." He cups my shoulder with his hand. "Then you'll spin to me."

I do a double turn inward toward his body before he catches my hand in his.

"Now zig zag, and then drop into a half-split." I sink to the floor, sliding one leg out to my side while he's still supporting my back. I'm already starting to breathe heavy and we haven't even completed an entire eight-count.

I continue to follow his lead, allowing him to change choreography as he realizes what's working and what isn't. I'm almost surprised once we get over halfway into the song and I have to stop for a water break.

"What were you struggling with, again?" I ask him with a laugh. "Your choreography is beautiful." I take a swig of my water and set my bottle down. "And fast."

Theo takes the bottle from my hands and takes a long pull. "It's coming together now. I probably just needed an assistant, but you know I don't like dancing with anyone but you."

I smile at his sweet words. Words I understand far too well. I don't have as much leeway in my career when it comes to who I dance with, but when it's not Theo, I get anxious. Performing intimate steps with anyone is something I don't take lightly.

"Well, I'm glad I found you then. Want to get back to it?"

He nodded. I could already sense his urgency to finish, and it felt like we were almost there. We walked through the routine slowly, from the top, and then once again with music before he started to add on to his choreography.

It took two hours for me to learn the entire fast-paced routine, before we started running it again and again, until I was breathing just as heavily as Theo was. And even though he'd taught me the entire dance, he still looked like he's struggling. "What's wrong?"

He growled and shook his head. "Something is missing. The routine is there. I'm happy with it. But I'm just having trouble connecting the emotion of the dance to the lyrics."

I nodded in understanding. "What do the lyrics mean to you?"

Theo shrugged. "Finding yourself, I guess. Struggling through your journey and pushing past all the bullshit to rise above it.

271

Overcoming hardships. Understanding life is about more than the adversity that stands against you."

The corners of my mouth turned up slowly as I listened to him speak. I always knew Theo was a genius, but it was something more to witness to one of his creations. He put everything into his art. It was what made him the best.

"So one person will represent rising above adversity. And the other?"

He shook his head. "Maybe I'm turning you away from the darkness and leading you into the light. Toward enlightenment."

I bit the inside of my lip, following along. "And I'm fighting against your pull. I'm torn."

His lids widened excitedly. "Yes, you're split. One of you is fighting against the pull, and the other is ready to follow me."

I could feel my smile stretching my cheeks. "I love it, Theo. Let's do it."

His eyes were so bright, I could tell it was all finally clicking together. He nodded and walked quickly to the stereo just under the window while I took my spot in the center of the room.

"Let's do it."

WATCH: Natural

I ended the dance in Theo's arms, our bodies pressed together, the remaining daylight from outside gone and replaced with a solid stream of whitish-blue light from the moon. My eyes locked on his, but before I could say a word his mouth is on mine and a growl slipped from his throat and into mine.

"You know," he started after pulling away from me. "I've been at it all day, and it only came together just now dancing with you."

I was still dizzy from his kiss, but I managed a smug smile and a lift of my shoulders. "It's why you keep me around, Noska."

He flashed me a grin and pulled me back toward him with a yank of my shirt. "I can think of other reasons for keeping you around."

life as he rocked himself so deeply inside me, I swore I
stars. I was already teetering on the edge when he began,
take long to bring me back there. It didn't help that he
p for a moment—not until I could feel his warm fluids
klessly inside me. And then I was meeting him with my
. I pulsed around him, tightening and releasing as a
light filled my lids. This is what heaven felt like. I knew,
It it every time I was with Theo. Like nothing more
rene could possibly exist whenever we came together.
led me around and moved his lips tenderly against
breaking the rules with you Alexandra Quinn."
against his sweet lips. "And I love breaking the rules
eodore Noska." I could feel my wicked smile growing at
"Let's do it again."
uckle, he swept me up in his arms and carried me
oor. "Deal. But first, I'm taking you home."

I could practically feel my insides purring. Theo and I had been living together for over a year now and one would think that meant we spent every waking minute together, but our reality couldn't be further from that truth. Theo had a million responsibilities that extended beyond choreographing a concept video for an investor. He had to be the face of all high-profile business decisions at Gravity, but not only that. He was also committed to coordinating appearances and dance class schedules at the community recreation center in LA. And if all that wasn't enough, there was my schedule too.

I had been lucky enough to stay around LA for most of the opportunities I had been getting, but that didn't mean my hours synced well with Theos. When he was sleeping, I was dancing, and vice versa, so it seemed. I missed him, and I missed the heat of his body while we're wrapped up in the sheets together. I'd been looking forward to doing just that tonight.

Theo must have had the same idea about me, because the next thing I knew, he was lifting me onto a nearby crate and pressing his body between my legs.

"What are you doing?" My words were airy with exhilaration and laughter combined. It had been a long time since Theo plopped me on a surface like this one. "Someone could walk in. I didn't lock the door."

He grinned, as if the thought of being caught turned him on even more. "Oh yeah?" He slid his hand over my shoulder and swept back a lock of hair. "What do you say we break a few more rules tonight?"

I swallowed, my skin heating with his words. Words that reminded me of our very first time, when intimacy between us had been forbidden and our every desire was being tested while we had been bound to the terms of a contract.

Focusing on his thick lips and disheveled blond hair, I slipped my hand beneath his shirt and tugged it in my direction, earning me a greedy, lustful gaze. "I'd say you better make it worth my while."

He chuckled and pressed himself into me further, his dick clearly just as hungry as his eyes. "Oh, I intend to, Lex."

A hand slipped down my back. A gentle caress, but the deliberate meaning behind it is all there. He may have been moving slowly, but Theo was not about to take his time with me. Not tonight. I could see the ravenousness in his gaze. The desperation in his breathing. He was still worked up from dancing, and even more so because he finished choreographing the number.

I didn't think I had ever imagined myself dating a dancer, but now I couldn't imagine anything different. The power behind every touch Theo made, and the passion behind every movement. It all just brought our connection to an insanely intense level. I found myself craving him when we were apart, and unable to keep my hands off him when we were together.

His fingers moved down my skirt, slipped beneath the fabric, and then moved back up my legs. I couldn't help but notice his pace was quickening by the second. He gripped my tights and pulled them down, leaving my panties, but pushing my skirt up to my waist.

He licked his lips, slow and steady while his glowing eyes examined my wet flesh like it was dessert. And then his mouth was on me. His warm tongue moved between my slit while my heart performed its own Paso Doble in my chest.

Heat rushed over my skin while I fell back onto the crate, my palms catching me from lowering down completely. I was propped up just enough to watch Theo devour me with the same fierceness he'd just danced with. When he pulled my clit between his lips and sucked, I was done for.

A moan shot from my throat as he buried himself further between my thighs. He didn't let up. Not when I dug my nails into his scalp. Not when I cried out my impending release. And not when I squirmed against him, forcing him to stay on me like he would one of those mechanical bull rides. And when everything grew hot—my mind, my skin, my core—Theo slipped two fingers deep inside me to finish me off.

I moaned out my release, my arms losing their strength as I

quivered and gave up completely. Bu
He pulled me up, slamming his mou
cock into me in one insatiable thrust.

In my orgasmic bliss, I hadn't ev
down, but there he was, fucking me
crate and easing me onto the stereo
He slowed down only to lift my sp

He groaned as the pad of his th
nipple. His hooded gaze lazily floa
away from letting go, and I could
down just to make it last.

"Don't you dare slow down, T
me. Give me everything you've g
missing while I've been away."

His gaze darkened as he acce
thrusts. His strong hands grippe
between pleasure and pain was
I only knew I wanted more of it

"I'm so close." He panted th
A panicked feeling filled m
Theo slowed as he nodded
setting my feet as he pulled ou

I swallowed, and turned a
floor-to-ceiling mirror was rig
telling me the studio was on
behind me, pressing his har
my hair as his palms roamed
squeezed. A growl followed

Instead of instructing m
himself to lift my left leg, b
stretching it out and placin
forward slightly and drew

"You ready to watch m
He didn't wait for my
this time from behind. I g

on for dea
was seeing
so it didn'
didn't let u
spilling red
own releas
bright whit
because I fe
blissful or s

He swiv
mine. "I lov

I smiled
with you, Th
a rapid rate.

With a ch
toward the d

ABOUT K.K. ALLEN

K.K. Allen is a USA Today Bestselling and award-winning author who writes heartfelt and inspirational Contemporary Romance stories focused on "capturing the edge of innocence." K.K. graduated from the University of Washington with an Interdisciplinary Arts and Sciences degree. She currently resides in central Florida, works full time as a Digital Producer for a leading online educational institution, and is the mother to a ridiculously handsome little dude who owns her heart.

www.kkallen.com

AMELIA WILDE

CHAPTER ONE

PERSEPHONE

WINTER IS different in the mountain.

At my mother's house, winter wrapped our small house in fluffy snow, muting the outside world and drawing everything in close. Want to go out? Take a coat and pull up the hood, Persephone, it's bitter out there. And if any man talks to you, if he so much as looks at you, know in your heart that he will kill you.

In the mountain there is no mother and no heavy fall of snow. I mean—it's there. It's snowing. It's winter. But it doesn't pull the world close. The world is already close.

Hades is already close.

He shouldn't be able to shake the mountain, and maybe he's not. Maybe it's just me, being attuned to him, that makes it easier to tell when he's nearby. It translates into my skin in small tremors. He's coming; he's coming. The door shifts in its frame, subtle and small— other doors in the mountain are opening. There is a series to cross through before he reaches his bedroom, where I wait for him. Nervously. A small *clink, clink, clink* announces his dog Conor's collar. I'm listening so intently.

Because I'm afraid of him?

A part of me will always be afraid of him.

A secret: I like being afraid of him. It's a luxury to fear him. I can do it wholeheartedly because I know he'll never harm me. Except in ways that make me wet. I love those ways.

I love the news out of the city a lot less. I'm not much for hiding since I came to the mountain. Since everything happened, since the past and prophecy rolled over me like a deep wave. When I resurfaced, I was a new woman. I am a new woman. But today, my old anxieties banded around my lungs and squeezed. So I draped myself in a shawl and tucked myself in next to the window, and now I am watching the snowfall in the valley and waiting.

I let myself think that the worry is about Hades' imminent approach and not anything in the outside world.

The door to the bedroom bursts open, and I startle despite all the warnings I've given myself, despite all the intense listening I've done, with a little gasp that releases some of the pressure in my lungs. Hades stalks toward me, tall and strong and indestructible, eyes sweeping over me in a way that I might have mistaken for ice cold when I first met him.

Now I see the fire there, too, hidden until he's very, very close.

Hades' phone hits the wall and falls to the carpet, forgotten, and then he's kneeling by my chair. He reaches out and takes my jaw in his hand like he owns me, which he does, and tilts my face the way he wants it. Hades is a deliberate man. When he kisses me, it's with savage deliberation. His tongue reminds me that I'm here for his pleasure, and his teeth remind me that he'll take it however he wants.

Hades only pulls back when I'm very, very reminded of all this. His eyes trace my lips while he watches me struggle to control my breath. How am I supposed to breathe normally when he's the way he is? Tall and muscled and cruelly beautiful?

"Oliver says you haven't come out of the room today."

Oliver, his head of security, a man with a mysterious past and a scar on his face. Oliver, who guards us in the hours when we're the most vulnerable. He ratted me out.

"I was anxious."

"So you decided to hide under a blanket and starve yourself all day?" The warning in his tone is clear as a bell and cutting as a newly sharpened knife. It makes my nipples peak to hear it. "You know better than that."

"There's so much bad news, though." I've opened the floodgates of my fretting, and I can't stop them again. I won't. Because indulging in my fear like this, openly and in front of him, is a luxury. "The things happening in the city—"

"Will never come here," he says firmly. "I've closed off the mountain. And I'm about to tell Oliver to close off these rooms, too."

"Why?" Another fist of nerves at the base of my throat. "Is something in the hall?"

His hand tightens around my face. "I'm in here, Persephone. Nothing is more dangerous than me." Then he leans in, tilting my head to the side as he does so, and kisses the place where my pulse bangs against the delicate skin under my jawbone. "There's nothing in the hall," he whispers, "but you've been disobedient, and I won't have it." Hades pulls me off the chair and bends me over the bed in one movement.

"Head up." The command is cold, rough. "On your elbows."

It's hard, with my feet flat on the floor and my pussy already craving him, but I arrange myself over the bed while he goes back out into the hall and comes back with something he sets down with a metallic ring on the table near the bed.

Then his hands are on me again, and my mind ejects everything I was worried about before. His touch erases the news out of the city. It obliterates the twin fists of anxiety around my lungs. Everything narrows down to the way he tests me, fingers skimming along the nightgown I'm still wearing and reaching down to the hem. He flips it up, a cool rush of air meeting bare flesh. Hades reaches between my legs and tests me there, too, and it's mortifying how wet I've gotten in only the short time since he's entered the room.

A luxury.

Then his hand is gone, and I let out the smallest possible whine. Whining doesn't get me anywhere with him. It only gives him the opportunity to punish me harder, the way he's definitely going to.

My soul needs him to be the way he is—solid to the core and harder than diamonds. If he's still standing, then nothing in the world can be as bad as all that.

"Not good enough," he says, almost to himself, and then the fabric of my nightgown stretches and rips with a sharp tug against my skin. He yanks it out from under me, leaving me undone and naked, still trying to keep my head up. It's made me so aware of how heavy my hair is and how little I've worked the muscles between my shoulders. I've never been more conscious of the space between my nipples and the covers. I can't get them any closer, but I want that sensation. I want more.

He walks away, but I keep my eyes straight ahead. A moment later, his hands come down in front of my face, and he uses a thumb to open my mouth. I think he might put his fingers there and order me to suck, but instead, he presses a piece of fruit between my teeth.

Melon, sweet and fresh, with a flavor that reminded me of mornings at boarding school. They always had melon there, and the other girls never wanted it, but I loved it.

"Bite."

I sink my teeth into the flesh of the melon, and some of its juice runs down my chin, but Hades delivers a slap to my ass that has me tensing, freezing in place.

"Keep it there. Don't bite through, or we'll start again."

Start what? I want to ask, to plead a little, but doing that will end with my teeth together and the melon on the bed, and Hades will be even more displeased.

I can't wait.

CHAPTER TWO

HADES

PERSEPHONE IS AN IMPOSSIBLE DISTRACTION. I'm here in my bedroom instead of behind my desk because the moment Oliver came to me with the news that she hadn't come out to make her usual visits or read in the library, it ripped away my concentration and flung it into the fire. I can't work when she's like this. I especially can't work when she's refusing to eat. We've had our fun with pomegranates, but this is supposed to be an object lesson, not a game.

Yet it's always a bit of a game, isn't it? I can't help but play with her when she's wet for me and trembling from the moment I walk into the room.

I steady her with a hand to the small of her back and work two fingers inside her pussy, adding another to make her arch. It can't be easy to hold that melon between her teeth. That's why I chose it. An apple would have been sturdier. An apple would have been a kind choice. But I have never pretended to be kind.

I thrust my fingers into Persephone at a leisurely pace and watch her while she struggles to stay still. Such a good girl, except for the part when she found it acceptable to let her worries get the best of her. I don't care if she spends the day in bed, but she's not going to neglect herself while she does it.

Fuck no.

She throws her head back, clutching at the bedspread, and I pull my fingers out and follow it with a sharp slap across her ass. A second. A third. Her skin turns pink, then red.

I wait for the tears.

I always wait for the tears.

Both because I like the taste, and because Persephone wants to cry.

It's not long after the tears that her chin shakes, and her teeth slice through the melon. A part of it falls to the bed, and I catch it in my fingers and put it into her mouth. Then I cover her lips with my palm and bend close. Closer. "Eat."

Her face is sticky with the juice and slick with tears, and it's obscene to feel her jaw work this way. Obscene for her, too. Finally, she swallows, and I take my hand away.

"You are the most precious thing on this mountain," I tell her, "and you'll treat yourself as such, or I'll teach you this lesson again."

"But you'll make it worse," she cries. "You will."

"So much worse." I nip at her earlobe with my teeth. "Count on it."

I stroke a hand down her back and feel it—the minute release of tension in her shoulders. The slight give to her arms. The release. Whatever happens out in the world, things will always be the same on my mountain.

My little queen, my little slut, needs more from me, so I step behind her and undo my belt. Shoving my clothing out of the way, I enter her in a hard stroke that forces a short breath from her lips. "I-I was afraid," she manages, "of what's happening in the city."

"We're not in the city." I play a hand down her belly, creating space between the bed and her hips, and search for her clit.

"The trains—"

"There are men at the station." If she wants to be reassured that I have thought of everything, then I will fuck that knowledge into her. "Nothing comes off the train that we don't control."

"Something could slip through." The shake in her voice could be more worry or the sound of Persephone on edge. From the clench of her cunt on my cock, I think it's closer to the latter.

"And if it did, what would it be to you? Do you think I would let anything from the city touch us? If it's my brother you fear, then don't bother. He has his own concerns."

"Other—things—" I'm driving into her with such force that she can hardly get the words out. Sweet pressure wraps itself around the head of me and squeezes tight, spreading out to the base like lightning. "I'm afraid of other things. Things we don't see. Things we can't—plan—for—"

The small circles on her clit, courtesy of my fingertips, have caught up with her. Persephone trips and falls into her orgasm, giving a startled cry, her muscles pulling me in.

"Who do you belong to?"

"You."

I answer her with a vicious thrust. I'm close, too, and the animal act of fucking her like this brings me back to myself. To the body and mind. It drives away the ever-present ache in my head from the day, from the harsh lights we've been using to inspect pieces of jewelry. Three more strokes and pleasure made sharp by desire pulls my lungs to my ribs, filling them with dark urges and air. I stroke Persephone to another orgasm, this one ragged, and a third, because there is no better punishment than to make her come again and again while I use her. She loves it, even as it verges on pain.

"Nothing will ever touch you that doesn't have my permission. Does the news from the city have my permission, Persephone?"

"No," she gasps.

Another slap on the heated flesh of her bottom. "Do your worries have my permission?"

"No, they don't—"

I spank her again and she cries out, the sound ringing beautifully in my ears.

"Who has permission?"

"You." A choked-off scream becomes a moan and a sigh. "Only you."

You, you, you. Her voice strips the last of my control from me and my own release winds tight, so tight it shatters. I empty myself into her with abandon, holding her down on the bed, and Persephone tries her best. She knows, the filthy thing, that I prefer a bit of a struggle. She prefers it, too. It's proof that I'll always win. Always.

I haul us both up onto the bed, onto the pillows, and curl her into my chest so she can catch her breath. Her hair falls against my chest and I lean down to kiss the top of her head. "You have my permission to sleep now," I tell her, and she stretches against me and settles in. "You can rest. Oliver is guarding the door, and I'm guarding you."

"For how long?"

"Forever."

She's already relaxing, drifting off. "What happens when I wake up?"

"We start again." I grip her ass tight enough to bruise and she sucks in a breath. "Count on it."

ABOUT AMELIA WILDE

Amelia Wilde is a USA TODAY bestselling author of steamy contemporary romance and loves it a little too much. She lives in Michigan with her husband and daughters. She spends most of her time typing furiously on an iPad and appreciating the natural splendor of her home state from where she likes it best: inside.

www.awilderomance.com

MANDI BECK

CHAPTER ONE

DEACON

"Princess!" I call as I take the steps two at a time, my legs like Jell-O after my run. When she doesn't answer, I wander down the hall looking for her. It's too damn quiet for the kids to still be awake. The pink-painted door to Gigi's room is open, so I peek my head in and find Frankie tucking our daughter into bed. With a finger to her lips, she shoos me back out into the hall, flipping the nightlight and closing the door behind us.

"How was your run?" she asks, standing on tiptoe to peck a quick kiss on my lips.

Not enough. Doing my best not to get her covered in my sweat, I snatch her hand to stop her from retreating down the stairs and place a kiss on the inside of her wrist before bending to take her mouth in a deeper kiss. "Mmmmm, you taste good," I murmur against her soft lips.

"That's called sangria. I needed a glass, okay, maybe two, after playing teacher and then bath time with the twins tonight. Gigi especially. That girl is going to be the death of me." Frankie chuckles.

That brings a smile to my face. "What, your mini-you is giving you a run for your money?" I feign shock.

"Shut up. Nobody asked you," she retorts with a playful punch to my gut.

"I know that hurt your hand more than it hurt me." I flash my abs at her, flexing. "I'm made of steel, baby!" Frankie runs a painted fingernail down the center of my muscled stomach, dipping into my waistband and popping the elastic back into place before she comes in contact with any *real* steel. "Tease," I groan. "You know shit like that will get you fucked."

"I am aware," my saucy wife answers. "Go take a shower. I have a couple of things to take care of, but I'll be in soon." She raises on her toes again for another soft kiss, this one not as chaste as the first. One that comes complete with an ass grab before she saunters off down the hall. Oh yeah, she's definitely getting fucked. I'm really enjoying all of this alone time with my wife.

With our dads in Cali and my brother in Boston taking care of our bigger gyms, there's nobody to barge in on us. Usually, the house is always busy with people in and out, but right now, it's more like our own little bubble. We go to the gym so that I can work out and Frankie can live stream her dance classes, but we're the only ones there, and then it's right back home. The world outside might be a mess with the virus that has us all on high alert but not in here. We're safe at home, just the four of us, and aside from missing our people, I'm taking advantage of having my wife to myself. A whole lot of advantage. Between teaching the twins, doing video calls with teachers, friends, and our family, and all the other shit we're doing to keep things as normal as we can, Frankie and I have been spending as much time as possible naked. As far as I'm concerned, we can stay locked down long after this is all over if this is how we're gonna get down.

Showered with a towel knotted low on my hip, I come into the master bedroom, expecting to find Frankie there waiting. When she isn't, I set out to find her again. There's a light and music coming from the office, which is more like a library now since my wife has taken it over. Untying the towel from my waist, I toss it aside and throw the door open. "Princess! Where you at? I wanna make a baby!" I say loudly, my arms above me gripping the doorframe, leaving myself open and making sure there's no question that I'm completely naked except for my ink and wedding band. I never know what to expect when it comes to my wife. She's constantly surprising me, so she might be splayed out on the desk waiting, for all I know. What I definitely did not expect was a chorus of gasps and giggles and a very Indie-like "Oh my god, I'm gonna puke!"

"Deacon!" Frankie screeches, her head whipping around, blue eyes so wide they're about to fall right out of her head. "I'm on a group video call!"

Oh shiiiit. "Hi, ladies!" I greet with a wave, making no move to cover myself. It's too late for all that shit, and I have nothing to be ashamed of. "I'd cover up, but my hands aren't big enough." I raise my hands so they can see for themselves.

"Put some freaking clothes on, you exhibitionist!" my wife's snarky best friend yells. A couple of the others chime in with, "Leave him alone," and "He doesn't have to if he doesn't want to."

Frankie is doing her best to shield the camera on the computer while she fiddles with keys, muttering, "Where is the damn end call button?" I'm far enough away that they're not getting the view that they could be, but they're for sure getting the gist.

"Now, Princess, don't go ending your video thingy on my account." I can barely keep the laughter from my voice as she clicks away, gulping her sangria and sneaking appreciative glances my way all at the same time. Poor thing is frazzled. I should put her out her misery. "The baby maker and I will be in the room waiting for you. Don't take too long, though." I turn and walk away, towel still discarded, flashing them my ass as I do. Go big or go home, right? Before I make it to the room, I hear her friends' babbling chatter.

"Oh my god, so gross!"

"How do you get anything done being on lockdown with *that?*"

"Seriously, Frankie. It should be against the law to be married to a man that hot."

The last thing I hear is my wife giggling like the Catholic

schoolgirl who she was. "Lock me up and throw away the key then, ladies. Apparently, I gotta go. My husband wants to make a baby! Byyyeeeee."

CHAPTER TWO

DEACON

LYING in my room with my arms folded behind my head, I wait for Frankie to bring her fine ass to bed. I wasn't kidding about making a baby. I've been thinking about it a ton lately. The twins have started kindergarten, and although we are all home together trying to homeschool them during this crazy time, it's made me realize just how much I have missed having them home all the time. Now that I'm retired from the EWF, having won all the titles I could there, and running and expanding the gyms full-time, I'm home more than I've ever been. I've been working on convincing Frankie that this is a solid plan and the perfect timing, and although I think she's on board, it might take a little more convincing. I'm up to the challenge. *Literally.* As if my thoughts have conjured her, my wife appears in the doorway. Her wineglass dangles from her fingertips as she looks me over. I'm lying, hard and naked, with my leg cocked and falling to the side, giving her a clear view and letting her look her fill.

"Deacon, you just showed my friends all of your bits. You realize that, right?" It's clearly a rhetorical question.

"Frankie, your five-year-old son has bits. I have a cock."

She pulls her lip between her teeth, trying to keep her smile at bay. It doesn't work.

"And what a fine cock it is."

"It is. And it's all yours. They just have more to be envious about now. Besides, I'm used to standing in front of people nearly naked with a hard-on for you."

"Wh-what?" she sputters.

"Every weigh-in before every fight, I had to stand up there in my underwear in front of a whole auditorium of press and people. Nine times out of ten, it was with a hard-on…for you." Had she never noticed? *That's ridiculous*, I admonish myself. Of course, she noticed.

"That was for me? I thought that was because you were excited about—whatever you were excited about." She laughs a little self-consciously.

"Yeah, I was *excited* about you. Just like I am now."

To prove my point, I take my cock in my hand. Drawing her attention, I give it a tight squeeze, sliding up the shaft, around the throbbing tip, and back down to the base. My eyes never leave hers as she watches my every movement. Nearly seven years later, and the heat between us is hotter than ever. All that bullshit about married couples not having sex is for pussies. In the Love house, we fuck like beasts. Not sure how much more of her eye fucking I'll be able to withstand, I pat the bed.

"Come over here, Princess. Let's play a game." Her eyes flick to mine, a knowing glint making the blue glow brightly in the dimly lit room.

"Let me guess, a little game of *Just the Tip?*" she asks, her raspy voice laced with laughter.

"You know it's your favorite," I tease.

A smile steals across her face. "What if I want more than the tip?"

"I'd say you're gonna get it," I promise as she makes her way over to the bed. Once she reaches me, I stand. At six feet three, I tower over her, but with just a look, she can, and often does, bring me to my knees. Taking the wineglass from her, I place it on the nightstand because she's going to need free hands. "Can I help with theses?" I ask casually as I lower myself to kneel in front of her. Frankie slides her fingers through the long strands of my hair, raking against my scalp as I slip my hands inside the waistband of her yoga pants to be met with bare ass. With a low, appreciative growl, I squeeze hard before sliding them over her hips and down her legs, kissing each inch of bared skin. Deeply inhaling her scent as I bend to release first one foot, then the other, her hold on my hair tightening to steady herself. Before standing, I place a kiss on the tattoo encircling one thigh, then over to the other, pausing in the middle to linger. "Mmm...how ready for me are you, Princess?" Mouth on her bare mound, I look up at her even as my hands drift up her legs to land on her ass once more.

"Why don't you check?" my wife challenges.

"Not yet." I can't help but smile when she's the one who growls, not out of appreciation but frustration. As I stand, I grab the hem of her shirt and bring it over her head, throwing it over my shoulder. In front of me in nothing but a bra, it's my turn to be the one doing the eye fucking. My wife's body is the answer to every one of my prayers, the star in every fucking fantasy and hotter than anything I could ever conjure. She gave me twins, the evidence of that left behind perfectly. Dancer's legs, toned abs, and tiny white lines leaving me a map to explore every dip and curve. With deft fingers, I remove her bra and fling it the same way of her shirt, then backing her up until she's forced to sit on the bed. Before she can lie back, I slip my hands under her back and legs and position her on the bed just how I want her, with her long ways, her head hanging over the side closest to me, and her legs splayed to make room for me. "You know that you have to make it up to me for calling my cock 'bits,' right?" I ask huskily, taking my dick in my hands and tracing over her lips with it.

"Are you going to make it up to me for flashing my friends?" My answer falls away as she opens her mouth and takes me to the back of her throat. The angle in which she's lying allows me to thrust even deeper before slowly pulling out.

"If I say yes, will you do that again?" Voice gritty with need, I push against her lips, watching as I slide over her tongue into the heat of her mouth once more. In and out gently to allow her to find her rhythm. Every one of her moans vibrates over the sensitive flesh of my cock. Not able to hold back, I palm her throat, squeezing just enough to feel her constrict around my shaft. With each slide in and out, she takes me deeper, her tongue swiping over my sac before I pull out and press back in. My insides tremble, begging for release, as I reach forward and trail my other hand over her nipple that feels hard against my fingers. I squeeze and watch as she bucks, knowing that her nipples are a straight line to her pussy. Scissoring her legs, she swirls her tongue over the head of my cock, swallowing it once more, faster now, urgency for some kind of release, whether it's mine or hers.

"Easy, baby. Not yet," I order. Pulling away just slightly, I force her to slow. Just long enough for me to pull my hair into a knot atop my head and secure it with the tie around my wrist. It doesn't stop her from the sweet torture she's making me endure. She uses the space to take me in her hands, running them up and over my shaft as she nibbles and nips my balls gently, murmuring appreciatively against the throbbing flesh. If I stand and watch her much longer, I'm going to come all over her face, and as much as I would fucking love that—fuck, would I—I've tortured her long enough. As difficult as it is, I tear my eyes away and glide my hands down her chest and across her tits, stopping only long enough to allow myself to tease each stiff peak with a pinch, following the map that leads me right to her thighs and the treasure waiting between them. "Open." My voice is rough, gravelly with need, tone demanding. Her legs fall aside on a sigh, her hand never stilling on my cock. The glistening wetness coating the insides of her thighs is the answer to my question earlier. I didn't have to ask; Frankie is always ready for me. Wet like this. Needing me as much as I constantly need her. Lightly, I brush my roughened hands across her silky skin.

"Deacon, fuck, Deac. Don't be sweet," she whispers pleadingly.

With a chuckle, I land a slap right on her pussy, her hiss against the head of my dick an invitation to do it again, this time harder. Fingers now covered in her arousal, I slick them through her folds before I dip inside, crooking my fingers and twisting on my retreat. "So wet," I murmur, landing another sound slap. Not ready for her to come just yet, I slide my hand through her arousal once more. Slowly, I take my cock from her grasp, taking it in my hand. I circle the head, spreading the sweet, sticky come from between her legs over the velvety tip and down the smooth shaft. After I coat it entirely with her scent, I guide it back into her mouth. Greedily, she pulls me in, sucking me so deep I see stars. This was supposed to be a distraction to keep her from coming too quickly but, with each pass over her tongue and down her throat, I can see it's become a race. Widening my stance, I thrust my hips, finding her rhythm and matching it with my fingers. First one, then two, dipping deep inside her and searching for that sweet spot I know is there. Time is closing in on me as she digs her nails into my ass, holding me in place and then releases, encouraging my thrusting. My fingers curl into her, my thumb slipping up and around her clit over and over in cadence as I work her over. Fucking her face as she rides my hand, knowing we're both so close, I fight back the heat sizzling a path down my spine. As soon as her legs start trembling uncontrollably, falling wider apart before slamming shut to trap me, I know that I can finally give in to my release and do so on a roar.

"Jesus fuccccckkkkking fuuucckkkk, Frankie." With my hand on the back of her neck, I watch as her throat works, trying to swallow every last drop. Unable to hold my own weight anymore, I reluctantly slide out of my wife's magic porn star mouth and climb on the bed next to her. With a tug, I pull her from the edge and into me, anchoring her there with an arm banded across her chest. My orgasm makes me feel like liquid. Like if I were not in this bed, I would be a puddle on the floor.

My wife sighs, eyes closed with a euphoric smile across her devilish lips. "You know that's not how you make a baby, right?" She giggles softly.

"That was just the beginning, Princess. I'm just getting started."

CHAPTER THREE

DEACON

WARM AND CONTENT with my wife's naked body pressed against my back, I sink deeper into the covers, reaching behind me to draw her closer. She sighs in her sleep, melting against me. Her warm breath fans over my skin, causing goose bumps. Thoughts of all the filthy things we did last night play through my mind. I should let her sleep because we didn't get much last night, but I'm not sure that I can, though, not with her soft, pliant body wrapped around me. I'm just about to turn and wake her up the *proper* way when our door creaks open, and two little bodies come running and hurl themselves on top of me.

"Oof!" My legs shift quickly to protect myself from the knees and small harmful limbs that always seem to make painful connections. "Easy, you two animals. You're going to wake Mama." I don't tell them they're also about to maim their father because then I would look like a pussy, and you can't show these two any weakness. Especially Gianna.

"We're hungry, Daddy," my son says as quietly as he can, which is not quiet at all.

"I told him that I could make breakfast, Papa, but he didn't listen," Gigi says, her long blond hair in a pony that is all askew and her blue eyes bright with fire. Sass on high already this morning. Noted.

"Gianna, you can't cook things on the big stove. Only on your baby stove, and I don't want any fake pancakes." J-Roc is getting heated, which means Gigi is about to lose her shit. She doesn't like to be told what she can or can't do, and she especially doesn't like to be told by her twin brother. Knowing that I need to defuse this situation before they start really fighting, I pull myself to a sitting position, careful not to let the blanket slip, so they don't get a show like their mama and her friends did.

"Okay, okay. No fighting outside the cage, remember?" I remind them.

"I remember."

"Yes, Papa." They answer simultaneously, shooting daggers as they do.

JR, with his dark brown hair like mine and blue eyes like Frankie's, stands a couple of inches taller than Gianna, but what she lacks in size, she makes up for in sass, much like my wife. When they really get going, I'll let them work it out in the cage, but they have to hug and make up before leaving the mats and can't bring their anger past the door of the octagon. It's a strategy my dad used on my brothers and me that always worked. They're so little that it just looks like a couple of monkeys rolling around and sitting on each other. They aren't in there to hurt one another, just to have a healthy outlet for their anger. Plus, it's super fucking adorable and always ends in them laughing and playing.

"JR, you want pancakes?" He nods enthusiastically, his curls dancing around his face. "What about you, Gigi?"

"Yes! But I want no bananas, and he wants some bananas," she explains to me. They might not always get along, but they always have each other's back.

"Got it! You go get the bananas out, and I'll be down in just a second, and we'll make them."

"Are you sending us out because you don't have your pajamas on?" Gigi asks, arms crossed over her little chest, judging me.

"Daddy and Mommy never wear pajamas, silly. Daddy says they itch," JR tells her with an eye roll at her lack of parental knowledge.

The bed begins to quake gently as my now, clearly awake, wife buries her face in my back to smother her laughter.

"Gianna, I'm a grown-up. I don't have to wear pajamas if I don't want to, so I don't...because they itch," I lie. Or maybe they do, I wouldn't know because I haven't worn any since I was a kid.

"Well, when I grow up, I'm not gonna wear any either." She harrumphs.

"Oh, you're gonna wear them. They won't be itchy to you." My voice carries a bit of panic at the thought of my daughter, A: being a grown-up, and B: well, I'm not thinking about B. Ever. "Now go on, I'll be right there." This time, they listen, racing each other out of the room as I turn on my traitorous wife and pin her beneath me in a tangle of sheets.

"How are you going to let me navigate that on my own? That was fucking torture!" I admonish. "And you better have a talk with your daughter. She needs to get used to wearing those old lady nightgowns now. You know, with the buttons and shit all up to her neck."

Frankie just laughs harder as if I'm not dead ass serious. "I would have given anything to see your face when she said that." She lets a little snort slip, which just causes her to go into breathless fits of laughter now.

"You are not funny, woman." All her writhing beneath me has me wishing that we had time to do some real writhing, but there is absolutely no fucking way that Gigi wouldn't come up here demanding her pancakes. With a sigh, I heave myself off my beautiful, sexy, naked wife and get out of the bed. Frankie lies there, head propped up on her hand, and watches me as I slip into clothes. "You keep looking at me like that, and you know what's going to happen," I warn as I always do.

She sighs deeply. "Unfortunately, there's no time for your *Love moves*," she teases. "You have to go make breakfast, and I have to wash all this sex off me before I hug my children." Frankie smiles coyly at me, her hair a just fucked mess as it tumbles around her shoulders. The sheet falls to the floor, and I watch, mesmerized, as she sashays her fine ass into the bathroom. Disappearing and leaving me there envisioning her wet in the shower…alone. I take a step to join her when I hear my name being called at the top of my children's lungs from downstairs. A groan rumbles from somewhere deep within me. We'll just have to practice our baby making when the kids go down for a nap. With that to look forward to, I turn and head to the kitchen. It's daddy time. Feed the kids, love on them, do some alphabet shit, love on them some more, and then nap time. Life. Is. Good.

Stick and move. Stick and motherfucking move.

ABOUT MANDI BECK

Mandi Beck has been an avid reader all of her life. A deep love for books always had her jotting down little stories on napkins, notebooks, and her hand. As an adult she was further submerged into the book world through book clubs and the epicness of social media. It was then that she graduated to writing her stories on her phone and then finally on a proper computer.

A wife, mother to two rambunctious and somewhat rotten boys, and stepmom to two great girls away at college, she shares her time with her husband in Chicago where she was born and raised. Mandi is a diehard hockey fan and blames the Blackhawks when her deadlines are not met. Ask her who her favorite hockey player is and she'll tell you that he calls her...mom.

www.authormandibeck.com

A WICKED TAHOE Retreat

PIPER LAWSON

CHAPTER ONE

"You're going to kill Jax Jamieson." My best friend's voice is blunt, and my gaze meets Serena's in the mirror over my shoulder. "The world's most infamous rock star will be dead thanks to you."

I inspect the lace bra, still on its hanger with the price tags on, and the matching panties. "There's barely anything to them."

"Exactly," she says.

I grin and turn, crossing to the mine-for-now walk-in closet.

The house Jax and I rented in Tahoe for the week and invited Serena and her boyfriend, Wes, to isn't as big as our house in Dallas, but the six-bedroom lakefront estate has wood, glass, and sweeping views from everywhere, including the master bedroom.

I'm surprised the closet doesn't have a view.

The house is opulent, but though I try to appreciate the details, I'm mostly here for the escape.

"Thank you guys for coming," I toss over my shoulder as I retrieve the black dress in its garment bag.

"This is perfect. Wes and I could use a few days away from New York. But we didn't need to intrude on your second anniversary."

"Are you kidding? It's no intrusion. We're happy to be adults for a few days. What's your second anniversary anyway? Paper?"

"I think that's first. Tin? Anyway, I'm pretty sure Jax is going to do better than that."

"He doesn't have to. I got him." My chest swells with love.

"Don't ever tell him that. His ego's already larger than most island nations. But when was the last time you and Jax went for a romantic dinner?"

"Months," I say, wistful. "The restaurant is supposed to be spectacular, and Jax had the chef make something special. Thanks for looking out for Sophie tonight."

"She has Jax's eyes and your hair and smile. She's the cutest mini I've ever seen."

I cross to the four-poster bed that's somehow made modern thanks to rough-hewn beams and white linens and drop onto it, the dress and lingerie in my lap. "She is devilishly adorable, which she gets from her dad. She's also exhausting," I admit.

Serena lays a hand on the beam, glancing toward the ceiling and pushing experimentally. "Just making sure this isn't going to bring down the house if you two break the bed tonight."

I grab a pillow and toss it at her, and she laughs and ducks out of the way. "All right. I'll let you get dressed." With a wink, she heads out the door.

I strip out of my light summer dress and plain underwear.

It feels as if my husband and I have been drowning in "real life" lately, and though I'm so grateful for our careers and family, I'm beyond ready for a few days of fresh air and grown-up company that's not trying to twist Jax's arm to do an appearance or endorsement. Life will never be the same as it was before we were married, but I want to feel those early days when I wound up on Jax's tour and every experience was shocking and terrifying and eye-opening—and not in the way diapers are shocking, terrifying, and eye-opening.

The way it felt to travel with the biggest rock star on the planet, to look up from working at the soundboard or joking with the band to find his heady, thrilling attention on me.

I'm tugging the fancy lace bra on after the panties when the sound of shrieking down the hall makes me freeze.

Oh, boy. Sophie's started.

I hurry to put on the black cocktail dress. Thank goodness I did my hair and makeup already.

I head down the hall, looking over the railing to the great room below. "Everyone okay?" I call.

The shrieking has turned to crying.

When I get downstairs, my dressy sandals in one hand, I follow the sounds to the main-floor bathroom.

The scene that greets me is familiar and heart-rending.

Sophie's sitting on the white granite counter, red and tear-stained.

My husband is in front of her, wiping at her cheeks.

"Soph's not feeling well." Jax's voice is resigned as he casts a look over his shoulder.

I should be entirely focused on my kid, and part of me is.

But my breath still catches in my throat at the sight of my husband in his off-white dress shirt, the top two buttons undone, rolled up at the sleeves to reveal tattoos. The trim pants hug his strong legs.

He's gorgeous.

But I can't linger on him because Sophie's gone from sniffling to bawling again.

"Did you take her temperature?" I ask, switching into mom mode.

"Just did." He holds out the thermometer, and I glance at it.

Crap.

"A little high. But nothing to take her to the emergency room for."

"We can take care of her," Serena says from behind me. I turn to see her, arms folded and brows pulled together, in the hall. Wes looms behind her, tall and serious. "You guys go for dinner. It's your anniversary."

I bite my lip. "Jax—"

"We'll stay."

He crosses to me. "I'm sorry about this, Hales. I had something special lined up." Jax's gaze drops down my body for the first time. "And so did you, judging by the dress."

Disappointment floods me.

"Why don't I take Sophie for a bit?" I offer, but he's already shaking his head.

"You take a load off. Have a drink with Wes and Serena."

I grudgingly agree, meeting them in the main kitchen that's all slate counters and chef-grade stainless appliances.

"I'm sorry about your evening. Jax told me he had quite the dinner organized," Wes says, and I grimace as I lean over the beautiful island, my bare arms resting on the cool slate.

"I know. Parenting has zero nights off." My stomach growls, and I realize we don't have a backup plan for food. "What were you guys planning for dinner?"

Serena shrugs. "We were going to order a pizza."

The wheels in my head turn. "I have a better idea."

I call the restaurant, and the chef volunteers to send food over for all of us. By the time I hang up, I'm feeling slightly better.

"Hales." I turn at the sound of my husband's voice. My kid's on his hip, her tired face on his shoulder. "Think she's ready to go down, but she wants you."

"I'll put her in her pajamas."

"I put out the purple ones she likes earlier."

I shift her weight into my arms, sharing a smile of understanding with my husband on the way. "You're the best dad, you know that?" I murmur.

His eyes crinkle and the expression on his face has me tingling all over.

I head upstairs before all my willpower slips away and I jump on my husband.

I take each polished wooden step carefully. Sophie's weight is comforting in my arms.

I knew things would be different when we had our first child together. Jax already had custody of Annie, but she's off to college and their relationship was established long before I met him.

This was new territory for both of us. While it hasn't always been smooth, I wouldn't trade a second of it.

I get Sophie ready for bed, giving her fresh water from her sippy cup before I lay her down. Her tears have faded, and she's not protesting anymore when I turn off the lights, brush a hand through her soft, dark hair, and check that the monitor's on and working.

When I come back downstairs, the table in the kitchen has transformed.

"This is beautiful." I can't get over the spread of food.

Serena's getting wine, Wes is setting out cutlery, and Jax crosses to me. "Not what I had in mind, but we'll make it work for now," he murmurs, brushing his lips across my cheek in a way that makes me tingle.

"For now?" I reply under my breath.

His gaze drops down my body again. I almost forgot I was dressed up, but the way he looks at me, I'm aware of everything I'm wearing.

"Glad you like the dress," I whisper.

"Gonna like peeling it off of you more," he replies so easily I have to press my thighs together to fight the sudden tingling.

We sit with our friends, and Wes and Serena tell us about New York, their apartment, and work. She's at a marketing firm, and he's a biologist and science teacher. I love their chemistry, how attentive he is to my wild friend.

We finish our prime rib. "Ready for dessert?" Jax asks.

But the monitor crackles to life before we can.

"Dada!"

"It's cute that she's started talking," Serena comments.

"Bet you wish she wasn't so specific." Wes's comment is directed at my husband, who grins wryly.

Jax is out of his chair. "That's me." He drops a kiss on my cheek that leaves me warm before heading out of the room. The feel of his touch on my shoulders lingers after he's gone, and I press my thighs together under the table.

"So, are you guys having kids?" I ask, a brow lifted. "Because I'm sure we're doing a good job of selling you on the perks."

Serena laughs, and Wes shakes his head. "Maybe someday. But not yet. Are you having more?"

"We've talked about it."

"You make great parents."

"We weren't sure at first," I admit. "With Jax's work taking him all over and mine keeping me busy, it's tough. But we make choices."

A sound comes from the monitor still on across the kitchen and my heart melts.

Serena's eyes round on mine. "He's playing guitar?" she whispers.

My throat swells up as the sound of the instrument streams through, followed by low singing overtop.

I melt.

I will never get used to the sound of his voice, of his music.

I knew Jax's voice before we ever met, not to mention fell in love, but hearing him like this—in a way that's deeply personal—it gets me every damned time.

"I can cut that torte if you like?" Serena offers, snapping me out of it.

"Thanks. I'll take it to go."

I plate a piece of the rich chocolate mousse cake and put two forks on it, then pad upstairs in my bare feet.

At the doorway of the room next to ours, I lean inside. It's all dark except for a small light by the crib.

Jax is on the edge of the rocking chair, guitar in his lap as he plays.

My breath sticks in my throat.

He's the most gorgeous man I've ever seen—not smooth and polished, still rough and a little dangerous. The fact that he's serenading a toddler doesn't make him weak.

It makes him the most masculine thing I've ever seen.

I think I might've ruined these panties.

Jax looks up and catches me staring. His fingers play a final chord, the sound dying out and leaving us in silence.

"She's asleep?" I whisper-mouth.

He nods. His strong jaw and amber eyes draw me in.

He lifts the guitar over his head and sets it on the floor before crossing to me.

The way he moves—controlled, deliberate—has the hairs standing up on my neck.

"I brought you dessert," I murmur.

Jax's gaze drops but only flicks over the cake and lands on me. "Yes, you did."

Every part of me goes liquid at the expression on his face, and I swallow. "You're still hungry?"

It's a tease, and we both know it.

"Starving. Bedroom. Now."

I bite my lip. "It's eight o'clock."

"Then I have all night."

I step backward down the hall, and he's stalking me.

I wanted it to feel like when we first met, and here, in this strange house with only the lights coming from the great-room chandelier on the other side of the railing, it does feel that way.

He's all strength and purpose, confidence bordering on arrogance, the way only a man who's had millions of people want him can be.

"Sophie will probably wake up in an hour," I say as if calling it out will keep it from happening.

He continues forward as I back up, his hooded gaze never leaving mine. "When she does, I'll make sure she's okay and put her back to sleep." His voice is like the lace I'm suddenly feeling on every inch of me, soft and irritating at once. "Then, I'll come back to the bedroom and fuck my gorgeous wife again."

Shivers overtake me, but I fight falling under his control. I've never caved to him, and it's one of the things that makes us so well-matched.

But somehow, we are all the way to the master bedroom.

I reach past his shoulder for the light switch, putting the dimmer on so the barest warm glow fills the room, and I can see not only the outlines of his gorgeous body but the details of his face.

I hold the cake up between us. "So... that's a no to mousse?"

I swipe a finger through it and hold it up between us. When I suck the sweetness off my skin, his entire body tightens, but I pretend not to notice. "It's really good, Jax—"

He's got the plate, nearly tossing it on a side table before pressing me up against the wall.

His mouth claims mine, hot and desperate and possessive. His tongue insists on entrance, and I can only deny him for one heartbeat, two, because I want it every bit as much as he does.

Yes.

I need this. I miss this.

I know I'm his, but I like to be reminded.

It reminds me he's mine, too.

My fingers dig into his muscled biceps through the shirt hard enough to make him groan.

We live together. I shouldn't be starved for him, but I am.

God, I am.

The way Jax brushes my hair off my neck and runs hot kisses down my neck, as intense as if he feels this could be our last time— or our first—cranks up my arousal another ten notches.

My head turns to look out at the view, the gorgeous lake and trees.

"You worried someone will see us?" he mutters.

"No," I manage. "I'm thinking about the day we met."

He pulls back an inch, and I want to protest until he speaks against my lips. "I loved you then."

I snort. "You did not. I interrupted your recording session, and you were pissed."

Jax tucks a piece of hair behind my ear, stroking my neck with a thumb and making me arch for more. "I was startled," he corrects.

"Then you tried to kill me in the back of a limo."

Jax's gaze narrows. "You know what I remember about the tour? The night after the first show when you told me Leonard Cohen was better than me. And I reached in your pocket for my phone you were holding for me"—his hand skims up under the hem of my dress and right where that pocket would be, fingers tracing down my bare skin and the edge of my panties—"and I thought, 'This girl is going to ruin me.'"

Desire and love surge through me, twining together into an emotion so powerful I can't resist it forever.

But that doesn't mean I won't have fun trying.

I angle my face up. "You haven't even seen what's under the dress."

His gaze darkens, sharpens, and he's spinning me around.

My face meets the wall, smooth under my cheek, as my husband's hands unzip the back of my dress.

Cool air hits my skin as he yanks it down, and the garment falls around my feet.

There's nothing—no sound, no anything.

Nerves invade my stomach, and I stand in my bare feet and lingerie, counting my breaths.

Eventually I turn, uncertain as to what I'll find when I look up.

Jax is a god but a devout one. The expression on his face is tortured and reverent at once.

"Christ, Hales." The words are a prayer as his gaze runs over the scraps of lace, the same color as my skin, hiding barely anything from his view.

Not my nipples, hard from the cool air and his attention.

Not the apex of my thighs, bare for the first time in a while in anticipation of this trip.

"You're stunning."

The words have a breath trembling from between my lips. I've never felt so weak and so powerful. "I love hearing you say that."

He lifts me and carries me not to the bed, but to the giant chaise by the window.

It's still barely light outside, the sun setting over the lake.

He spreads my legs and strokes his hands up my thighs. "What's this?"

I glance down and curse. "Forgot to take the price tags off. I was thinking I might take them back."

Of course, now that I'm wearing them, I can't, but I was thinking of getting to my kid when I put them on and then forgot altogether.

He turns one tag over, and I grab for his big hand with my smaller one, suddenly embarrassed. "Don't! You're not supposed to see how much they are."

Jax's grin is devilish, cocky. "Hales, first, there's no price I would care about, but I'm guessing you bought them with your own damned money anyway." He's right. "Second... there's no way you're taking these back."

He rips off the tag, then does the same with the one on the bra, discarding them.

"The only place this lingerie will be from now on is on your body or on our bedroom floor. Got it?"

I sigh. "Mhmm."

The next second, he drags me to him and sucks my nipple into his hot mouth through the fine lace.

I gasp, fingers tugging on his hair. It's so good. The lace is rough and almost uncomfortable, but on the other side of it is him—and he's everything.

I need more.

He moves to the other side, giving it the same treatment.

Then he drags his lips south, down my stomach, between my thighs.

His fingers trace the panel of my panties. "When'd you get so wet, my beautiful wife?"

"When I saw you dressed up," I admit.

"With our kid screaming on the counter?"

I bite my cheek. "Maybe. Does that make me a bad mom?"

"You are the best mom and the sexiest fucking creature I've ever seen."

His mouth follows his fingers, and he dips his head to tongue me through the lace. My head falls back, and I groan.

His fingers sink into me, two at once, and I moan. "Every night I dream of this, of us, of you. Even when you're lying right next to me."

He stands and strips off his shirt.

I don't bother not to ogle his body, and from the expression on his face, he expects it.

He's hard and muscled, in as phenomenal shape as the day I met him, when he was still touring and the world still worshipped him as their god.

They can think he's theirs, but the truth is…

He's mine.

In private, he's all mine.

The perfect ink accentuating the lines of his body. The wicked expression on his face, like he's got enough control to take me apart before losing himself in me, chasing his own pleasure until we both destroy one another.

Jax makes efficient work of his belt, his pants, and the hard outline of him through his underwear makes my mouth water.

I'm on fire, and he's not even inside me yet.

I reach for the waistband, and he lets me strip the pants off his hips. He springs free, thick and hard and bobbing against his abs.

I want him everywhere, and I can't even think straight. I need to suck him into my mouth until his hand fists in my hair. I need to feel him so deep in me I know there will never be part of me he hasn't touched.

But first, I wrap my hand around him, his silky hardness making the buzzing between my thighs intensify.

Jax groans low in his throat. "I like seeing you on my cock. Your hand. Your mouth. Your pussy. It's all for you, and only you."

"Show me."

He shifts over me, hitching my leg around his hips and nestling himself between my thighs.

The thrill is familiar and new at once, like something we've forgotten in the months of everyday life.

It's not even about the house or the escape—it's about the fire within us, between us.

The one that's always been there if we knew where to look.

I know it's going to be so fucking hot, even before Jax nudges my slit with his bare cock.

"Tell me you want it, my wife." It's a request and a command.

"I don't want *it*." His gaze flares, combative, until I go on. "I want *you*."

Then Jax drags my mouth to his, swallowing my cry as he slides home.

All.

The.

Way.

He's been inside me a hundred times, but the first few moments are always a stretch.

I savor them, like the sweetest candy you know will melt on your tongue and be gone before you've had a chance to fully enjoy it.

Sure enough, he starts to move.

His strokes are hard and shallow at first, then smooth out.

Jax's abs are taught, his hips pistoning against mine, and it's the sexiest thing I've ever seen.

The visual stimulation alone is overkill—he's gorgeous and sexual and commanding and competent. He knows how to turn me on, make me beg.

But the fact that I can do the same to him—that I'm the reason for the tic in his jaw, the sweat on his brow, the way his amber eyes darken nearly to black—is what stops my heart.

"Jax," I moan.

"I gotta slow this down," he grunts, to me or himself.

I stare at him through half-lidded eyes. "Next time."

He fights himself, his attention moving between my eyes and my parted lips as he continues to fuck me.

"Next time," he decides.

Relief washes over me, but it evaporates in the same second, swept away by the tension beneath as he shifts over me, scooping up my hips to change the angle and hit me harder, deeper.

We're both hanging on. We've done this before, but there's always an edge underneath.

One I should be able to contain after being with this man for five years, but I can't.

I know it when the telltale shaking starts low in my stomach, when my breasts pull tight and my toes start to clench.

Jax pulls back to press his forehead to mine, not once closing his eyes, as if he needs to see this to believe it.

"You're so beautiful like this," he rasps, our breath mingling. "You're my everything."

"I love you so much," I whisper.

His corded neck vibrates. "I love you too, Hales. Then, now, always."

I can't hold it back anymore. The intensity it too much, and I go off, shaking, my head thrown back. "Oh my God. Jax!"

It's three strokes later that he starts to rock, too, the strong arms boxing me in beginning to twitch from effort.

He plunges into me one final time, deep and desperate, before claiming my lips with his. I swallow his sexy, endless groan as he comes for what feels like ages.

I memorize every moment. My fingers trace the hard muscles of his arms, his back, until he collapses onto his elbows so as not to crush me.

He moves us over so he can drop onto his side, his hand cupping my face as if he can't stand not to touch me.

"Happy Anniversary," I murmur, glancing down at the wet, disheveled lace still barely covering parts of my body. "Dinner was great, but I guess the lingerie was a bust." I bite my cheek and sneak a look up at my husband.

His gaze narrows playfully on mine. If I know my husband, the smug expression from knowing we just took each other apart—and that we're nowhere near done—will last well into tomorrow.

When he speaks, there's less cockiness and more gratitude than I expected.

"This is everything. You and me. Wherever you are is home, Hales. Whatever comes at us, we've got it covered. Whatever we are is perfect."

ABOUT PIPER LAWSON

Piper Lawson is a USA Today bestselling author of smart, steamy romance. She writes about women who follow their dreams (even the scary ones), best friends who know your dirty secrets (and love you anyway), and complex heroes you'll fall hard for. Piper lives in Canada with her tall, dark and brilliant husband. She believes peanut butter is a protein, rose gold is a neutral, and love is always the answer.

www.piperlawsonbooks.com

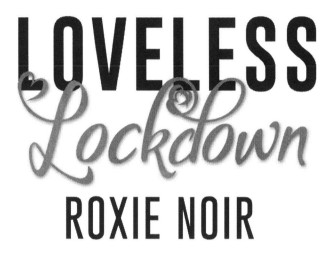

ROXIE NOIR

CHAPTER ONE

CHARLIE

THE MOMENT I touch the fire truck, its siren starts blaring.

"Shut up," I hiss through clenched teeth, flipping it over.

"Sirens blazing! I'm driving to the fiiiii—"

I find the switch on the underside, and the world's most irritating song cuts short, though it's too late for me. I'm going to have it stuck in my head for at least two full days now, and there's probably nothing I can do about it.

Gently, I put the fire engine into the bin. Then, I listen. I literally cross my fingers, but all I hear is the slight creaking of floorboards above my head, the familiar rhythms of my husband putting our ten-year-old to bed.

The eighteen-month-old doesn't make a peep, thank God. The kid is helplessly and utterly consumed with love for this fire engine — a gift from my sister, who notably neither has nor wants children — and if he woke up right now, it would take forever to put him back down.

With a sigh, I sink to the hardwood floor, lay on my back, prop my feet on the couch, and pull out my phone, because it's finally time for stupid phone games.

I'm still swiping blue diamonds into groups of three when

footsteps descend the stairs, then stop in the doorway to our living room.

Then they pause.

"Everything okay?" Daniel asks.

"Yup."

"You know you're on the floor, right?" he asks.

"I like the floor," I say, clearing a level. There's fanfare and confetti on my phone, and I switch it off, plop it onto my belly and look at him. "Also, Thomas has decided that his legs don't work and I have to carry him everywhere, so this feels amazing on my back."

"Ah," he says, then walks over and lays on the floor next to me, also propping his feet on the couch. "It's kinda hard."

I giggle, and Daniel just gives me a look that's half disbelieving, half entertained.

"That's what she said," I tell him, waggling my eyebrows.

"Ridiculous," he says, but he's grinning, and it just makes me laugh harder.

"You like it," I say. "And also, who texted who a picture of a cactus that looked like a dick last week?"

"That's irrelevant," he says, one arm behind his head.

"I don't think it is," I say, my head turned toward him. "I think it's extremely relevant."

"You didn't think the cocktus was art?"

"I think the angle and framing left something to be desired," I tease.

Daniel somehow scoots closer, and now our hips are brushing, his shoulder against mine.

"Tell me more about things you desire," he says, one eyebrow just barely lifting as his grin goes wicked.

My heart thuds in my chest. My thighs tighten together. Daniel and I have been married for almost three years now, and we're raising two kids together, but I'll be damned if that look doesn't *get* me.

"Tell me more about things that are kinda hard," I murmur, rolling in to nuzzle my nose against his.

He rolls in too, sliding a hand across my hip, squeezing my leggings-clad ass.

"I'd rather show you," he says, voice lowering. "And frankly, *kinda* is an understatement."

And then he kisses me, and it's gentle and demanding all at once, and it doesn't matter that we've kissed thousands of times before because my body still responds like it's the very first time.

Yes, we're on the floor, and yes, I'm pretty sure that I just crushed a Cheerio under my shoulder, but he grabs my ass harder and I slide my fingers under his t-shirt, playfully nipping at his bottom lip, and he growls at me.

"So the floor does it for you?" I ask, trailing my fingers up the soft fur on his belly as I hitch my knee over his hip, his big hand sliding to my thigh, locking in place.

"Sure, it's the floor," he says, that light in his blue eyes that I've come to know *so* well. "The floor, and not the fact that you spent all day bending over in skintight pants."

"They're comfortable," I say, rolling my hips into him.

"They're hot as fuck," he says, and pulls me in for another hard, hungry kiss.

On the floor. In the living room.

I push myself tighter against him, half thinking that we should probably go upstairs and half not wanting to stop for that long. It's our house, after all, and both the kids are—

"Oh. My *God*," says Rusty's voice.

We both jerk backward, yanking our hands away from each other like we've touched a hot stove.

Rusty's standing in the doorway to the living room, in her pajamas, staring at us as if we're a nest full of spiders atop a mound of elephant dung, surrounded by a moat of rotting brussels sprouts.

"You're supposed to be in bed," Daniel says with perfect calm, propping himself up on one elbow.

"What are you *doing*?" she asks. "Eww-*wuh*."

She says *ew* so hard she adds an extra syllable.

"Do you need something?" I ask, pushing myself to sitting.

Both knees crack. Getting older is not for the weak.

"I just wanted some water," she says, then turns and walks into the kitchen. "Gross," she mutters, loudly enough that we can hear it.

Daniel also sits up, running a hand through his slightly-floppy hair. He needs a haircut. I also need a haircut. Everyone needs a haircut, but we've been in quarantine for two months and have barely left our house, so we're all out of luck.

The tap in the kitchen goes on. Daniel gives me an amused, raised-eyebrows look, and I give it back, leaning my elbow on the couch. Rusty drinks, then fills the water glass again and heads back for the stairs.

"Yuck," I hear her mutter to herself.

"Goodnight, sweetheart," Daniel calls.

He doesn't get an answer.

"Can you believe she's gonna be eleven tomorrow?" he asks.

"Yes," I say instantly, still leaning on my elbow, sitting cross-legged on the floor. "I've never believed anything more easily, as a matter of fact."

He glances back at the stairs, and for a moment, he's quiet.

Then he turns to me and lowers his voice.

"She'll like the surprise, right?" he asks. "What if it's too dorky?"

"Well, we'd be the first parents to do something dorky, then," I say, and Daniel smiles.

"Point taken."

"She'll like it," I reassure him, rearranging myself, one hand on his knee. "Or at least, she'll tolerate it because it's the best we can do right now."

"That's probably all we can hope for," he says, turning himself to sit next to me, our backs against the couch. "Did you see the look she gave me when I asked how to do a TikTok today?"

"You brought that on yourself," I laugh, and he slings an arm around my shoulders.

"I'll sure never ask again," he says, his thumb rubbing my shoulder through my t-shirt.

We both go silent for a moment, leaning together.

"Can I ask you something?" he says, after a moment.

"Sure."

"How come you're still wearing a bra in quarantine?" he says, and now his voice has that devious, teasing quality to it that I know so well.

His fingertips skim across the tip of my breast, circling my nipple. "I mean, you don't need it, right?" he teases.

"Technically, no," I say, snuggling closer. "I'll be sure to take it off next time I walk through the background of your video meeting."

"Hmmm," he says, a low rumble, and then in one fluid movement he pulls me around so I'm straddling his lap as he leans against the couch.

I push my face against his, shift my hips as he grabs my ass again. He was right earlier. There's no *kinda* about this hardness.

"I could always try just letting them jiggle free all day," I say. "Maybe wear some really tight shirts, accidentally douse myself in cold water, jump on a trampoline?"

"Go on," he says, grinning, running both hands lightly over my breasts. My nipples prick up at the sensation, even through two layers of fabric.

"I'd rather go to a room with a locking door," I say.

Daniel leans in, captures my mouth with his. I rock against him as he slides his tongue into my mouth, kissing my lips until they feel slightly bruised and I'm a little breathless.

It's been longer than normal since the last time. I'll be the first to admit that being in the house with two kids 24/7 while trying to homeschool and work full time has put a slight damper on our sex life.

"You think she'll come downstairs again?"

"I think I don't want to pay for therapy," I laugh, and he nips at my bottom lip, then lightly smacks my ass.

"Bedroom," he says, in a voice that's half tease and half growl. I don't need to be told twice.

"Can you put this in, please?" I say, holding out a tiny damp t-shirt to Thomas.

He grabs it with two chubby toddler hands, then stomps over to the dryer and throws the t-shirt in like he's trying for a three-pointer. I press my lips together and force myself not to laugh, even though the way that toddlers always give a hundred and ten percent is both adorable and hilarious.

"Dryer!" he shouts, then comes back to me. I hand him another damp shirt, and he throws it into the dryer.

Is it the quickest way to get laundry done?

No.

Does it eventually get laundry done while keeping a one-and-a-half-year-old entertained?

Yes, it does, and right now 'child entertainment' is my number-one life priority because it's increasingly difficult to come by.

The playground is closed. Daycare is closed. The library is closed, the parks are closed, Grandma's house is closed. Every single thing that we do for fun is pretty much closed, so here we are, making a game out of putting clothes into the dryer.

Just as we toss the last item into the dryer, my phone buzzes.

Eli: The falcon is leaving the nest.

I frown at my phone as Thomas gleefully bangs his chubby hands against the side of the dryer.

"Boom! Thunder," he shouts.

"Why can't your uncles be normal?" I ask.

My only answer is more banging, and then my phone buzzes again.

Daniel: Are you the falcon?

Eli: Obviously.

Daniel: And you're leaving the nest to bring the cake over?

Eli: You're really killing my cool metaphor.

Seth: That was a cool metaphor?

Eli: If we had code names I would definitely be the falcon.

Seth: I'm not sure that's true.

Daniel: Eli, are you bringing the cake over now?

Daniel: Please focus.

Eli: The falcon is bringing the secret package over now, yes.

Seth: It's not secret, it's a cake.

Caleb: There's no way Eli would be the falcon.

Daniel: Can you park on the street and leave it on the back porch? She's on a classroom call right now, so I think she won't notice if you're quiet.

Eli: Yes. The falcon is a swift and silent hunter.

Caleb: You're thinking of owls.

Eli: Falcons are also silent.

Seth: Don't falcons scream?

Levi: Caleb is right, you're thinking of owls. Falcons have a very distinctive cry and lack the serrated primary feathers that make owls so quiet when they fly.

Levi: Is there a reason I'm in this group text?

I'm sitting on the floor and Thomas comes over, plops himself into my lap, and reaches for my phone.

"Turtles," he demands.

"Not right now, kiddo," I say.

"Turtleeees!"

Recently, I've been making the mistake of alleviating boredom by showing him wildlife videos on my phone once in a while. Of course, now that's all he wants to do, ever.

"No turtles right now," I say as my phone lights up with more texts from Daniel's brothers. "Let's get up and go—"

I go silent as Daniel appears on the stairs, obviously sneaking. Thomas is still grabbing at my phone, and Daniel points at Rusty's room, then makes a question face.

I nod. He taps his wrist and makes the question face again. Thomas squirms.

"Noon, maybe?" I whisper as quietly as I can. "Is today Wednesday or Thursday?"

He has to think about that, then shrugs and jerks a thumb over his shoulder.

"CAKE," he mouths, and just then, Thomas finally sees him.

"Daddy!!" he squeals, jumps out of my lap, and hustles for Daniel, only stopping when he bonks against his leg.

"Hey, buddy," Daniel says, keeping his voice low as he lifts Thomas. "Want to come help me do a fun secret thing for your sister?"

"Daddy beard," Thomas says, and pats Daniel's chin.

"Are we good to go?" I whisper at Daniel, standing from the floor.

"Yeah. You're in the group text, right?"

"Yup," I say, turning the dryer on. "If you've got him for a while I'll go..."

I glance at Rusty's closed door.

"Get the other thing together," I whisper.

Daniel just flashes me a thumbs-up, and then my guys head back down the stairs together. I take a deep breath and try to pull my brain together, just a little, though that's been harder and harder these days.

"Okay," I say, completely to myself. "Wrap the model, get the plans. That's all."

Still in my hand, my phone buzzes.

Seth: I think Eli is more of a mockingbird type.

I snort, put my phone back in my pocket, and head for my workshop in the garage.

CHAPTER TWO

DANIEL

AT THE EDGE of the forest that surrounds our back yard, the trees shiver. They crunch.

Then, improbably, the trees curse.

"Shit," a big oak tree hisses, moments before my older brother Eli emerges from the light green tangle that heralds spring in the Virginia mountains. On the back deck, Thomas stands up straight, a twig in each fist.

"Just like a falcon," Eli whispers, holding up a round cake carrier. He's wearing a black face mask with purple lightning bolts, undoubtedly made by his wife Violet.

At least, Violet made all our face masks, including the rainbow unicorn one I've got on right now. Rusty thinks it's hilarious and Thomas loves it, so it's fine with me.

"Sure, a falcon," I say, and lift Thomas into my arms. "Who's that?" I ask him, pointing.

Eli waves. Thomas frowns and says nothing. The masks tend to throw him off.

"It's your Uncle Eli," I say, as Eli puts the cake on a table and waves back. "He's bringing Rusty a surprise cake for her birthday."

That gets his attention, and his eyes go wide.

"Cake?!" he says. "CAAAAAAKE."

"Hey, can you whisper?" I ask him, whispering myself, because a toddler shouting "CAKE!!" doesn't make for a great surprise.

"*Caaaake,*" he whispers in the loudest whisper I've ever heard.

On the other side of the table, Eli is cracking up.

"You did this to yourself," he laughs.

"What kind is it?" I ask him, over Thomas's repeated whispers of *cake. Cake. Cake.*

"It's a rose-pistachio sponge, and the base frosting is vanilla-almond," Eli says, leaning over the cake container. "The red flowers are raspberry, the purple ones are lavender, the blue ones are blackberry, and the yellow ones are pineapple."

My kid squirms in my arms, and I just stare at my brother for a long moment.

"It's pretty good," he says, smugly.

"I was expecting chocolate and funfetti," I admit, and then look down at the cake again. Thomas squirms more, so I flip him upside down.

He shrieks with delight.

"Rose and pistachio?" I ask, jiggling the toddler, who shrieks more.

"Your kid's got fancy taste," he says, laughing. "Don't tell Charlie, but last week when she made brownies from a mix, Rusty texted me to complain."

I flip Thomas right-side-up and sigh. I know that Rusty is bored, trapped at home, hasn't seen her friends in two months, and it's only natural that she's taking her frustrations out on us, but come *on.* Who complains about brownies?

"Thank you for this cake that befits her station," I say dryly. "She'll love it. Icing flowers are always her favorite."

"Yup," says Eli, a little too nonchalantly. "See you in three hours?"

"You got it."

"Unless I get lost and die in your woods."

"Our neighbors are about three hundred feet away, so if you get lost and die you've got more problems than I can help you with."

He just laughs, then points finger-guns at Thomas.

"Later, little man," he says, and then he walks off our porch and disappears behind a tree.

"When's that book report due?"

"Next week," Rusty says. "I already read the book, it was okay. Kind of dumb."

She doesn't move from the couch where she's lying on her back, holding the iPad over her face. I'm on the floor with Thomas, who's pushing around his fire engine and slowly getting annoyed that it's not making any sound.

Someone must have turned it off. How terrible.

"What book was it?"

"Hatchet."

"I liked that book," I say, as a fire truck drives up my leg. "I thought it was pretty good."

To be honest, I have no clue whether or not I ever read *Hatchet*. Fifth grade marked the first time I ever got detention and also the first time I ever sneaked out of my house at night, and I'm honestly not sure I read a single book the whole year.

Rusty doesn't need to know any of this.

"It's *fine*," she sighs. "It's just, like, who cares? I'm not in the wilderness."

"That doesn't mean you can't enjoy it. You're not in the wilderness, but, you know, it's still good to think about the value of perseverance and patience," I say, taking a stab at some of the things *Hatchet* probably touches on.

Finally, Rusty turns her head, and gives me a look that could probably melt lead with its sheer teenage-ness.

"I've thought *plenty* about patience," she says, then gives Thomas a pointed look and goes back to whatever she's watching on the iPad. I take the hint and don't say anything else. She's clearly in a mood right now, and if I'm being honest, I can't blame the poor kid. It's her birthday and she's stuck inside with a toddler and two totally lame adults, and all she gets is a boring family party later.

Well.

She thinks.

Just as Thomas pushes the fire engine up my torso and onto my face, grinning like a fiend, my phone dings in my pocket.

Charlie: The eagle has landed.

Charlie: Eagles. There are many eagles. And a falcon, apparently. They've all landed.

I glance quickly at Rusty, who's totally absorbed in whatever she's watching.

Me: Excellent. Operation Hatchling's Birthday can commence as planned.

Charlie: We need to talk about naming operations before Thomas's birthday.

Moments later, the front door opens and Charlie leans in, her curly hair in a high, messy bun. She's trying not to grin.

"Hey, Rusty," she says. "Can I get your help with something out here?"

"What is it?" Rusty sighs.

"It'll only take a minute, I swear."

"Does it have to be right now?"

Charlie and I share a look, and she smiles and rolls her eyes at the same time.

"Yes. Please?"

Rusty heaves a deep sigh, then shuts off the iPad, tosses it at the other end of the couch, and heaves herself off, her own curly hair sticking out at wild angles. Even though she and Charlie aren't related by blood, people assume that she's Charlie's biological daughter all the time. These days, Rusty corrects them less than she used to.

"Okay," she says.

"Out here," Charlie says, and disappears through the front door again.

As soon as Rusty follows her, I push myself off the floor, pick Thomas up, and follow them.

When she gets to the door, Rusty stops. She stares.

"Huh?" she finally says, taking a step onto our front porch.

"HAPPY BIRTHDAY!" everyone shouts, very much not in sync. A car horn honks. Someone whistles so loudly that I flinch. Several girls' voices *wooooo!!* excitedly. Glittery signs on poster board wave. Pom poms swish. A kazoo… kazoos.

Best of all, Rusty grins.

Then she starts laughing.

"Hi!" she shouts at the collected cars and people, waving.

Everyone cheers again, and the second time is even more raucous. Levi, sitting next to his wife June in the bed of his pickup truck, is spinning a noisemaker with one hand and June's the one with the kazoo. In a lawn chair on the front yard, my brother Eli has two metallic pom poms, and his wife Violet is holding up a HAPPY BIRTHDAY RUSTY sign.

Caleb and Thalia and my mom are also in lawn chairs, all making various noises and shouting. Seth and Delilah are sitting on the trunk of his Mustang, and finishing up the party are three sedans, each with a parent inside and a pre-teen girl yelling her head off and jumping up and down outside.

Everyone is wearing a party hat.

"Madison!" Rusty yelps. "Sofia! ELLIE."

"Rustyyyyyy!" they squeal. "Happy birthdayyyyyyyyy woooooo!"

In the next moment she runs down the stairs and then she's plowing over the front lawn. The adults in chairs get a breathless *hi* as she runs between them, then stops a good six feet away from Madison.

"I forgot to give her a mask," I mutter to Charlie.

"What a horrible parent," she mutters back, looking out at everyone. Rusty and her friends are shouting something at each other, slightly too far away for me to understand what they're saying, but it doesn't matter.

This is how it is now. This is how it's supposed to be, if you parent a kid right: they grow beyond you and you're left behind, hoping that you gave them all the tools they need and not too much of the baggage they don't.

Meanwhile, Charlie and I sit on our steps with Thomas, who stomps around in the grass and tries to escape my clutches repeatedly. Finally, Seth starts playing long distance peekaboo with him, and that seems to do the trick.

"She's happy to see her friends," Violet finally says.

"And you," I say, and they all just laugh.

"You get points for trying," says Eli.

"She said *hi*," laughs his wife, Violet. "What more do you want?"

"Nothing at all," Eli says, leaning back in his lawn chair. "I'm grateful simply to be acknowledged."

"Oh, please," says Charlie. "You're still on the *pretty cool* list. Daniel and I are somewhere between lawn clippings and soap scum."

"No, you're not," Levi says, sitting on the tailgate of his pickup. "She talks about you like she likes you when you're not around."

There's a squeal, and I glance over at Thomas just in time to see him launch himself at Seth, who catches him and swings him around.

There goes that social distancing, I guess. Toddlers don't really understand the concept of *please stay six feet away from your cool uncle*, and I took my eyes off him for about three seconds there.

"You're breaking *all* the rules right now," Seth is saying to Thomas, who's looking at him adoringly while giggling. "You're gonna be a handful, aren't you?"

"Never," says Delilah, coming up to them and leaning in, one arm on Seth's shoulder as she grins. "You're gonna be sweet as peach pie."

"My money's on both," calls June, and everyone laughs, including Thomas. I'm pretty sure he doesn't get the joke, he just likes to laugh when everyone else does.

"Sorry," I tell Seth, even though it's way too late.

"I'll take my chances," he says, half to me and half to Thomas. "Luckily, I just read that you're not contagious if you're upside down!"

He flips my kid. My kid shrieks in delight.

"I'll make you really good chicken soup if you get sick," Charlie says, patting my arm.

"Will you?" I tease.

"I'll *obtain* really good chicken soup?" she says, laughing. "I'm pretty sure I can make *perfectly fine* soup."

"Chicken soup can heal near anything, you know," my mom chimes in. "I've told you the story of your Granddad, right? He got measles, scarlet fever, and the mumps all at once. Doctors said he wasn't gonna make it, but his momma gave him chicken soup and he lived to be ninety-four."

"I don't think mine will be that good," Charlie says.

"I sure didn't learn it from her," my mom laughs.

We hang out in the front yard like that for another half-hour, easy. It's a beautiful, sunny April day, and even if everything is a little strange, it feels good to see my family again. I'm not even sure when the last time I saw them all in one place was — between life getting in the way and then quarantine it's been months.

Thalia excitedly tells us her research. Levi shares his plans to build an addition on their house. Eli and Violet tell us all about the

344

fantasy world tour they're going to take when they're allowed to travel again.

At one point, I look over and Delilah's got Thomas on her shoulders, holding him steady as he grabs a tree branch and shakes the hell out of it, both of them laughing.

After a while, Rusty's friends drive away and she stands next to the road, waving, until their cars disappear. A quick pang of guilt stabs through my chest. I know none of this is my fault, but all the same, I feel awful that she has to spend her eleventh birthday stuck here with her parents and little brother.

"Hey guys," she says, coming back onto the porch and sitting next to me. "Thanks for coming by. I like your hats."

"You want one?" asks Charlie, who reaches behind herself and grabs a bright blue, metallic hat.

"Uh, sure," says Rusty, who clearly thinks the hat is kind of dorky, but decides to go with it. "Can I have a pom pom too?"

"Anything for the birthday girl," says Charlie, and hands them over to Rusty.

I lean back on my elbows on the steps and adjust my own hat.

"Let us know when you're ready for presents," I tell her casually.

That gets her attention.

"There are presents?" she asks, and in response I just point to the small pile of wrapped gifts on the porch.

"Go for it," I tell her, and she jumps to her feet, then practically dives into the pile.

"Oh, and a picture," Rusty says, entering the living room.

I turn, sitting on the couch, but she walks on past, iPad held in front of her face.

"My uncle's girlfriend made it, it's got a dragon fighting a unicorn while a bunch of other monsters watch from the sidelines," she says, giggling. "It's pretty awesome…"

Her voice fades as she heads into the kitchen. A few moments later, I hear the telltale sounds of silverware and plates that probably mean she's getting more cake.

I let her. It's her birthday, and the cake is *really* good. I go back to scrolling the news on my phone, because even though I know I need to go do the dishes and clean up the kitchen and clear the toys from the living room, sitting down feels good.

So, *so* good.

I'm still scrolling, and Rusty is still in the kitchen, when Charlie comes downstairs and flops next to me, heaving a deep sigh.

"You can do a surprising amount of bargaining with two-word phrases and a lot of pointing," she says.

"I thought you weren't negotiating with terrorists."

Charlie just snorts.

"He gets me every time," she says. "It always starts out reasonable, like *more water*, and then before I know it we're hashing out in detail which of his trucks he's allowed to sleep with at night."

She sighs, then turns and looks at me.

"How did your parents have *five* of you?" she says.

"Well," I start. "When a mommy and a daddy love each other very much…"

Charlie snorts. A moment later, Rusty leans through the kitchen door frame, a horrified look on her face, which only makes Charlie laugh harder.

"Sorry, sweetheart," I call out.

"I'm just saying, if I were your mom, you wouldn't exist," Charlie says. Rusty's face disappears.

"You'd want Levi and Eli to be your entire legacy?" I tease. "*Them?*"

"Look, we both know you were an accident," Charlie laughs.

"You're thirteen months younger than Eli. There's no way that was on purpose."

"But then I was so great that they went on to have two more," I say.

Charlie just leans into my shoulder and pats my leg. I think about all the other tasks I should be doing right now — the dishes, tidying the living room, there's probably laundry to do — but I'd much, much rather sit here in silence with Charlie.

After a few minutes, Rusty comes out of the kitchen, the iPad tucked under her arm, and heads for the stairs.

Then, a moment later, she heads back, standing to one side of the couch.

"What's up, kiddo?" I ask, and Rusty pushes one hand through her hair, like she's thinking. Then she clears her throat.

"Thanks for the party," she says, standing on her left foot and tapping the toes of her right on the floor, like she's thinking. "It was really nice to see my friends again. And also everyone else. I'm really excited about the treehouse."

For a moment, it's quiet enough to hear a pin drop.

"I'm excited too," Charlie finally says. "I think this is gonna be a really fun project. And we can change the plans, if you want. What Levi and I drew up is just preliminary."

Rusty balances on the other foot, still fidgeting.

"Maybe?" she says. "I'm not sure, I've never had a tree fort before."

"Well, this one is all yours," Charlie says.

Rusty just grins, and I push myself off the couch.

"You're welcome, kiddo," I say, wrapping her in a tight hug.

"Dad, you're squishing meeee," she says, her voice slightly muffled in my shirt.

I squish her harder.

"Charlie, help," says Rusty.

"Like this?" Charlie asks, grabbing her from the other side and wrapping her arms around me.

"Noooooooooooooo," Rusty intones, even though she's giggling.

We give the Rusty sandwich one final squeeze, then let her go. She sighs dramatically, then gives us both a look.

Then she shrugs and heads upstairs.

"So it's a tree *fort* now," Charlie murmurs.

"What kind of defenses are in the plans?" I murmur back. "A moat at least, right?"

"We could probably set up a platform for the trebuchet," Charlie says, stepping forward and into my arms, resting her head on my shoulder. "What could go wrong?"

Yes, Rusty has a trebuchet. It's a small one. Her interests are diverse.

We stand there like that for a long moment, and for once, I think about nothing at all except the woman in my arms. I think about how lucky I am that she's my life partner, how lucky Rusty and Thomas are that she's their mom.

"I hate quarantine," Charlie finally says. "But I'm glad I get to spend it with you."

"Likewise," I say, and kiss the top of her head. "Love you."

"Love you too," she says, and tilts her head back for a kiss on the lips. She's warm and inviting, and even though I've probably kissed her thousands of times by now, it still makes my heart beat a little faster.

"That said, the moment this over I'm chucking both of these kids at their grandparents and we're going somewhere for the weekend," she says, laughing. "Alone. Just the two of us. I won't even accept phone calls from the kids."

For a moment, I let myself fantasize: just Charlie and me in some romantic cabin, in the middle of nowhere, with a great view and a huge bed. Even though we've been trapped together for two months now, the idea is still inviting.

Especially the part where there are no kids and a huge bed.

"I'd love that," I say, and I kiss her again.

ABOUT ROXIE NOIR

I love writing sexy, alpha men and the headstrong women they fall for.

My weaknesses include: beards, whiskey, nice abs with treasure trails, sarcasm, cats, prowess in the kitchen, prowess in the bedroom, forearm tattoos, and gummi bears.

I live in California with my very own sexy, bearded, whiskey-loving husband and two hell-raising cats.

www.roxienoir.com